Civil War Life

by

Judy Sharer

A Plains Life, Book 3

Civil War Life

COPYRIGHT © 2020 by Judy Sharer

Cover Art by *Diana Carlile*

The Wild Rose Press, Inc.
PO Box 708
Adams Basin, NY 14410-0708
Visit us at www.thewildrosepress.com

Publishing History
First American Rose Edition, 2020
Trade Paperback ISBN 978-1-5092-3470-7
Digital ISBN 978-1-5092-3471-4

A Plains Life, Book 3
Published in the United States of America

The blast from guns, the smoke of the powder, horses' bodies clashing, and screams from the wounded punctuated the chaos around them on the battlefield. Mark heard a sudden shout. The voice was his own. Looking down, a stain rapidly spread on his right pant leg. His foot warmed as his boot filled with blood. He grabbed his leg and called out, "Billy, I'm hit!"

Billy raced to his side and cried out for JJ to fall back and stand guard.

Ripping the sleeve off his shirt, Billy wound the bandage tightly around Mark's leg to staunch the flow.

"It burns." Mark gasped. He grabbed at his shaking leg to steady it while Billy managed to wrap the wound and tie a knot.

Mark grimaced as he turned Ruby back toward the fighting.

"Hold up, Father. You're not going back in," Billy insisted. "Keep pressure on your leg and head back to one of the medical stations. Don't worry, JJ and I'll find you when the battle is over."

Mark nodded and reluctantly turned Ruby back toward camp.

"Come on, Billy," JJ shouted. "Remember, we're both getting home in one piece."

"Yes." Billy grinned. "In one piece."

Then suddenly, a loud cheer went up. Billy saw more Kansas militia reinforcements join the fight, giving the Union soldiers on the front line a renewed surge of courage and energy to finish the battle. The Union army outnumbered the Confederates.

Previous Books in the Series
A Plains Life

SETTLER'S LIFE — Book One
Released September 2018
Available in Paperback, E-Book, and Audio Book

~

SECOND CHANCE LIFE — Book Two
Released October 2019
Available in Paperback and E-Book

~

Purchase through on-line retailers
wherever books are sold.
Published by The Wild Rose Press, Inc.
Cactus Rose Division

Dedication

To my husband
for all his patience, understanding, and encouragement,
with much love and gratitude

Chapter One

Spring 1863, the Third Year of the War

Sheriff Sloan didn't visit the Hewitt farm often, but they knew when he appeared on their doorstep, there was a good chance trouble would accompany him. One sunny April afternoon while working in the barn with two of his sons, Mark looked up to see the lawman riding in. He led a horse carrying a woman and two young girls riding bareback. Mark guessed the girls' ages at six and eight, not much older than his adopted son Steven. With worn clothing, disheveled hair, and the youngest girl clinging to her mother, the fugitive slave family was clearly in distress. He opened the barn door wider and said a quick prayer as he gestured them to enter.

Sheriff Sloan took the mother's hand and helped her down then lifted each girl from the horse.

"You're sure your husband is coming?" he asked the woman.

"Yes, sir, pretty sure," the mother said in a barely audible voice, her eyes lowered. "He stayed behind 'til he was sure we got away. He did catch up and sent us on ahead again to keep us safe. But I know he's comin' iffin' they don't catch 'em." Her shoulders sagged.

"My deputy knows to send him here," Sloan said to assure her then addressed Mark. "The father should

1

catch up in a day or two if everything goes as planned. Can you hide these three until he arrives? I told the bounty hunters hired to retrieve them they're headed north and they lit out after them, so I brought these folks west. There shouldn't be any trouble but keep watch. I never know if those bounty hunters believe me or not. They could double back in a day or two."

"We'll be happy to help them, Sheriff." Mark called for his wife Sarah who was hanging the weekly wash with his daughters Lydia and Johanna to come to the barn. "Please take this mother and her daughters to the safety of the root cellar and show them where to hide."

With a kind smile, Sarah took the mother's hand and led them away.

When they were out of sight, Mark posed the same questions he asked every time anyone visited from town. "What's the news? Any military fighting on Kansas soil? How about the bank? Any robberies lately?"

Digging in his saddlebag for a recent newspaper, the sheriff filled him in. "Even though Lincoln promised emancipation for all slaves, they aren't free yet. They're still struggling to get free like this family.

"The fighting continues with no end in sight. No military action in Kansas yet, but there's bounty hunters and strangers passing through. Fights between true Kansas Free Staters and slave owners are happening more often at the saloon too. I have three deputies now and we're doing our best to protect the townsfolk. There was an attempted bank robbery, but we caught 'em before they opened the safe." Sheriff Sloan took off his hat and rubbed his brow. "Mark, you can keep the horse they were riding. I found the poor thing about twelve miles back. There's no brand, so if you want her, she's yours."

"Thanks. We can always use another horse." Mark handed the reins to his son Jack who led the weary animal to a stall. "And thanks for the newspaper, Sheriff."

"I stopped at Billy's farm first so he could harbor the runaways, but he was nowhere around, so I brought them the rest of the way myself," Sheriff Sloan said.

"Billy's helping us clear land. We're trying to get a head start on our fields since he'll be getting married the tenth of May and then planting a couple acres of his own this year." Mark shifted his stance. "We'll see you at the wedding, I hope. Consider this an invitation, Sheriff."

"I'll be there with pleasure. Billy already mentioned the date. You have a good man in that son of yours."

"Yes, we'll all miss him around here."

Sarah appeared with two sacks of food. Handing one to the sheriff she said, "This is for your return trip, Sheriff."

"Thanks, Sarah. Guess I better be heading back. A deputy is covering the office, but I can't be away too long. Townspeople get suspicious awful easy these days," Sloan said shaking Mark's hand. Tipping his hat to Sarah, he mounted his horse and set out on the day-and-a-half trip back to Dead Flats.

Mark took the other sack of food and a jug of milk to the root cellar and tapped on the door. "Here's food for you, ma'am. I'll always knock on the door, so you know it's me. I suggest you go out only at night if you must, and be quiet. We never know who might be watching the farm."

"Thanks for helping us, mister. All the folks we've met been kind. We be quiet. Thanks for the food." The woman curtseyed, but couldn't make eye contact.

Mark took her hand and cupped his other hand on top. "You're welcome, ma'am."

A few streaks of light filtered through the cracks in the wooden door illuminating the family's new quarters as they dug into the welcome vittles.

****

Later that night, Mark sat at the kitchen table reading while the rest of the family slept. He was about to turn in when he heard a faint knock. Grabbing his rifle, he peered out and saw a black man bent over and breathing hard.

Guessing this was the father, Mark quickly helped him into the house.

Barefooted, exhausted, and wearing torn clothes that barely covered his body, the man whispered breathlessly, "I come for my family."

"You found the right place. Your wife and girls are safe in the root cellar behind the house." Mark poured the man a drink of cool water then set out hot coffee, sliced bread, and filled a bowl with warm venison stew. "Sit and eat. You should stay the night if you think you haven't been followed. You can rest during the day and leave tomorrow night."

The man paused from devouring the food and took a gulp of coffee. "Nobody followed, mister. I promise, we leave in the mornin'."

"No, stay and rest. It's safer to travel at night. I'll bring food at first light and again at dusk for your journey. Then you can be on your way."

The man finished the stew, mopping the bowl with another thick slab of bread. With his belly full for the first time in days, he nodded his thanks to Mark and the two men went outside to the root cellar. Mark knocked on the door to let them know it was him and then opened the door slowly, causing the hinges to creak, and motioned for the husband to step inside. Standing in the cool, dark, dampness outlined by the moonlight through the open door, the father whispered into the darkness, "Are you here?"

Leaping from the shadows, his wife flung her arms around him, and his daughters wept as the family clung to each other. Mark stepped back and let the reunion unfold.

"Oh, Leroy, we was worried you couldn't find the farm, or that you got caught. The sheriff said there's a bounty on us," the wife whispered between sobs.

"We prayed you was all right, Pa," the older girl said.

The younger daughter added, "Please, don't leave us no more."

Clasping his wife's face in his hands, he wiped away her tears with his thumbs. "I'm here now." He kneeled and hugged his daughters. "We're safe and together, at least for now." He kissed the girls' tear-streaked faces. "The farmer will fetch us food in the morning and then at day's end. We'll leave tomorrow night."

Holding him close, the wife said, "Leroy what happened? Your clothes are damp and you're shivering."

"I had to hide in the creek under a tree root till

dark. Thought I heard riders earlier in the day and figured I was close to the farm and might get caught, iffin' I didn't stay hidden."

Huddling together in the cool quarters to keep warm for the night, Leroy assured his family, "We're gonna be free one day. We'll get north and find a town that accepts our kind. I'll get me work. Get some sleep, my family. Tomorrow night we head north to freedom."

That said, Mark returned to the house knowing he had done the right thing telling the sheriff the family could stay.

****

After sunset the next day, Sarah packed a feed sack with enough food to last the family a few days and included a jug of milk. Mark left the items at the root cellar door including a shirt for the husband, knocked, and walked away. He heard the door creak open but didn't look back. Although he had great compassion for every runaway who showed up at the farm, for the safety of all, he didn't want to know names or any specific information.

The following morning when Mark checked the root cellar, all traces of the parents and girls were gone. Mark said a silent prayer for their safety. His family had done all they could to help in their perilous bid for freedom. He was especially thankful no harm had come to them or his family. The three families he helped previously had not been caught while on his watch, and he prayed with dangerous times looming ahead, none ever would. But he knew it might only be a matter of time.

Mark was aware that lawless bounty hunters could be ruthless with anyone who harbored slaves. His stomach churned every time he recalled the day he found Billy tied like an animal to the wagon of a peddler named Rusty. The boy sat cowering and unable to fight back against a man who bought and used him like a slave. Sheltering slaves on the run was Mark's way of helping break the unjust yoke of slavery.

****

Sitting around the kitchen table with the family that morning, Mark said, "Our guests are on their way. We were lucky once again that the bounty hunters didn't show up. We all agree freedom is everyone's right. The color of a person's skin shouldn't matter. Having enough wealth to own land doesn't give anyone the right to own another human being."

Sarah added, "We all know the danger we're in every time we give safe harbor to runaways. But helping slaves to better lives outweighs the risks. But, we still must be careful."

"We know, Ma," Jack said. "We aren't to talk about slaves or politics, especially when we're in town."

Lydia added, "And bounty hunters might be watching the farm, and could ransack us at any time. If anyone comes around that we don't know, we're to get to the house as quick as we can."

"And I'm not to tell anyone if I see a black person. It's none of their business." Steven crossed his arms and nodded his head like an adult.

"No tell, no tell," Johanna said, crossing her arms like Steven.

"That's right. We don't tell anyone, not even our friends or neighbors," Mark affirmed.

Billy sighed. "With all the abolitionist talk in town,

it's too bad the country came to blows three years ago. How much longer can this war last? And slavery isn't the only issue. We need a unified country. One where everyone has rights and can make their own decisions. I'm willing to fight for the Union if it comes to that, but I sure wish the war would end. Being a free state and a border state, the fighting could get worse before it gets better. I'm marrying Elizabeth, but I don't believe she has the same opinion on slavery as we do. Keeping our secret won't be easy."

Sarah closed her eyes and prayed aloud, "Heavenly Father, please watch over our family and guide us. Please keep us safe as we help those in danger. We pray for their safety on their journey to freedom. Be with those in the battlefields and those waiting for them to return. May they all come home safe and soon. We ask this in Jesus' name. Amen." A chorus of "Amens" followed with a delayed, enthusiastic "Amen" from Johanna.

Chapter Two

While the church bell rang, guests filed in and took their seats. Almost as a relief from the situation in the country, the room overflowed with relatives and friends dressed in their Sunday best. Many of the men wore suits with vests showing off their pocket fobs with pride. A top hat finished off the outfit of those that owned one. The women paraded about with spring-colored finery, the hems of their skirts flounced and they carried matching drawstring handbags and wore flower-bedecked bonnets. Some women even brought a parasol to use at the reception for shade.

Elizabeth gazed at her handsome husband-to-be waiting for her at the altar. He wore the new suit and shirt she helped him pick out. Soon she'd be Mrs. William Henry and all her dreams would come true. She'd have a good-looking husband, a new last name, the home he built for her, and hopefully a baby to call her own in the near future. The courtship of four years would climax into the life she'd dreamed about. She wanted the perfect, romantic life that she read about in romance novels.

Everyone stood as Mr. Parker walked Elizabeth down the aisle toward Billy. Her ruffled dress had an heirloom brooch pinned at the collar. The brooch had belonged to Billy's birth mother. He gave Elizabeth the brooch six months earlier on her nineteenth birthday to show his intentions. Elizabeth wanted to marry Billy, but with the fighting such a threat, her father had demanded the couple wait. Finally he gave in to Elizabeth's constant pleas and today was the big day. With every measured step, Elizabeth's dress bobbed front to back as she walked down the aisle and took her place beside Billy.

"Dearly beloved, we are gathered today to witness the marriage of Elizabeth Sue Parker to William Paul Henry." As the minister read from scripture, a calm surrounded Elizabeth that blocked out all sound as she gazed into Billy's eyes. She knew Billy was the man she would marry after they shared their first dance and his kiss left her breathless and wanting more, so much more.

The minister stepped closer and instructed the couple to hold hands.

"Elizabeth Sue Parker, do you take William Paul Henry to be your husband, to have and to hold from this day forward till death do you part?"

"I do, with all my heart," she said as she squeezed Billy's hand.

"Do you, William Paul Henry, take Elizabeth Sue Parker to be your wife, to have and to hold from this day forward until death do you part?"

Billy answered, "I do. With all my heart."

Finally, the words, "I now declare you husband and wife. You may kiss your bride!"

Elizabeth embraced Billy who kissed her deeply, then picked her up, twirled her around, and set her down gently as he sneaked another kiss.

The congregation stood as piano music rang throughout the church, and Mr. and Mrs. William

Henry turned to their audience, grinning with delight, and walked toward the door to exit as man and wife.

Mark stood with one arm around Sarah's waist, leaned over, and whispered in her ear, "I'm as proud of him as if he was our own."

"He *is* ours, Mark. Billy became family the day you brought him home. And when he found his little brother Steven in Kansas City, we opened our arms wider and he became our son too. We're blessed to have all our children." Sarah gave Mark a quick kiss then looked at Lydia who had tears running down her cheeks. "I hope those are happy tears," Sarah said.

Lydia wiped her eyes. "Yes, Ma, happy tears. But I'll miss Billy and Steven when they leave to live on their farm with Elizabeth."

"We'll all miss them," Jack said, lifting Steven onto the bench so he could see.

"There they go," Steven said as he leaned out into the aisle.

"Yes, you're right, Sarah dear. We are blessed. And now we've gained a daughter-in-law." Mark chuckled and caught the eye of Mr. Parker across the way. He was smiling too, as was Mrs. Parker. Mark could tell by the expression on their faces that Billy was a good choice for their daughter.

****

"Come join us for a reception in the grove," Billy announced once everyone was outside. On the sun-filled spring day in May, family and friends followed the happy bride and groom to the grove beside the church. The newlyweds mingled with guests under the shade of the elm trees. An emboldened few guests made veiled references to when they could expect a child on the way. The couple cut the two-tiered cake and the mothers of the bride and groom chatted as Sarah plated cake slices and Bertha Parker ladled cups of punch.

When everyone had a plate and cup, David Parker, Elizabeth's father, raised a glass and said, "I'm sad to see my little girl all grown-up and married, but I'm glad to see my only child with the man I know will make her happy."

Everyone toasted and cheered, "Here, here."

After the toast, Billy kissed his bride in front of everyone, took her hand, and said, "Thank you all for your blessings. We'll make a good life together, and we'll make you proud of us."

A tug on Elizabeth's dress made her look down. Steven, his face bearing crumbs of wedding cake and a smudge of icing, wanted her attention. Elizabeth bent over and gave him a kiss on his cheek. "Yes, you're a part of our family too, young man." Smiling, she left him with Billy and rushed to talk to her friends.

Billy and Steven walked over to keep Mark occupied while Sarah slipped away to the Postal Office to check for mail, Jack had found Abby, and Lydia talked with friends.

Sheriff John Sloan approached Mark and gestured for Billy to join them. "Would you two be interested in helping the abolitionist cause today?" he asked in a low voice.

Mark nodded. "What do you need?"

"Well, right now, I need eyes and ears. I figured this wedding would be a good reason for people to gather and talk. The rumor is a group favoring slavery is planning a raid on abolitionist farmers. If you hear anything about forming a raid, I'd like to know." Sloan tipped his hat.

Mark ran his fingers through his hair. "Let me handle this, Billy. You enjoy your day. I'll keep watch and let you know, Sheriff. I'll stop by the office before I leave today."

"Thanks," Sloan said and walked away.

"Can I talk to you for a minute, Father?"

The two men sat in the grass beside Steven.

"I can't thank you enough, Father, for everything you and Mother have done for Steven and me. We wouldn't be here today if you hadn't rescued me from Rusty. That good for nothing peddler still makes me angry when I think of him," Billy said and tousled his little brother's hair.

"I'm proud of you, son. It's been quite a journey since we met four years ago and we both have much to be thankful for. I couldn't be happier for you and Elizabeth. You're always welcome in our home, and I hope you know that if you ever need help, advice, or want to talk, you can always bend my ear. You and Steven are family same as Jack, Lydia, and Johanna."

"Thanks, Father, you and Mother mean the world to me." Billy put his hand on Mark's shoulder then pulled him in for a hug.

****

Mark walked among the wedding guests. A group of men talked about the topic that was on everyone's mind since March third when the Enrollment Act went into effect. "My son turns twenty in August," one farmer said. "The newspaper said The Act covers every male citizen and those immigrants who had filed for citizenship between ages twenty and forty-five. That means my son and I might both get drafted. Who would take care of the women folk and my farm?"

Another jumped into the conversation. "The only way out of the draft is to pay three hundred dollars or find someone to take your place. Who can afford three hundred dollars, and nobody is going to want to take your place to fight?"

"Yes, the controversial act stirred up quite a storm," the first man added. "The headlines, *Rich Man's War, Poor Man's Fight*, says it all."

Under the shade of a nearby elm, ladies were also talking about the draft issue. "Did you hear Ada Johnson's boy got shot and killed? She received a letter last week," one woman said shaking her head in disbelief.

Another commented, "To lose a son at such a young age. I can't imagine. Children shouldn't die before their parents, but this war will make sure that many of our husbands and sons never come home. All the unmarried men are to be called up first, but our husbands will be soon to follow."

Mark wished he could give the ladies hope, but knew their fear of impending violence was valid. Opposing political parties and their opinions hung over the people of Dead Flats like a fog. Several fathers and sons were already fighting in the East, leaving wives and children behind to run the farms. Many men had already come home injured or not at all. Mark prayed the fighting would never reach Kansas soil.

****

As the afternoon cooled, the celebration ended and both families helped carry leftovers and decorations back to the Parkers' house. With everything cleaned and put away the Hewitts were ready to depart. They had agreed to take Steven home with them and give the newlyweds three weeks alone before the little boy joined them.

Climbing into the wagon, Lydia gave Billy a kiss on the cheek and said, "I worried you might not get the words out for a second. But I know how much Elizabeth means to you. Now that you're married, we'll miss you and Steven around the house. Life won't be the same, will it?" Lydia poked Jack.

"Nope, not the same." Jack grinned. "I'll have a bedroom to myself and Steven's little feet won't be following me around. But I won't have anyone to talk to, and I'll have more chores to do again. No, really, brother, we'll miss you and Steven."

"When you're in town, please drop in and say hello," Bertha Parker called out.

"We will. Take care now," Sarah called as they drove away with everyone waving and Steven's little hand doing double time.

"I've got to make a quick stop at the sheriff's office before we leave town." Mark used the excuse that he had forgotten to tell him something, then the family headed to the old oak tree campsite.

****

The newlyweds walked hand in hand to the hotel for their wedding night. Elizabeth was a little nervous when Billy asked for the key, but once in the room, she couldn't wait for this night. Finally alone with her man who treated her as gently and caring as she dreamed he would.

Elizabeth lay resting her head on his chest and whispered, "I don't want this night to end. The wedding, the reception, and the entire day, were perfect.

Now, my husband, promise me we'll be together always."

"I'll stay with you as long as I can, but we both know if the fighting comes to Kansas soil, I must go fight in the war. Mark and I already discussed enlisting together so we could look out for each other."

"I don't want you to go," Elizabeth pleaded. Tears started to flow as she clung to Billy.

Billy held her tight then kissed away her tears. "I might not have a choice, Elizabeth."

"Promise me you won't go unless you absolutely must." Elizabeth held him tight.

"I promise." Billy said the words she wanted to hear, but knew his chances of escaping the war altogether were slim. He wanted to do his part for the Union. He worried about Elizabeth becoming pregnant and what would happen if he had to leave. He knew she could stay with the Hewitts. Jack would be home, too young for the draft, and would care for the family and do what he could to take care of the farm. But until that time arrived, he and his bride would live as complete and happy a life as possible.

****

The next morning after breakfast at the hotel, the newlyweds walked to Elizabeth's house to load trunks full of her precious belongings plus the wedding presents they had received. After loading the wagon, Elizabeth said to her parents, "You must come to visit us soon and see the house and property."

"We'll try, dear. You know your father can't get away for too long, and your farm is too far for a day trip. But we'll do our best."

Good-byes were said, then Mrs. Parker asked,

"You'll be back for the Fourth of July celebration, won't you?"

"Yes, and we'll stay with you," Elizabeth assured her.

Mr. and Mrs. William Henry drove off to begin their new life.

****

The house that Billy built stood on a piece of property a five-hour ride by wagon from Dead Flats and three-hours from the Hewitt farm. He and Mark had traveled to the land grant office in Ogden for its purchase. With Mark and Jack's help, Billy began building last year knowing he might need to leave to fight against the South at any time.

The first thing the men did was to dig a well. Water bubbled through the ground when they were less than thirty feet down, a good indication that water would run all year long.

When the newlyweds arrived at the house, Billy carried his bride across the threshold. Still holding her in his arms, they shared a kiss. When her feet hit the floor, Elizabeth danced through the house taking in every detail. Billy's parents' furnishings added a homey feel. As she peered into the loft over the last rung of the ladder, a giggle escaped. "This loft is large enough to divide into three rooms for children! We're going to have a big family, aren't we, Billy?"

"As many children as you want," Billy said.

A hearth and chimney built of native limestone stood against the back wall of the main floor. In the corner was a door to an enclosed bedroom. There was a tilled garden plot awaiting seeds. Planting and harvesting a garden would be new to Elizabeth, and she wasn't excited about the thought of having to dig in the earth and getting her hands dirty. Living self-sufficiently on a farm would be a completely new experience, and she was a bit hesitant about the responsibility.

Elizabeth had been to the house last fall when the windows were being placed but had not seen their home since. When she opened the door to the bedroom and saw the chest of drawers, the wardrobe, night table, and the bed made with new linen sheets, blankets, and pillows, she fell onto it. "You thought of everything, sweetheart. I love our new home. We can grow old together. It's all ours, and I know we'll be happy here."

"Yes, it's all ours, and as long as we are together nothing can hurt us." Billy stretched out on the bed and pulled her to him.

After a playful interlude, flushed cheeked Elizabeth asked, "Was that your stomach growling, husband?"

"No, that moan came from yours, but I'm hungry too. Let's get supper cooking. Actually, I'm starved." Billy tucked a stray hair behind his wife's ear and once more kissed her breathless.

Elizabeth discovered a note on the table from Sarah that read, *Enjoy your new home.* She found a basket full of vegetables, tins of tea, and sprigs of dried herbs. Opening the dry sink, she noted dishes, and in a sideboard drawer there was silverware from Billy's parents. Six crocks arranged neatly on a side table contained flour, cornmeal, salt, sugar, dried corn, and peas.

"Billy, remind me to thank your mother for fetching in supplies. Would you like soup and cornbread?"

"Sounds great. That'll give me time to take care of the horses." Outside stood a hen house and a large lean-to with the west end and sides enclosed so tools, wagon, and horses would be out of the weather.

During their first meal together in their new home, Elizabeth said, "Our next trip to town, we'll have to get chickens."

Billy replied, "I already thought of that. When Mark and Jack drop off Steven, they will also drop off chickens. Until then, we'll make do. I'll go hunting tomorrow, and there's a stream nearby that has plenty of fish. Jack said he'd come this summer and help dig a root cellar. We're going to need one to store our garden produce for the winter."

"What about a milk cow?" Elizabeth asked.

"We'll get one when we go to town for the Fourth of July. That's only a few months away. Life on our farm won't always be easy, but we're together now and that's what matters."

Chapter Three

There were two letters from her mother when Sarah had picked up the mail in Dead Flats after the wedding. She had read them to Mark and was waiting for a good time to share them with the children. As the family sat relaxing one evening, Sarah fetched the letters from her bedroom and returned with the news. Paraphrasing, she read her mother's letter:

"We had a wonderful growing season here. Aunt Emma and her husband Abel are both doing well and their money crops flourished.

"Aunt Mildred is still working for Doc Davis, and Emma works at Gibson's boarding house helping with the meals and cleaning. Abel didn't like her waiting tables because she was never home in the evenings so now they have more time together when he's home. He still makes a few trips a month to Pittsburgh logging, but farming is his real love."

Sarah paused and lowered her head then continued,

"Matthew joined the Union army. He and his friend John Folley left the beginning of April to meet up with the 113th Pennsylvania Regiment and Grandma hadn't heard from him when she sent her first letter right after he left, but in this letter to us, she had received a letter saying he is fine and not to worry.

"Of course we will all worry and keep Matthew in our prayers."

Sarah turned the paper over and read,

"He is only to serve for nine months, but if I know Matthew, he won't come home until the fighting is over. Mr. Reed at the newspaper told him he had a job waiting whenever he returns.

"We pray every day that this great rebellion between the North and the South will be over soon. Grandma said he wasn't drafted, but knew he could be at any time so he enlisted rather than wait. Able could also be drafted any day. Emma worries this might happen and doesn't want to think about the possibility. Of course she would come back home with us until he returns. We also pray that Billy will not be called to serve. Why, with him and Elizabeth now married, I worry there is a chance he will be called up and be forced to leave his new wife and the home he built and go off to fight.

"All my love, Mother"

****

Every day Steven asked, "Where's Billy?" And, "Why isn't Billy home?" Everyone attempted to explain the concept of marriage and he seemed good with the explanation for a while, but the next day the questions started all over again and never stopped.

"When you grow up you'll learn all about marriage, Steven. But at five years old I guess you're allowed to ask so many questions," Lydia said as she gave him a hug.

The following day, Sarah and Lydia started packing Steven's belongings.

Steven asked, "What are you doing with all my things?"

"You're going to live with Billy and Elizabeth at

the new house that Billy built. We're going tomorrow," Lydia said as she plucked his books from the shelf.

Jumping with excitement, Steven said, "I can't wait. Let's go now."

"You must wait one more day, then we'll all go with you tomorrow." Lydia kissed his forehead.

After reading two bedtime stories instead of the usual one, Steven's eyes were heavy with sleep. The next day, as his pa and Jack loaded his toys and clothes into the wagon, he ran up the ladder to the loft to hide. After a few minutes, Lydia found him in bed.

"I thought you wanted to see Billy and live with him again?" Lydia wrapped her arms around the boy as he buried his head in her chest.

"I want to see Billy, but I don't want to leave you," Steven managed to say between sobs.

"Don't worry. I'll come visit and you'll come back to visit us too. You'll see; you'll like your new home. I'm sure Billy misses you and can't wait for you to get there. Elizabeth will be there and the two of you always have fun. I know she likes to read you stories, and we packed your books and building blocks. Lucky is there too. You remember Billy's horse Lucky? I bet he's missed you."

"Lucky?" a muffled voice whispered.

"Yes, he's waiting for you and Billy to take rides together again." Lydia kissed the top of his head. "Come on. It'll be fun. You'll like your new home. There will be chores to do every day and you can help Elizabeth plant the garden, set the table, and fetch firewood. Living on your farm won't be that different from living here." Lydia held Steven's face in her hands. She knew when she had to leave him with Billy and Elizabeth, letting go would be difficult. "Remember, I'll always love you." She took Steven's hands and led him to the ladder. "You'll be back to visit soon, and your bed will be right here with Jack," Lydia promised.

Jack walked with the little boy whom he loved like a brother to the wagon and lifted him into the arms of Sarah. Everyone would miss Steven and Billy, and each family member would deal with the changes in their own way.

On the ride to Billy and Elizabeth's, Steven talked to the chickens to keep them from squawking. He did have a way with animals. Next, Lydia read a story to him and Johanna. After the story, he sat with Jack as they looked for wildlife along the path. Then he sat on the bench seat with his ma, pa, and little sister for a spell. Sarah told a story about everything Steven would do at his new house. Tired from all the distractions, the little boy crawled in the back, snuggled under a blanket, and napped. Johanna joined him. They both awakened when the wagon dipped into the creek bed and up the other side.

Steven suddenly became talkative again, anxious to see Billy and Elizabeth. The jostling of the wagon ruffled the chickens and he soothed them again telling of the new home they would have, repeating what his family said to convince him everything would be all right. He was a bright young boy. He could write his name as well as many of the letters in the alphabet and count numbers to twenty-eight. Lydia taught him to count while they collected eggs together and how to use the pyramid counting, adding, and subtracting method. She made learning numbers a game, and he enjoyed the repetition of counting. He was already to the eighth row on the pyramid ending with number twenty-eight. (Note: See Math Pyramid)

****

Waiting for his family to arrive, Billy said to Elizabeth, "I'm a little worried how Steven will react when the Hewitts leave. He loves his family and will miss them all terribly. Whenever he needs anything, he always goes to Lydia. He helps her collect eggs and feeds the chickens every day plus helps with little Johanna every chance he can. He liked to sit with Johanna in Ma's rocking chair and sing loudly, so Lydia taught him to hum. I hope he'll call this place home soon, but we may have our hands full until he gets used to the three of us under the same roof."

"Don't worry, sweetheart, he'll adjust. He'll like living here. You fret too much," Elizabeth said as she set the table and prepared a salad of wild greens while fragrant loaves of bread baked in the oven. Billy caught fresh fish that morning to fry for dinner.

When the wagon pulled in, they rushed out to greet their family. As soon as the wagon stopped, Jack lifted Steven to the ground, and he ran full out into Billy's arms.

While the men and Steven introduced the chickens to their new home, Elizabeth showed the house to Sarah and Lydia. She had rearranged the furniture that Billy brought from Kansas City to add her own touch and couldn't wait to show off some of the wedding presents they received. The three she especially liked were a Regulator clock hanging on the living room wall, a beautiful pink opaque glass oil lamp she placed on a small table next to the bed, and a quilt folded at the end of the bed that her aunts and mother made her with the wedding ring appliqued pattern, done in shades of pink and blue scrap fabrics.

After an excited Steven talked through the entire meal, the Hewitts said their good-byes. A few tears were shed, but for the most part the departure went well with promises made to visit again soon. The family of five headed home with a three-hour drive to endure and chores to complete when they arrived.

****

When bedtime came, Elizabeth told Steven a story about their new life on the farm and showed him where he'd sleep in the loft. Billy's rope bed that Mark and he made together, and that Steven slept in many times, sat in the corner of the loft. At the end of the bed was a trunk with his clothes and against the wall stood a small chest of drawers that Billy used growing up. Steven would be sleeping by himself now without Jack or Billy beside him. He had been up and down the ladder steps to the loft several times during the day. The ladder wasn't the problem. Sleeping in the loft by himself was the problem.

Steven listened to the murmur of Billy and Elizabeth talking and fell asleep. Not until everyone was asleep did Steven wake and became frightened. The house was dark. Where was Jack? He sat on the bed for a few minutes. He was at the new house, but being by himself frightened him. After his eyes adjusted to the darkness, he climbed down the ladder and made his way into Billy and Elizabeth's bedroom. Afraid if he woke Elizabeth she would send him back up the ladder, he pulled the quilt from the end of the bed, cuddled on the floor, and fell asleep.

At dawn, Billy awoke first and discovered Steven on the floor. He put him back in the loft bedroom, covered him, and kissed his forehead. Steven stirred a little and fell back to sleep. This happened a few more nights until Steven got used to sleeping by himself in his bed upstairs.

****

Sarah had brought smoked meat and canned goods from her root cellar to help tide the newlyweds until harvest. Elizabeth, pleased to have hens, fixed a breakfast of eggs and smoked sage sausage. Afterward, with the ground warm enough to plant, the little family worked in the garden. They sowed enough to fill the root cellar they'd build and would have additional produce to sell in town for extra money. The next day Billy planted a small field of corn, then oats, and wheat. A pasture of clover and grasses for the milk cow they would acquire soon was the last seed sown.

Elizabeth soon learned, to her dismay, that Steven always wanted her to play. He wanted her to read to him, take him for walks, or let him help her make a sweet dessert. He did help with the chores, but his constant demands took much of her time, much more than she expected. Weary of housework, cooking, the burdens of the garden, and taking care of Steven, Elizabeth was ready for a change. Mid-June, she asked Billy if they could go to town to get a milk cow so Steven could have milk. Elizabeth indicated the trip as intended to benefit Steven, but the reality of the life she chose when she married seemed like all work, and she began chafing against the severe restrictions. She hated that her hands were red and chapped from washing clothes. Being cooped up away from her friends and family was taking a toll on her. Running to the dress shop for new clothes was now a thing of the past. She longed for the life her friends and mother had in town, the life she left behind while caught in the romance of being married and starting a family.

Billy finally agreed, sensing something was annoying or bothering Elizabeth. *Maybe she needs to talk with her mother?* They would buy a cow and return home the next day so the chickens wouldn't go without feed and water too long. He'd take along bushel baskets and buy feed until the crops produced and the clover field grew lush enough to pasture the cow.

Chapter Four

Arriving at the Parkers' house, Billy dropped off Elizabeth and Steven and picked up supplies and Elizabeth's list of food staples before heading to the stables to look for a milk cow.

"Surprise, Mother, I'm home. I hope it's all right. Billy wanted to come to town for a milk cow and we needed a few supplies."

"You're always welcome to come home. You know that, sweetheart. Your father will be glad to see you. And Steven, my you have grown."

"I'm going to run out for a while. Will you watch Steven for me?"

"Of course. Where are you going?"

"I want to find Katie and Mary Jane. I have so much to tell them."

After looking in a few stores the girls liked to frequent, she located them at the dress shop. They talked and caught Elizabeth up on the town news, sharing that a classmate returned wounded from fighting in the East and he'd asked about her. Elizabeth kept one eye on the clock and scurried home before Billy, without him knowing she left.

"I planned on a roasted chicken supper tonight when your father gets home. I hope that sounds good," Mrs. Parker said.

"Sounds wonderful." Elizabeth rushed to take her

things upstairs and unpack.

In her old room that she would be sharing with her husband for the first time, she opened the closet, but all her things were gone. The bed was made but didn't have her favorite covering. Her hairbrush set that always sat on the bureau was now in her own home and she forgot to pack additional shoes, so had only the pair she wore. And she had already been seen in her dress once today. She'd hoped to ask Billy to take a walk through town after dinner and now she'd be seen in the same outfit. Next trip she would pack more.

Living on the farm, she didn't care how she looked. In fact, some days she probably looked like a farm girl and not the lady she was raised to be. There weren't friends to come visit, so she didn't have to dress a certain way. Maybe she could ask her friends to visit her new home, but they would never venture that far alone. She'd talk to Billy and see if he'd bring her to town more often. Certainly, she could find enough reasons.

Billy walked in the door and called to Elizabeth at the top of the stairs, "I'll take Steven for a walk and give you and your mother time to talk."

****

Billy and Steven walked to Cain Gibbs' blacksmith shop. Billy and Cain became friends one day when Billy ran over a large rock, putting a dent in the tongue of the wagon. He couldn't return home with the dent, so he went to Cain's shop for help. They hammered out the dent together good as new, and Billy repaid him by helping as an assistant occasionally. When Billy would come to town courting Elizabeth, he'd spend the night at Cain's blacksmith shop. Nothing fancy, a straw bed out of the weather and a safe place to sleep. Cain arrived at four in the morning to get the coal furnace going. The two became good friends. Sometimes Billy helped Cain with projects and slowly learned the trade over the years.

"Good to see you again, Cain." Billy shook his hand. "And this is my little brother Steven."

"Nice to meet you, Steven." Cain stretched out his hand to shake, but Steven didn't budge. His eyes were fixed on Cain's large, rough hand. Cain stood six feet two and weighed more than two hundred and seventy-five pounds of pure muscle.

"It's all right, Steven, Cain's our friend. You can shake his hand. He won't hurt you."

Cain knelt on one knee and put out his hand again. This time Steven accepted.

"Thanks for coming to the wedding. I was glad to finally meet your wife and son."

"Ah, you're welcome. My wife enjoyed the day. What brings you to town so soon?"

"We needed a milk cow and a few supplies. We'll be back for the Fourth of July, and the Harvest Festival, then not again until next spring. How's business going?"

"I keep busy. There's always something needing fixed, shod, or made."

"I see you haven't gone to fight?"

"No, and I hope to never go, but if I do, would you want to go along as my helper? I figure they'd want me to work my trade taking care of the wagons, horses, gun barrels, and whatever else might need made or fixed."

"My father and I were planning on joining together if they make fighting mandatory, but as long as we stayed with the same regiment, I'd be glad to work with you," Billy replied.

"Good, that makes me feel better. I'll have your back and you'll have mine, and we can both watch out for your father."

****

After supper and the dishes were done, Elizabeth approached Billy. "Why don't we walk to town? We don't need to buy anything, only take a stroll and maybe visit with friends if they're out. I'm sure Momma won't mind watching Steven for us. We won't be gone that long."

"Sure. It's a nice evening. Grab your shawl."

She had a snag in her wrap where she caught the yarn on a piece of splintered wood in the chicken coop. She hadn't repaired the raveling and so said, "The evening air isn't that cool tonight. I should be fine. And if I do get cold, you can put your arm around me."

The town bustled with people on the lantern-lit Main Street. Elizabeth held Billy's arm with one hand and clutched her dress with the other, swishing it back and forth as she walked. Attention. Attention was what she wanted. She was back and wanted everyone to see her and her new husband happily walking together.

Billy said hello to a few people he knew, but Elizabeth couldn't believe she didn't see any of her friends. Someone must be having a party and she wasn't invited. Katie and Mary Jane didn't mention a party. Wait until she saw them the next time. Walking the length of the street and back with no acquaintances in sight, they headed back toward the house. But not wanting to take care of Steven for the rest of the evening, Elizabeth turned toward the church grove.

31

"Remember when we first met, sweetheart?" she began. "You were the most handsome boy on the dance floor and I had to meet you. If you hadn't come and asked me to dance, I told my friends I would ask you."

"Then it's a good thing I got my courage up and asked you first," Billy said. "I'm not sure I'd have said yes to a girl asking me."

"I love you, Billy Henry."

"And I love you, Elizabeth Henry."

The long kiss they shared reminded Elizabeth of their first kiss with Billy holding her tightly, Elizabeth's feet left the ground and, after a couple twirls, she was back to earth.

"You're chilled, Elizabeth. Come on, I don't want you to take sick." Billy took her hand and they walked to the house. For a moment, Elizabeth forgot all about living on the farm and enjoyed being a new bride again.

****

Early the next morning, the Henrys headed home. Billy was surprised they passed two wagons and several riders on the road usually deserted. Back at the farm, Billy, with Steven's help, unhitched the horse and untied the milk cow. Leading the cow into a stall made for her, he asked, "What should we name our new milk cow, Steven? I know. How about Buttercup?"

"I like Buttercup. She looks thirsty." Steven grabbed the pail and hauled it to the well.

After chores, Billy practiced with his rifle, the one he bought for his trip from Kansas City after finding his little brother and parents' portrait three years ago. He'd try his hand at the best shot contest again this year. Last year he took third place and Jack fourth. If the family came to town this year, he'd compete against Mark and

Jack. Billy could always use another gun at the house and, if he did go to war, he'd have another reliable gun to take along. He wanted to win, but if either Mark or Jack won, that would be all right too.

Chapter Five

At the Hewitts', Jack and Mark were busy cutting and stacking a cutting of natural grasses to feed the cows before trying to clear and till the land to extend their fields. Sarah and Johanna were busy baking. Lydia sat in the rocking chair making a swimming outfit for Johanna. If they were able to go to town for the Fourth, Johanna would need something to wear swimming.

Last year, Johanna loved the water when Sarah took her in, so this year she would learn to float.

With the holiday fast approaching, Mark and Sarah questioned whether or not they should go to town with all the conflict brewing in the country. Also, would Seth and Emily want to go or would they let the Hewitts pick up supplies for them and take care of their animals in exchange? Sarah considered riding to the Frazers' herself to ask them. Then she could see Ethan, their two-year-old son, and catch up on news. She couldn't wait to tell Emily about the wedding, but she didn't feel safe journeying that far alone, and she didn't want Jack to go alone either. She could handle a gun well enough for a day, and she'd pray nothing would happen when Mark and Jack rode to the Frazers' to ask if they were going to town or if they'd take care of the animals while they were away.

"What do you think, Mark? Should we chance a trip to town for the July holiday this year?" Sarah asked.

"Well, we need supplies and I know everyone would love to see the married couple and Steven. I'm sure they're planning to attend."

"Let's chance it," Jack said.

"Yeah, I want to go," Lydia added.

"I've been thinking, and if we do go, there are rules that everyone must agree to," Sarah intoned.

"Rule one: Nobody goes anywhere alone. You must tell your father or me where you're going and about when you'll be back. I realize you're old enough to decide what you want to do, but you'll be safer with a friend.

"Two: I'll need help with Johanna. You know how she likes to venture off. You can't put her down without holding her hand, and you must always keep an eye on her.

"And three: We don't talk politics in town. If someone asks you a political question, politely say, 'I don't discuss politics,' and walk away. No fighting amongst yourselves or with others. If you see a fight, walk the other way. You're not being a coward; you're being smart.

"Any questions?"

"No, ma'am," they answered in unison, even Mark.

"Good. We're going to have a good time. I need your help with Johanna, and you must be smart about situations.

"Mark, will you and Jack ride to Seth's and ask if he'll care for the livestock while we're away?"

"Of course, dear. We can go tomorrow and then we can make our plans accordingly."

****

Arriving at the Frazers' place midmorning, Jack rapped on the door.

Seth greeted them. "Hello, nice to see you. Please, come in and have a seat. We were talking about you the other day, wondering if you'd be going to town soon."

"We'd like to go. That's why we're here, Seth, to see if you'd watch after the livestock and to ask if we could pick up any supplies you might need, unless you plan on going yourselves." Mark took his hat off and sat down.

"No, we're not going." Seth sat down beside Mark. "But we could use some items, plus I have a favor to ask. Would you mind taking this gold dust to the assay office for me? As I'm sure you already figured out, I pan a little and occasionally I hit a good spot. It's not much, but it should pay for the supplies with a little leftover."

"Sure, I'll do that for you, Seth. I've heard folks around here say there's gold, but I was skeptical. So, I guess this proves them right."

"I head due west. It's a three-day trip one way. There's a big lake with several tributaries. I've traveled different spurs panning and sometimes I have luck. I don't go as often now that we have Ethan. I don't like leaving Emily alone that long. I'm thinking of taking them with me for a couple weeks and see how we make out. The extra money never hurts any."

Mark tucked the pouch in his pocket for safekeeping and asked, "Jack, didn't your mother send something for Emily?"

"Oh yeah, I'll go get it." Jack rushed out and brought in a sack of fresh peas from the garden and a loaf of apple bread.

Handing them to Emily, Jack got down on the floor to play with Ethan. "My, has he grown since the last time I saw him. Mother wanted to come herself, but decided it wouldn't be safe. She said to tell you she can't wait to fill you in on Billy's wedding and tell you all the news."

"Tell your ma we'll come the week after you get back, and I can't wait. Thank her for me, please, Jack." She held out the sack and loaf of bread. "I'll cut the bread and fetch some cool tea."

After a good visit, Mark and Jack were on their way knowing Sarah would worry if they didn't return before dark.

****

In the morning after the men had left, Lydia ran into the house calling, "Mother, come quick! I found a fresh chicken carcass out behind the barn! We can't afford to lose our chickens. What should we do?"

"It could have been a number of critters looking for an easy meal. We'll keep our eyes open today and be ready to scare off anything that comes around." Sarah brought the gun to the kitchen and placed it out of Johanna's reach.

Midday, Lydia looked out the kitchen window toward the barn and saw a fox run from the barn to the coop. "Mother, get the gun."

Sarah didn't think twice about what she must do. She set Johanna in a chair with orders to stay and grabbed the rifle, flung open the door, and raised the gun to her shoulder in time to get off a shot at the blur of red. The bullet hit the dirt underneath the fox sending pebbles flying as the animal raced off.

"You missed him. What if he comes back?"

"Let's hope it scares him away until your father and Jack get home. Then they can deal with it." Sarah put the gun back.

"Did you aim to miss, Ma?"

"No, I meant to kill the chicken thief. I must not have aimed high enough."

"You would have killed the fox, Mother?"

"Yes. As you said, we can't afford to lose our chickens."

"But I thought you could never kill anything."

Sarah reasoned her family needed the chickens for food as much as that mother fox. This was the first time she ever attempted to kill anything except a pesky insect. "Yes, I would have killed the fox if it meant saving the chickens that we count on for eggs and meat. But I'd never kill anything that wasn't food unless it harmed our food supply or, of course, one of our family."

When the men returned, Lydia couldn't wait to tell about the fox, and Jack reported on how much Ethan had grown.

Chapter Six

With plans to attend the Fourth of July festivities
and owning a milk cow now, Billy couldn't be away
from the farm longer than overnight. He thought about
asking one of the neighbor boys if he could do the
milking and feed the chickens, so Billy and Steven set
out on Lucky, Billy's horse, to the neighbor family's
farm about an hour away.

He talked to Mr. Morgan about one of his boys
doing the chores and they agreed on a price of three
cents a day for Peter, age fourteen, to take on the task.
As part payment, the boy would take home the days'
milk and eggs. Billy paid six cents, a fair price for two
days of the boy's time, and headed home. Now they
wouldn't worry about the animals.

The Henry family left early Friday morning to
return Saturday evening. This gave Billy time to shoot
in the contest, he and Elizabeth could go to the dance,
and enjoy a leisurely morning before heading back.

****

In Dead Flats, Billy peered down the main
thoroughfare. In the road near the sagging boardwalk
sat a small Conestoga wagon with the crude rendering
of a native medicine man painted on the canvas. Above
the image he read, "Doctor Hollingsworth's Magic
Elixir." There was no mistaking this wagon. Rusty was
in town.

Approaching slowly, Billy wondered, *Was Rusty in the wagon? It's too early for him to stop off at the saloon.* Visions of the peddler tying his hands to the side rail of the wagon flooded Billy's memory. His hands clenched the reins and beads of sweat dampened his forehead. His body trembled with rage.

Billy wanted to jump off the wagon and beat the daylights out of Rusty for the way he'd treated him. But he drove past not wanting to upset Elizabeth and Steven. There'd be time to confront Rusty when they weren't present.

Leaving Steven with Elizabeth at the Parker residence, Billy needed to register for the Best Shot contest at the sheriff's office. As he turned the corner, he couldn't help himself and looked down the street. The wagon was still there.

The registration line for the shooting contest was out the door of the sheriff's office and he saw Mark and Jack in line a few men ahead of him. He tapped Jack on the shoulder. Both men turned around. "I wondered if you'd shoot this year, Father. It's good to see you."

Jack and Mark shook Billy's hand. Mark said, "It's good to see you too. How's married life going?"

"Yeah, and how's Steven?" Jack asked.

"All's well and Steven can't wait to see you. Are you in the usual spot in the church grove? We'll find you after the shooting contest and go to the picnic with you." Billy took off his hat as he stepped through the door of the office.

"Sounds good. I know your mother and the girls can't wait to see you too." Mark reached over and tousled Billy's hair. "And she wants to get another family photo taken right after the shooting contest and before the picnic."

"I'd like a photo of our family this year too!" Billy gave Jack a nudge.

Jack registered, then Mark.

Jack spoke up, "I hope there isn't a three way tie."

"No, I plan on winning with my first score." Billy patted Jack's shoulder.

"Well, I'll show you two youngsters how it's done," Mark boasted.

Billy signed his name, paid his fee, and they headed their separate ways. Billy walked directly to the painted wagon. He threw back the flap. With clenched fists poised to fight he discovered Rusty slumped over a crate. The man looked older than Billy remembered. That tall, stout, red-haired man once dressed in an elegant suit was now much thinner, his face so drawn his cheekbones were prominent, his rough hands now skin and bones. He looked as though he hadn't eaten for quite a while.

Billy called, "Rusty?"

No response.

Billy called louder.

Lifting his head he growled out a reply. "Do I know you from somewhere? Your voice sounds familiar."

"Yes, you know me. My name is Billy Henry."

"What do you want?" Rusty said, cowering

"I wanted to use my fists to pay you back for all the pain you caused when you treated me like your slave, treated me like an animal. But now you're nothing but a has-been old man. Fighting you wouldn't give me any pleasure, because you can't even fight back. When was the last time you ate?"

"I don't remember. Without handouts, I wouldn't be alive. I've sold everything except my wagon and mule."

Billy scanned the interior of the wagon, and the old man had told the truth. But in a corner of the wagon sat four boxes of elixir bottles. He pointed to them and asked, "Are those full or empty?"

"Empty, of course. If I had elixir to sell, I could start over. Get on my feet again."

"You get yourself clean, shave, and buy a new shirt. Here's two silver dollars." Billy flipped him the coins. "Eat something at the roadhouse and meet me back here after the shooting contest."

Billy couldn't stand to see an animal suffer. How could he let another human suffer if he could help? He thought about the little dog he and Jack happened upon a few years back that died because they found him too late to save. He had to try, or at least get Rusty back on his feet again. His father always said, "You never kick a man when he's down."

****

Excitement rose as everyone gathered for the contest. Jack shot well until the second bottle. He pulled a little to the left and missed, but then went on to hit the farthest bottle at three-hundred yards. Nobody had a perfect score yet.

Mark shot next. His paper target hit the X, but didn't shoot out the center and he had a clean sweep on all three bottles. He crossed his fingers his score would be good enough to win if Billy didn't shoot a perfect score.

When Billy took his turn he shot clean until the last bottle which he rocked, but didn't shatter.

The threesome located their families in the crowd and waited out the rest of the contest. The winner was determined by who was the closest to the X on the paper target.

Making his way through the crowd the sheriff announced, "We have a two-time winner here, friends. This man also won three years ago. Mr. Hewitt, come get your prize."

Mark didn't realize he was holding his breath until he exhaled with relief and accepted the rifle.

The crowd cheered. He heard Jack's and Billy's hooting and hollering above all the others.

With the rifle held high in the air, he walked toward his family, heart beating in his throat. "Here, Jack, this is for you with one condition. When you win this contest and your own rifle you give this gun back."

Billy slapped Jack's shoulder. "I figured that's what Father would do if he won. Now we each have a good rifle of our own. God knows we may need them with this war hanging over our heads. Come spend some days at our house and we'll go hunting," Billy offered.

Mark gave Sarah a kiss on the cheek. She in turn whispered in his ear, "That was sweet of you to give the rifle to Jack."

****

Sarah had arranged for the photo ahead of time so when the family arrived for the sitting, no time was wasted. One new member of the family was included in this year's photo, Elizabeth, and next year's photograph could look very different.

Sarah ordered four tintypes. Billy ordered one of the entire family, and then had a photo taken with only

43

himself, Elizabeth, and Steven, and ordered two. One of them to give to Elizabeth's parents and the other for their home. "Here's the money for our photos, Mother. Will you get ours when you get yours?"

"Of course, dear." Sarah took the coins and put them in her pocket.

"The photos will be ready in the morning and three will be wrapped for mailing," said the photographer.

"Wonderful, we'll be by at around eight then be on our way." Sarah was delighted to have her entire family together again and couldn't wait for the family back East to meet Elizabeth.

****

Heading to the church grove for the picnic, Billy announced, "I must run an errand. I'll meet everyone at the picnic. Don't wait for me to eat. I'll be there as soon as I can."

Billy walked to the Dry Goods Store first. "Eight quart jars of canned beets and a pound of sugar, please."

The clerk didn't question the order. Billy paid, then walked across the street to the saloon toting the bulging sack and asked the bartender, "Can I have three bottles of whiskey?" The man behind the counter looked him up and down. Billy slapped the money on the bar, and the man turned and returned with three bottles. He'd never forget the recipe for the elixir. He'd mixed so many batches he had the ratios memorized. Grabbing the bottles off the bar, he returned to Rusty's wagon and began mixing the ingredients in the right proportions. Anxious to return to the picnic, he wasted no time.

Rusty returned, clean-shaven and wearing a new

shirt when Billy finished bottling the last box. "Well look at you. You cleaned up real good, old man. Do you remember your sales pitch? I'm sure you do, like I remembered the recipe."

Finishing the last bottle, Billy corked them all and returned them to the crate. "Now, you have four boxes to sell. That should surely get you back on your feet again if you stop drinking."

Billy stood and walked away as Rusty started to say, "Thank you."

Joining his family, Billy grabbed his plate and headed to the food tables. Jack went along for a second piece of cake.

"Hey, what was so important that you couldn't eat with us?" Jack cut a wedge of cake and flopped it on his plate.

"Oh, I had to help out an old man with a project, but it's done now." Billy added meat, vegetables, and salads to his plate until the food was piled high, then snatched a roll and the two young men made their way back to the quilt.

Steven and Johanna played together while Billy finished his dinner and everyone talked about local news and of course the topic on everyone's mind, the war.

Mr. Parker stood and said, "I'm not feeling well. I have a headache."

"Since we won't be returning for the dance, Steven can stay with us tonight, if you'd like, Elizabeth," Mrs. Parker offered.

"That'd be great," Elizabeth said, before Billy could speak. "Then we can dance every song and not worry about him."

Heading back to the Parkers' house for Elizabeth to freshen up before the dance, Billy heard a familiar voice gathering people to his wagon. Rusty stood on the makeshift platform at the back of the wagon to perform an evening show after the picnic dispersed.

Billy stopped to watch with his family.

The man orated in as loud a voice as he could muster, "Brought to you from Chicago and parts east, the one, the only, Hollingsworth's Magic Indian Elixir! Only one dollar a bottle! My new supply just arrived by stagecoach. Are you rundown, tired of feelin' poorly due to hard work or lack of sleep? A small measure daily will increase manly vigor, aid in sleeping, and banish aches due to arthritis and rheumatism. Friends, I tell you, this elixir will cure female complaints as well as colic and fevers in infants!"

A small group of townsfolk gathered around.

THE BEST IN THE WORLD read the sign on the wagon.

"It's made from secret ingredients Dr. Hollingsworth himself learned from a Cherokee Medicine Man on his deathbed." The Irish peddler's voice rose. "Only one dollar!"

As Billy watched Rusty perform the familiar spiel, the hatred inside of him for the man melted away. *If Rusty stays off the booze, he could start over. This is his chance.* When Billy caught the old man looking at him, he nodded, smiled, and walked away with his family. He could put this shame-filled part of his life behind him now with no regrets.

Chapter Seven

Mark spotted Joe Spencer and his wife Martha and joined them to talk.

"Good to see you." Joe slapped Mark on the back.

"Sarah's at the food table with Johanna if you ladies wish to catch up." Mark pointed in Sarah's direction. Martha made her way through the crowd.

"We weren't sure if we should come with all the fighting among the Free Staters and slave owners we heard tell about, but we need to order seed for next year and get supplies, so I brought the family for a treat." The words were barely out of Mark's mouth when shouting started behind him.

Two men were in a heated argument about the war. "The rebellion is about slavery," one man shouted.

"No, Lincoln said those who had 'em could keep 'em," shouted the other as punches were thrown.

Mark and Joe got out of their way. Others gathered cheering on the scrabbling until the sheriff and his deputy arrived to break up the fight.

"I'd have been surprised if there wasn't a fight tonight," Mark said to Joe as they joined the ladies.

"I'm not in favor of this war." Joe exhaled. "Not because I don't believe in the cause, but I sure don't want to leave my family behind while I go fight. I'm not going until it's required by law."

"I'll go if I must." Mark sighed. "I want one of the

boys to stay back with their mother and the girls. I agree with the cause, and I'm not afraid to fight for my beliefs, but those we leave behind have the real war to fight. They'll be fighting to stay alive as much as the men in the battlefields."

Martha spoke up, "It looks like the jail will be packed tonight. Heard tell there was a fight earlier between a Free Stater and a slave owner. The sheriff has already hauled off four men."

"Have you seen Seth and Emily Frazer lately?" Joe took off his hat and scratched his forehead.

"Why, I bet their son is keeping them on their toes," Martha added.

"Jack and I visited them last week. They're all doing well and Ethan is growing like a wild weed. Seth feeds our livestock when we come to town and we take home supplies for them. Oh, that reminds me. I have something to do for Seth tomorrow before we leave. I mustn't forget. He's counting on me. Remind me in the morning will you, Sarah?"

"Of course, dear." Sarah, holding Johanna, passed the little girl to Mark. "We probably should have picked up our items today, but with the excitement of seeing Billy's family and the shooting contest, we didn't get there. I hope the store isn't sold out."

****

Lydia's friend Ben, the boy she liked to dance with, found her with her friends and asked her to dance. He boasted of his plans to one day own a plantation with hundreds of acres. "I'll have slaves to work the soil. I'll become rich and maybe someday run for governor." Ben puffed out his chest.

"Where did you get this notion? You're only

sixteen." Lydia knew she wasn't to talk about these things, but she was curious about his answer.

"My grandmother told me I have family in the south. One uncle owns a plantation. If the fighting gets too close here, I'm going to head out for Arkansas. That's where he lives."

"What about your grandmother? Will she go too?" Lydia asked.

"No, she said she's too old to travel that far," Ben said.

"So, you'll leave her alone? It's only the two of you isn't it?"

"Yeah, but Gram said she'd rather I be safe and that I should leave iffin' the fighting gets bad. I'll send word to let you know where I am. When the fighting is over, you can come and we can start a life together. At least that's what I thought."

They danced another song and Lydia thought about Ben's ideas. Walking off the dance floor she said, "You do what you must if fighting gets close. Write me if you still want, but I fear if you leave, we'll never see each other again. I'll miss you if you decide to go. Be safe and I pray you find what you want when you get there. Now, I must fetch my little sister so my parents can have a few dances." And with those words, she hurried to find her ma and pa. She wasn't sure she wanted to associate with Ben anymore if those were his hopes for the future.

While Lydia held Johanna and swayed to the music, a slower song started to play. Mark asked Sarah to dance, and Joe and Martha followed them to the dance floor.

****

49

Judy Sharer

Jack nudged his girlfriend Abby Proctor with his elbow, and when she turned around she propelled herself into his arms.

"I was so proud of you today, Jack Hewitt. Your shooting keeps improving. You'll win that rifle one day." Abby hugged him close.

"Gee, thanks. I'm glad to see you too. May I have this dance?" Jack twirled her out onto the dance floor.

"I wasn't sure you'd come." Abby moved closer.

"Well, we needed to order seed and get supplies, so my folks said we'd take a chance on the town being quiet for a change. After that fight broke out, I wasn't sure we'd stay, but I see my parents talking to friends so we must be staying until morning. By the way, I brought you letters."

"I have letters for you too, but they're at the house. I'll fetch them when you walk me home. I'm not allowed to go anywhere unless I'm escorted. My parents almost didn't let me come tonight, but I promised I'd stay close to friends and come home right after the dance."

"Don't worry. You're safe with me, and I'll walk you home."

"A friend and I came together, so you can walk both of us home."

"That's fine, as long as I get to kiss you goodnight."

Jack and Abby spent the entire evening talking and dancing.

****

When Billy and Elizabeth arrived, Elizabeth's friends told them about the sheriff breaking up a fight and hauling the offenders to jail. Billy remained on alert the rest of the evening. After several dances together, Elizabeth said she wanted to talk with friends, and Billy visited with Mark and Sarah. He watched as a man walked over and spoke to Elizabeth. The next thing Billy knew, Elizabeth was on the dance floor with him.

He excused himself from the conversation and walked to the dance floor in time to confront the man he knew only by his first name, Quinn.

Surprised to see Billy, Quinn's lip turned up at the corner as he handed Elizabeth off, not saying a word.

Elizabeth had to admit to herself that she liked Quinn's attention. The fact that she was now married did little to dispel her pleasure at being the subject of two men's attention.

Billy took Elizabeth's hand and rejoined Mark and Sarah to finish his conversation about coming to the family farm to help extend the corral. Before the dance was officially over, the young couple returned to the Parkers' house. Steven was already in bed. Billy announced, "We'll be leaving right after breakfast. We're going to meet my family and follow each other until we get to our turn-off. Thanks for watching Steven for us, Mother Parker. Goodnight, Father Parker."

****

Elizabeth said nothing, but sensed something upset Billy or they wouldn't have left the dance so early. She briefly thought about returning to the festivities, but her mother wanted to chat and so they talked awhile. When Elizabeth tiptoed into the bedroom, she assumed Billy would be sound asleep. But he surprised her when he rolled toward her, fluffed his pillow, and said, "Goodnight. Sweet dreams."

****

The next morning, the Hewitts stopped and picked up all the photos from the traveling photographer. Sarah addressed the three wrapped for mailing and ran them to the Postal Office with three quick notes she had written last night.

Mark drove the wagon and left it in front of the Dry Goods Store and waited for the owner to open the doors. "Jack and I'll order the seed and then meet you here to load the supplies," Mark said to Sarah.

"And don't forget you have an errand to do for Seth," Sarah reminded him.

Lydia looked after Johanna while Sarah shopped for items on her and Emily's lists, slipping in a few surprises for Christmas.

"Can we afford any fabric this time?" Lydia asked, but only received a sad look from her mother.

"Go ahead." Sarah flicked her wrist. "You can select five skeins of yarn if you want. That will give you something to keep you busy this winter."

Sarah finished both lists, helped pack the items into crates, and the clerk tallied the bill when Jack walked in.

"Father will be along in a few minutes. I'll load the wagon for you, Ma. And there's one supply I need to buy." Jack lifted the lid on the salt bin and scooped out two ten-pound sacks, paid for them with his own money, and carried the sacks to the wagon. "Have Father pick me up at the Butcher Shop. He knows what I'm doing." Jack hurried down the street.

The smell of coffee wafted from the backroom, and he heard men talking. Jack shouted to the men enjoying their morning coffee, "Do you have any cowhides I can buy?"

A man walked through the door and lifted his brow. "You want cowhides this early in the morning? What for?"

"I plan on tanning them and making leather products to sell." Jack put his hands in his pockets.

"Yeah, I think I can rustle some for you, young fella. You want the heads too I s'pose?"

"Yeah, of course, heads too."

"How many you want?"

"How many you have?"

The man called over his shoulder. "Bring me out ten of those larger cowhides we finished this morning. Roll them up and put them in a few feed sacks for this young man. They'll stiffen pretty quickly so you'll need to tend to them right away. Here's some sacks, you can get the heads from the scrap pile outside. Take as many as you want."

"Oh, I will. What do I owe you, mister?" Jack pulled his hand out of his pocket with coins clenched tight.

"Well, I usually get five cents a hide, but seein's that you're here to get 'em and I know you'll use 'em, you can have 'em for two cents each."

"Gee, thanks, mister. I assure you they won't go to waste." Jack handed the man two dimes. He took the sacks of hides, and filled other sacks with the heads, and made a few trips, dragging everything to the street.

****

Mark walked out of the assay office with a surprising two hundred forty-two dollars in his pocket that he was sure Seth and Emily could use. Walking to the wagon, nobody was on the street near him, and he prayed nobody saw where he had been. He didn't need

53

any trouble while doing a favor for a friend.

Mark stopped the wagon for Jack to load his sacks and they continued down the street to the Parkers' house. Billy's wagon was packed and ready to leave.

Steven asked, "Can I ride in Ma and Pa's wagon until we get to the turn off?"

Billy looked at Sarah and Lydia who were both smiling approval and said, "Sure, you can. Maybe you can sing songs along the way."

Steven ran to stand beside Jack.

"Here are your photos, Billy," Sarah said.

Elizabeth stood on her tiptoes to look over his shoulder to get a glimpse.

Steven ran to Billy's side to get a peek.

Billy handed one to Elizabeth who in turned handed it to her mother and said, "We had our photograph taken yesterday and this one is for you and Father."

"It's very nice, sweetheart. We'll place it on the mantle. Thank you for thinking of us," Bertha Parker said, holding out the photo for her husband to see.

As Mr. and Mrs. Parker stood in the doorway waving, they called good-bye.

****

Billy had been cool with Elizabeth that morning, speaking mainly to her parents. Now, alone in the wagon, Elizabeth asked, "Is there something wrong? We left the dance early, and you went straight to bed."

"Well, since you ask. I was surprised to see you in another man's arms with not even a feather's width between you. Do you know how embarrassed I was?"

"What do you mean 'embarrassed'?"

"If you looked around while you were dancing, you

would have seen everyone looking at you. I'm not willing to share you with Quinn or any other man. We're married and your life is different now."

Elizabeth looked at Billy for a moment then broke into tears. "I'm sorry if I hurt your feelings. You're right. You're my husband now. I love you, Billy." Elizabeth hugged his arm which he slid around her waist to hold her close.

"Everything's all right, Elizabeth. We have the rest of our lives ahead of us. As long as we love each other, we'll be fine."

****

Reaching the turnoff in the road, both wagons stopped and everyone got out while Steven gave each Hewitt family member a hug and a kiss before heading toward Billy.

"I know you plan to go to Marysville next month to buy horses," Billy said to Mark. "How about if I bring Elizabeth and Steven to the house the second Monday in August and you and I ride there together? I'll help you get them home, and Elizabeth and Steven can stay at the house while we're gone."

"Is that all right with you, Jack?" Mark put his arm around Jack's shoulders.

"Sure. You'll only be gone four or five days. I'll have plenty to do tanning my hides, and I can look out for the family." Jack lifted Steven and set him on his hip. "You can stay and help me take care of the family. We'll set the rabbit snare and maybe we'll have rabbit stew for supper one night."

"I'll help." Steven grinned.

"Good, then its settled. I'll see you the second Monday in August." Billy shook Mark's hand and took

Steven from Jack. "Come on, Elizabeth, time to get home."

Back in the wagon, Steven talked about everything he saw in town, the shooting contest, the picnic, what he did with Elizabeth's parents, and finally settled down to sing softly when Elizabeth covered him with a blanket.

Chapter Eight

Seth, Emily, and their son Ethan, arrived right on time to pick up their supplies.

Mark greeted Seth with a hearty handshake. "Let's go inside." Mark handed Seth the pouch he took to town. "I hope you're pleased with how much the gold fetched."

Opening the pouch, Seth counted the money. "Holy scuds. I wasn't expecting this much! There's enough to buy a new workhorse, chickens, fabric for Emily to make a new dress, and still have money for seed next year. If you're going to the Harvest Festival, would you be willing to pick up a few items for us? On second thought, maybe Emily will want to go. We haven't been to town since she arrived."

"Even if the whole family doesn't go, Jack or I must order seed. We'd be glad to pick up supplies and order your seed. You talk with Emily and let me know your pleasure," Mark said.

Emily greeted Sarah by leaning in and taking her arm. "You must tell me all about Billy's wedding. We have a lot of catching up to do."

While the children went out behind the barn to play with the cats, the ladies walked to the house where Sarah's delicious muffins were baking and hot tea and coffee awaited their arrival.

"Look, sweetheart." Seth jingled the pouch of coins

and tossed the pouch to Emily. "It's more than we expected. We have enough for everything we talked about and will still have money left over. My being away on those trips paid off."

"Oh, Seth, I'm so proud of you! I knew the Lord would take care of us one way or the other." Emily wiped away a tear of relief.

"Billy and I are riding to Marysville in a few weeks to buy horses. Seth, would you like to come along?" Mark offered.

"Emily and Ethan are welcome to stay with us," Sarah added.

Seth stepped back. "Would it be too much to ask for you to pick out a horse for us?"

"No, not at all. I'd be glad to do that for you." Mark motioned Seth to go outside so they could talk and leave the ladies to their own conversation.

"Now, tell me everything, Sarah. Start with the wedding and don't leave out any details." Emily sat and Sarah poured them mugs of tea before sharing all the news.

As the women chatted about everything that happened since they last were together, they shucked peas and snapped beans for dinner. Before long, they called everyone to the table.

Mark, Seth, and Jack took their plates and drinks outside to eat, making space at the table for the others.

Jack asked, "Did Mark tell you he won the Best Shot contest? He gave me the gun until I can win my own."

"He didn't mention a new gun. You must show it to me. I didn't know you were such a good shot, Mark." Seth raised his glass to take a drink.

"I can hit the target when it counts. I wanted Jack to have a nice rifle in case I must leave with Billy and fight for the Union. We've never discussed it before, Seth. Where do you stand on this great rebellion between the states?" Mark asked. "I know we don't talk much about it, but what will you do if the draft hits Kansas or you're called up for the militia?"

"I'll go of course, but I'm not sure what good I'll be. I don't think I can kill another person, but there are things I could do to help our country other than fight. I'd hate to leave Emily and Ethan. Even though we live alone, far away from town, we still get our share of passers-by and you never know who's friendly or not." Seth took a bite of chicken.

"I know what you mean. People are still traveling west, some to escape the war, others to loot the families whose husbands and sons are off fighting. If we must go, I'm sure Sarah would be happy if Emily and Ethan stayed with our family."

"I agree, Father," Jack added.

"If the time comes, Seth, you're welcome to join Billy and me when we go to Fort Riley. Jack will do the best he can to keep the farm running and take care of the family. He's pretty good with a gun, and I taught Sarah and Lydia to shoot too. Do you have an extra gun for Emily?"

"I have a fifty caliber muzzle loader and a pistol. She can handle the pistol at close range, but is afraid to shoot the other. I'll need powder and lead balls your next trip to town. I sure do appreciate you getting supplies for us. I spoke to Emily, and she prefers to stay home. Before we leave, I'll give you a list."

"We're happy to help you, Seth," Mark said,

shoveling the last bit of chicken and biscuits into his mouth.

****

"Come on," Jack said. "I'll show you my new gun, and I've got something I'm working on in the barn for you to see," Jack said, eager to show Seth.

"What's with all the cowhides, Jack?" Seth asked, and Ethan wrinkled his nose.

Jack responded, "I'm thinking of going into business tanning my own leather and making things. My pa and I did some leatherwork as a hobby, and I'm pretty good. I finished the belt my father started and gave it to Mark and discovered I really enjoy working with leather. I'll make belts and holsters then sell 'em in town. Fancy leather tooled belt and holster sets sell anywhere from ten to twenty dollars at the Dry Goods Store. Some cost even more. I checked out what the men were wearing in town at the shooting contest and I know I can make them as good. Even better! Come next spring, I hope to have belts and holsters ready for sale. If my work is good, I can make a name for myself."

"Well, I wish you luck," Seth said.

****

The following morning, Mark shook Seth's hand and helped him pack the wagon for their trip home. "You can come for the horse anytime, or you can get the horse when you come for your supplies when we get back from the Harvest Festival, if that's all right?"

"That sounds good. Again, our sincere thanks," Seth said as he handed his supply list and money to Mark.

From the back of the wagon, Ethan blew a kiss to Johanna who sent one back.

"So good seeing you all again!" Emily waved, as the Frazer family headed home.

Chapter Nine

Elizabeth bent over and sweated while working in the garden. She hoped the plants would grow despite her meager efforts. It got her outside and away from Steven, except when he insisted on helping. He had helped his ma weed the family garden and knew which weeds to pull. By the time the family would visit the Hewitts in August she'd have vegetables to put up. She'd take everything along and ask Sarah to teach her, so she wouldn't have to do all the work herself.

Elizabeth didn't enjoy living on the farm after having the convenience of town life, but she made an effort. Knowing that if she didn't make bread every week, they wouldn't have any, gave her conflicting feelings of pride and impatience. She never made bread while growing up. Using her mother's recipe, many sodden or hard loaves emerged from the wood-fired cook stove before continuity was established. If she didn't keep the fire going, the house got cold at night. She didn't like braving scratches on her arms and sunburned cheeks while picking berries to make cobbler and pies. Ah, pie crust! That was a feat in and of itself. She tried different recipes Sarah had copied for her. Although not everything was edible the first attempt, she persevered, always wishing for the comfort of the life she lived before. She gave up trying to impress Billy in the kitchen. Then, on top of everything,

Billy wanted to teach her how to milk the cow. Elizabeth wasn't sure this was a talent she wished to master.

****

The second Monday in August everyone helped pack the wagon with vegetables for their trip to the Hewitts'. Billy had Peter, the neighbor boy, tend to the animals while they were gone. Anyone seeing activity would think twice about looting or squatting.

The entire Hewitt family greeted them in the front yard upon their arrival. Billy helped Steven jump from the wagon. When his feet hit the ground he ran straight into Lydia's waiting arms. He couldn't wait to see everyone again and play with Johanna and the cats. "We brought lots of vegetables," he shouted.

"My, your garden has done well." Sarah wrapped her arm around Elizabeth's shoulders and gave her a hug. "We better get some of this canned tonight while the men are still here to help. Everyone grab a basket. Remember, many hands make light work."

While walking to the house, Mark said, "We'll leave in the morning for Marysville, Billy, and should be back in five days. I'm looking for good breeding stock, and four or five horses should give us a good start on building a herd. And Seth wants us to bring him back a strong workhorse for plowing."

Once the vegetables were in the house, the three men headed to the barn. Cowhides hung from the rafters.

"After they're dry," Jack explained, "I can start laying out the patterns Lydia helped me create to make leather goods. The thickest lengths will make belts, and the leftover pieces pouches and possible bags, and maybe even gloves."

"I'll order a belt and a pair of gloves," Billy said.

"Great, my first order." Jack grinned and slapped Billy on the back.

From the barn, the men walked to the corral and looked at the horses.

"I want to find a smaller horse for Steven in Marysville," Billy said. "He's old enough to handle his own horse. He loves to ride, and I promised him a horse one day. Having his own would mean a lot." Billy fell quiet for a moment recalling when he first made this promise sitting on the floor of the Fillmore's house when he met his brother for the first time.

"We sure miss you around here, Billy." Jack broke the silence. "Ma and the girls miss you and Steven something awful."

"I miss all of you too, but life with Elizabeth and Steven keeps me busy. It's different when you have a family relying on you. Steven tries, but he can't help with everything yet and is in the way more often than not."

"Give him a few years. He'll grow into a fine helper," Mark encouraged.

A young voice yelled from the house door. "Ma says it's time to eat." Steven ran out to meet the men who had started back to the house. "Momma fixed my favorite beef stew with vegetables from the garden. Come on! I'm hungry." Steven took Billy's hand and tugged to hurry him along.

After supper and the excitement of helping with the canning, Steven was all tuckered out. He climbed the ladder and crawled into Jack's bed like old times while the adults talked.

****

Billy and Mark headed out early and arrived in Marysville two days later. To Billy, the stagecoach incident that killed his pa and changed his life forever was a Marysville memory that he'd rather forget. Although the incident happened more than five years ago, as he walked past the sheriff's office toward the corral, the horrifying images of his father being pulled from the stage and lying on the ground flooded his thoughts. He remembered taking his father's watch and money clip out of his pocket and sliding it into his own pocket. He remembered the funeral like it happened yesterday.

Billy tried to push the incident out of his mind and wondered if he'd see Sheriff Kurtz. He knew he would never forgive the sheriff for giving him to Rusty.

At the horse corral, Billy spied a young gray and asked, "What do you think about me buying the one by the left fence for Steven?"

"He'll do fine, but I'd pick out a second and leave room to bargain."

Billy and Mark looked at the horses in two corrals and decided on those they thought were suitable, including a workhorse for Seth. Billy listened closely as Mark haggled over prices. When Billy got his turn, he used some of Mark strategies and arrived at a fair price on the gray for Steven.

Pleased with their dealings, the men strung the horses together and left them at the stable where they arranged for feed and water, and Billy bought a small, used saddle for Steven. Then the men walked to the local hotel for a hearty meal.

Taking a sip of coffee, Mark asked, "Would you

like to go to the cemetery and see your father's grave?"

"No. I'm not much on visiting the dead. When I was in Kansas, I didn't go to my mother's resting place. It's too painful."

"Well, we pass the cemetery on the way out of town if you change your mind." Mark dropped the conversation then said, "By the way, congratulations. You made a good deal on Steven's horse. He sure will be surprised."

Returning to the stables, the men walked past the sheriff's office again. Billy slowed and looked in the window.

"I sure would like to give the sheriff a piece of my mind, giving me to Rusty like he did. He should have sent me back to Kansas City when Poppa died." Billy's voice trailed off.

"I believe everything happens for a reason, son," Mark said. "If you'd gone back, we wouldn't have met. I can't imagine you not being in my life. You'd never have met Elizabeth either."

"Yeah, I guess you're right. And maybe I should stop and see my poppa's grave. I'll let him know I don't blame him anymore for leaving town the way we did, now that I know the truth about Momma and my brother who I thought died with Momma when he was born. I'd sure like him to know Steven and I are together now and that we're doing fine."

Billy led a string of three horses and Mark the same as they headed out of town. Riding down Main Street, Billy stiffened in his saddle when he caught sight of the sheriff talking to a man in front of the saloon. He pulled back on the reins then thought better. *Mark is right. The past is in the past and doesn't matter now.* Reaching the town cemetery, the men tied the horses to the gate and Billy walked to his poppa's grave alone. He walked to the exact spot where he lay buried beside a small tree, near the back fence.

Standing in front of the tombstone, Billy took off his hat, stood tall, and gazed down to read—*Jacob Henry, Died March 24, 1858.*

Everything happened so quickly after mother died. I didn't really know the exact date of your birth and couldn't remember what year you were born, so we only wrote the date you died. He committed the date to memory then started talking aloud to his poppa starting with, "I miss you, Poppa."

After reminiscing about memories of his life in Kansas with his parents, he got to the point. "I know you did what you thought was best, not telling me the truth about Momma and Steven. Don't worry about us. I'm married to a swell gal. Steven is safe and lives with us, but you probably already know all of this. I'm sure you're with Momma now. I'll raise Steven. He is a good boy. He behaves and is respectful. Momma can be proud of him. We have most of the things from the house in Kansas City in our new home. I own a farm now and everything I have is because of the money you left in the bank. I'm being smart about our spending and still have over half of your money saved. There's some in a bank and some at the farm for safekeeping.

"You and Momma would both like my new family. After you died, Mark got me out of a bad situation. Now I have a mother and father, two sisters, and two brothers, including Steven. I love them very much. Steven was well cared for when I finally found him. Mr. and Mrs. Weston helped me with all the arrangements to have Steven come to the farm with me.

"The woman that owns our old house is nice, but the house wasn't the same. I got to see Lilian Ross again. Her mother was the one who told me about Steven. I'm sure you know all this if you're watching out for me, and I believe you are.

"Well, I better go now. When I get back this way I'll stop again. Tell Momma I love and miss her. Heck you're probably standing together with your arm around her shoulders looking down on me right now."

He turned and walked back to Mark. "Thanks for waiting for me, Mark. I guess I did have things to say after all."

"That's all right, Billy. I'm glad we stopped too. Now we need to keep moving. We have a long ride ahead of us."

****

Mark had seen the sheriff on the street also and prayed Billy wouldn't stop. Billy wasn't the only one who'd had dealings with the sheriff. He could identify Mark as the man who collected the reward money for killing the two men who attempted robbery when really it was Sarah's first husband, Samuel, who saved Billy and the stagecoach driver that frightful day. Samuel was the real hero.

I'm relieved that Sarah knows the truth, now I worry what Billy would think of me if he ever learns the whole story that took place the day his father died. I pray Billy never finds out. If he learns the truth, everything I worked so hard to build with him: the trust, friendship, and the family Billy loves could be at risk.

****

Steven and Jack saw in the distance the puffs of

dust kicked up from the horses' hooves coming their way. They fetched water and were waiting in the barn when Mark and Billy arrived.

"One, two, three, four, five, six...six horses." Steven counted as he inspected each horse.

"Yeah, I thought we might afford three or four. You must have done some good haggling." Jack started untying the horses.

"These aren't all ours, Jack. Remember we picked up one for Seth, and Billy bought one of these horses." Mark ran his hands down the neck of the little gray.

Steven's eyes grew wide. "Which one is ours, Billy?"

Billy handed Steven the lead rope for the little gray and said, "This one's for you, Steven. Your own horse."

"Really? You mean it? It's all mine?" Steven was already hugging the horse's neck and petting the velvety nose.

"Yup, he's all yours." Billy grinned. The joy on Steven's face made spending the money worth every penny.

"Can I show everyone?"

"Sure, I'll run to the house and fetch them," Jack offered.

"Don't tell them what I got," Steven shouted after him.

"Don't worry, I won't," Jack yelled back.

Steven led the horse out of the barn and paraded her past the family. "Billy got him for me, and he's all mine." A smile from ear to ear covered his face.

"What are you going to name him?" Lydia asked.

"I don't know yet, but it'll be a good name. I get to take care of him and everything." Steven's smile was contagious.

Sarah said, "Congratulations! Now you can ride by yourself, but promise me one thing."

"I promise, Momma. What is it I need to promise?"

"Promise you'll be careful and take good care of your horse. Feed and water him every day and never put him away wet. Brush him as often as you can and no going fast until Billy says you're ready." Sarah put her hand on Steven's shoulder.

"I promise, Ma." Steven patted the horse's neck.

Billy placed Steven on the horses back. "How's that feel? We'll start out slow and when you're used to the saddle we'll take rides together. I got you a saddle too."

Jack and Mark took the other horses to the corral and as they were returning Lydia called, "Time for supper."

Stepping in the door, the smell of Lydia's fried chicken warmed everyone's hearts. The family was together again.

****

Packing the wagon to leave the following morning, Elizabeth said, as she handed a basket of canned goods to Billy, "Thanks for the help with the canning, Sarah. I'm not sure I can put up the rest of the garden myself, but I'll try with the help from the two men in my life. I'll let you know how we did when we see you at the Harvest Festival in September."

Mark spoke up. "I'm not sure yet if the whole family will come. It will probably be only Jack or myself. I'm sure we'll need a few items to tide us until winter. Regardless, whoever comes will check in at the Parkers' house to see you."

With the little gray tied to the back of the wagon, everyone said their good-byes and the Henry family headed back to their farm. With Steven chattering about his new horse and trying to figure out a name, Elizabeth explaining the canning process, and Billy telling about stopping to see his father's tombstone, the three-hour ride passed quickly.

Chapter Ten

Elizabeth reluctantly canned vegetables from the garden's bounty, and dried peas, beans, herbs, and mint for winter meals. She had an increasingly difficult time thinking about the isolation of being on the farm and not seeing anyone during those long, cold winter months ahead. *Maybe this time will allow us to start a family. I so want a baby of my own to spoil and show off in town. I expected I'd be in the family way by now. It's not because we aren't trying. Hopefully, by Christmas.*

Elizabeth still had much to learn. She no longer could walk to town when she needed things. Before, she never thought to use a knife instead of scissors to cut the herb stems. While making preserves one day, she didn't have a strainer and decided she would need to buy one, never thinking she could strain through cloth to get out the impurities as she had seen Lydia do. Elizabeth had a long way to go before she could handle living self-sufficiently. Sure, she had settled into a weekly routine of chores, but it seemed life was always work and not what she craved. There were no dances, social activities, or get-togethers with friends. She was bored. Where was the romance?

While at the Hewitts', Elizabeth learned Sarah baked for the entire week on Monday. Tuesday was butter churning along with sewing and mending.

Saturday and Wednesday, lamps were filled and wicks trimmed for both the house and barn. Thursday or Friday, depending on the weather, wash was gathered, scrubbed, and hung to dry, a long process that needed vast amounts of hot water. Add to that housework, caring for the garden, making soap, cheese, and butchering. All this, plus preparing three meals daily for the family. *Mark said they would butcher a cow for meat this winter during the last week in October and we should come. I'm not sure I want to learn, but I guess I don't have a choice.*

****

One evening, after Elizabeth and Steven were in bed, Billy heard a faint tapping. He grabbed his rifle and put the gun by the door, looked out the window and didn't see anyone. Then the tapping began again.

Billy opened the door to two young, barefoot, black boys wearing torn shirts and pants whom he guessed were brothers, about ten and twelve years old. Billy stepped outside and asked, "Where'd you come from?"

The oldest boy looked at Billy and said, "The sheriff brought us to the turn off road. Said you'd help us."

"Where are your parents?"

"They're coming, we hope. We haven't seen them in a couple days," the taller boy said.

"We got away first." The younger boy wiped a tear from his check.

"Go to the lean-to." Billy pointed to where the wagon was stored. "And I'll fetch you food and a blanket for the night."

The boys dashed to the shelter and Billy returned

with bread, a jug of milk, and a blanket. "You'll be safe here tonight, and tomorrow I'll take you in my wagon to the creek that you'll follow to the next farm. I'll bring food in the morning. You can sleep in the wagon but be sure to stay out of sight. Get some rest and don't leave this shelter."

Both boys nodded. "Thanks for the food, mister," the oldest boy said.

Before he was married, Billy had sheltered slaves a few times but this was the first since he'd married that the sheriff sent anyone his way. He knew Elizabeth wouldn't understand from comments she had made earlier about slavery. He recalled her saying, "They should stay where they're at until after the fighting." *I better wait for the right time to discuss this topic, but it better be soon, before the sheriff sends others our way.*

Steven had been with Billy the first time a black family stayed the night. Steven knew he wasn't to mention the fugitives to anyone and Billy trusted him not to mention the two boys to Elizabeth.

The next day, Billy announced, "If it's all right with you, I'm going to the neighbor's farm this morning and be neighborly. I'll be back in a few hours. I can take Steven along, if you'd like, Elizabeth."

"That would be lovely. It'll give me time to get things done plus have some quiet time to myself." Elizabeth smiled as she dried the last dish from the morning meal.

"Remember to keep the gun close. We'll return as soon as we can. Come on, Steven, I'll get food ready to take along, and we'll be on our way." Billy sliced bread and added butter and jelly to six slices. He grabbed carrots and beans and got a jar of peaches from the shelf before heading out the door.

Billy put the food and a jug of milk in the back of the wagon along with two crates, a couple of buckets, fishing poles, and some feed sacks. "Help me hitch the horses, Steven, and we'll be on our way."

About a mile down the road, out of sight of the farmhouse, Billy stopped the wagon and turned to Steven. "Remember when we had a family stop by who needed our help a few months back?" Billy asked.

"I remember," Steven said.

"Well, we have two boys who need our help and they're in the back of the wagon right now. Remember, we can't tell anyone that we helped them. Nobody can know but you and me. We can't even tell Elizabeth. We're taking them to the creek so they can find their way west.

"Their father or mother are coming to find them, but they had to leave when they could get free. They're coming west from Missouri for a chance to grow up without having to take orders from white people that treat them poorly. They can start a farm of their own one day and be free to work their own land."

"I won't tell anyone, Billy, I promise." Steven made a crisscross over his heart.

Billy opened the flap to the back and discovered the boys sitting on the crates eating some jelly bread. "You better save the rest for later. I wasn't able to grab much food, but it should be enough to get you to the next farm."

The boys nodded their heads in understanding.

"The creek where I'm taking you flows past a farm about a half-day's walk from here. That will be your next stop," Billy explained. "They are good people and will help you. Wait until dark to knock on the door. If you get there earlier, hide in the barn and stay out of sight.

"If your ma or pa comes here first, I'll let them know where you are so they can find you. Are you all right?"

The boys silently nodded.

"Sleep now while you can. I'll wake you when we get to the creek. You'll want to travel at night and find a hiding place to sleep during the day."

The boys nodded again and laid down to rest.

The creek was a good hour away. Billy and Steven talked most of the way, then about ten minutes from the water, Billy heard riders approaching from behind.

Steven, firmly holding on to the edge of the wagon seat turned around, looked, and said, "Four men are coming!"

"Quick," Billy said, "get in the back and keep them from opening the back flap. Boys, hide behind the crates and buckets and don't make a sound."

Billy kept the horses at a steady pace and waited for the men to catch up, slowing as the men flanked the wagon.

A man wearing a fancy six-shooter shouted, "Where you goin' and what ya got in the back?"

"There's a creek down the road a few minutes ride from here. We thought we'd drop a line and surprise the wife with some fresh fish if they're biting."

"Who's we?" the six-shooter asked.

"My little brother and me. He's in the back sleeping."

"I was sleeping," Steven shouted so he could be heard.

One of the four rode to the back of the wagon and was about to grab the flap to look in when Steven's head poked through the hole where the two flaps were gathered. "Hi, I'm Steven," the little boy said.

"How old are you, son?" a man with a big belly asked.

Steven stuck his whole arm out the hole with five fingers spread. Then he drew it back and poked his head out again to shout, "I'm five. You want to play a game with me?" His head ducked inside for a split second and then popped back out.

"No. That's all right," the man said and returned to the front of the wagon.

"Have you seen anyone along this road?" another man with a gruff voice asked Billy.

"Nobody at all," Billy replied, shaking his head slightly.

"We're looking for a black family. They snuck away two weeks ago. We got one of them, but there's three on the loose and we aim to fetch them back for the reward," a man with a beard and felt-brimmed hat explained.

"I'll keep my eyes open, but I haven't seen any blacks in these parts and hope I never do," Billy said taking off his hat and putting it on the wagon seat. "I don't go looking for trouble."

"Well, they're around these parts somewhere. Where's this road go?" asked the bearded man.

"It takes you about an hour west then dead ends at another creek. Not many folks live in these parts. It's too far from town. We're just here to fish." Billy wasn't sure if they believed him. "Well, we got to get going if we're gonna catch anything and get home before the midday meal."

Apparently satisfied, the four men rode off down the road.

Billy lifted the reins to nudge the horses forward. At the creek, Billy dropped a line into the water before checking to make sure the men had ridden on. The boys climbed out of the back of the wagon. Billy put food in a feed sack and tied another around the waist of the younger boy. He asked, "Do you remember what I told you?"

The boys nodded. The older glanced down, then gazed directly into Billy's eyes and said, "Thank you for not letting those men take us. We heard they got one of our parents, but they didn't say which."

Steven jumped to the ground to stand by Billy. "We don't have our ma or pa with us either. They both died, but we have each other. And you have each other."

The boys looked at one another then at Steven and Billy. "How long until we get to the farm?" one boy asked.

"Travel when the sun goes down and you should be there late tonight. Hide out and make sure nobody follows you. Remember to keep this creek in sight." Billy shook the boys' hands and said, "Good luck."

The boys, keeping low to the ground, hurried to the creek and were soon out of sight.

"You did real good back there, Steven, not letting them open the flap to look in the back. Those men wanted the boys and you helped save their lives. You may have saved all our lives."

Steven smiled at his brother and retrieved the fishing pole. "There's no bait on the hook, Billy. You can't catch a fish with no bait."

"We don't have time to fish today. I hate leaving Elizabeth by herself for this long. Those men may have stopped at the house. We better get back."

"But what if those men come back and we don't have any fish."

Billy smiled and patted his little brother's shoulder. "I guess you're right. Let's find some bait."

The fish were biting and the brothers caught four fish before returning to the farm.

"Any visitors while we were gone?" Billy asked stepping through the door.

"No visitors. Why do you ask?" Elizabeth replied.

"We passed four men on the road." Billy hung his coat on a hook.

"Look what we caught for supper!" Steven walked in holding a string of fish.

Chapter Eleven

The two barefoot boys did as Billy said and traveled upstream a few miles before hiding in a thick hedge of briers. Not long after, they heard horses' hooves pound the dry earth in the distance. As they got closer, the boys could hear men talking. Immobilized by fear, the brothers huddled in place until dark.

They traveled by the dim light of a waning moon, taking their time, and trying to slip soundlessly down the side of the path. The boys finally arrived at the Hewitt's, the farm Billy told them about. They waited hidden behind the well, until the house grew quiet before the taller boy tapped on the door.

Mark set his rifle nearby before opening the door.

The boy stepped from around the corner of the house and in a whispered voice said, "Will you help us, mister?"

"Do you think you were followed?" Mark asked in a hushed tone.

"Nope. My brother and I was careful."

Mark couldn't help but see their bare feet, torn clothes, and tear-streaked faces and said, "You're safe here. Come with me."

The boys almost stepped on Mark's heels as they followed him around the house to the root cellar. Once inside, Mark said, "I'll fetch you leftovers from supper and a blanket. You wait here."

Mark returned and the boys told him how they got there. The oldest said, "Can we wait here a couple days so our ma or pa can find us? One of 'em just gotta come."

Two days was Mark's limit. He didn't like putting his own family in harm's way. Knowing from experience that bounty hunters were always around tracking runaways and had not yet come to his farm concerned him. "Let's see what happens by tomorrow night, then I'll make my decision." Mark had sympathy for the children, but also needed to keep his family safe. "When you finish eating get some rest. I'll bring food in the morning. Remember, I will always tap on the door so you'll know it's me."

Mark told Sarah the next morning, "We had two late-night arrivals." Sarah made corn bread muffins and a large pan of fried potatoes, eggs, and sausage.

While Jack, Lydia, and Johanna were doing their chores, Mark took the food and a jug of milk to the boys and collected the plates from last night. "If you hear loud voices, hide under the bottom shelf behind the crocks and pumpkins. You're small, and they won't see you, but please be quiet. After dark tonight, I'll fetch you more food. Don't worry, if one of your parents comes, I'll bring them right away." Then Mark reached into his pocket and handed the boys each a piece of rock candy. "I know you're scared, but you're also brave to have come all this way by yourselves."

"Thank you, mister," the boys said in unison.

Mark went about his day until late afternoon, when four men quietly rode in, one from each point of the compass. Mark and Jack were in the barn when Jack caught a glimpse of one of them riding past the door of the barn and immediately alerted his father. When Mark and Jack walked outside the men gathered at the well and dismounted.

Each man had pistols around their waists and rifles attached to their saddle holsters. The man with the fancy six-shooter spoke first. "We're looking for slaves, and if you're lettin' 'em stay here it won't bode well for ya."

"How many got away this time?" Mark asked with a straight face, trying to conceal his concern for the boys in the root cellar.

"Four, but we caught the woman. We need the others, two kids and the father. You see any runaways around these parts lately?"

"No. Heard tell they head north to Nebraska when they get this far west. The farther north, the more refuge they get. We don't get many visitors this far from town."

"You wouldn't mind if we check out your barn if you've nothing to hide, would you?"

"No, go ahead." Mark made a sweeping motion with his arm and let them go first.

"Hey, any of you men ever tan your own hides?" Jack asked. "I'm only learning and I'd be glad to try new ways."

The gruff-voiced man said, "Yah, I done some. Let's see 'em, boy."

As Jack and the man talked, the other men checked out the barn and the loft. Satisfied, they walked outside.

"You wouldn't be hiding something in the house from us now would ya?" the bearded man said.

"Or someone." The man with the six-shooter drew his gun.

Mark walked toward the two men. "No need for a gun. You can go in if you'd like, but I'm asking that you leave your gun belts outside. I don't want my wife and daughters afraid of you. Would you like a cup of coffee? I think there's still some in the pot."

"That's mighty neighborly of you. I'd take a cup," the older bearded man with the felt hat said.

The man with the six-shooter started to say something, and the bearded man said, "Take off your gun belt." The men put their guns on the ground. "Remember, if we don't come out in one piece, my men have your son. They'll kill him if they hear a shot or even loud voices."

The two men in the yard drew their pistols and pointed them at Jack.

"I'll take a cup of that coffee now," the bearded man who seemed like the leader said.

"I'll ask my wife if there's any left." Mark started toward the house.

Inside, Mark said, "Sarah, these men are passing by and I told them there might still be hot coffee in the pot."

"Well, they're in luck." Taking two cups from the cupboard she divided the remains.

"You keep a clean house, ma'am. We're going to take a look around," said the bearded man.

"It's all right, sweetheart. They're looking for runaways. When they don't find any, they'll be on their way." Mark gave her a nod of approval.

Lydia and Johanna were sitting at the kitchen table working on printing Johanna's name, when the men barged in. When they heard what their father said, the girls immediately ran to their mother's side.

The young man climbed the loft ladder. When his head cleared the last step the man could see under the beds and with one more step he saw nobody in the loft. He slid down holding one side of the rail.

The bearded man opened the bedroom door and looked around. Nobody there, the man gulped the coffee and handed Sarah his cup. The young man did the same. "That was good coffee, ma'am," the older man said.

Both men walked out of the house with Mark stepping out and closing the door behind him.

Seeing everything was all right, the two men outside holstered the pistols they had drawn on Jack.

"When I rode in, I saw a root cellar out back," the man with the six-shooter said. He buckled his gun belt around his waist and headed for the back of the house.

"I'll go with you," Jack said. "Ma asked me to fetch her a couple jars of peaches. I sure don't want to forget if it means peach pie for dessert." As they rounded the corner of the house, Jack asked, "You from around these parts?"

"No, Missouri and parts east," the man said stepping back for Jack to walk past.

"I've never been to Missouri. What's it like?" Jack asked as he opened the door, stepped in, and reached for the peaches on the middle shelf.

"Not as flat as Kansas and there's a lot more people," the man said, stepping in and glancing around. Seeing nothing out of the ordinary, he stepped out.

Jack turned around and stood there momentarily before pulling the door shut behind him.

Jack and the man with the six-shooter walked back to where the other men were, watering the horses at the well.

"Fellas, I think I've been hospitable. Now, my son and I have work to do." Mark put his arm around Jack's shoulders.

The men mounted their horses and rode off with the man with the fancy six-shooter leading the way.

****

Mark debated. *Should I even try to get to the root cellar this evening? Maybe the men are still watching. Did they suspect anything?* He went to bed as usual and waited until after midnight to take the boys food. *It's been a long and trying day for the youngsters, and I'm sure they're hungry.*

Around midnight, Mark made his way to the root cellar. He tapped lightly so the boys would know he was at the door, and stepped inside. The boys crawled out of their hiding places where they had been since they heard the men talking earlier. They eagerly drank from the jug of milk and attacked the hearty food Mark brought.

"Everything's all right. I waited to make sure the men weren't watching the house."

"Was there four of them?" the older boy asked.

"Yes, four. They don't know it's only the two of you. They think your pa is with you which works in your favor. I'm sorry to tell you this, but they said they caught your ma and took her back."

The boys stopped eating, tears flowed down their cheeks, they embraced each other, and when they finally let go again, wide eyes gazed at Mark. "What about Pa? If they didn't catch him, he must still be out there. What if he can't find us?"

"Your pa will find you boys. I'm sure he's looking

for you right now. You better stay a couple nights to make sure the bounty hunters have moved on. That'll give your poppa a chance to get here. I'll fetch more food in the morning. If you must go out, only do it at night. Go now and I'll wait for you to return."

With both boys safely back in the root cellar, Mark returned to the house. Lying beside Sarah in the quiet of the night, he couldn't sleep. *This is the first time anyone looked for slaves while they were hidden on the farm. If it had been more than two young children hidden there, the family would have been caught. There isn't enough space to hide a family.* He had to rethink how to hide an entire family and find another safe location to hide at least two people. *I pray the father who is still free gets here soon. Those boys are scared and rightfully so.*

****

Sarah fixed a day's worth of food, and Mark took it to them in a flour sack, knocked, and left the food outside the door.

The second night Mark heard a faint knock. He grabbed his gun and held it to the side as he opened the door.

"Are my two young'uns here?" a deep male voice asked.

"Yes, 'round back in the root cellar." Mark heard movement. "Wait," Mark said. "You must be hungry. I have stew for you. The boys have already eaten." Mark ladled stew warming on the stove into a bowl and handed it to the man waiting in the shadows.

This man was also bare footed, his arms and legs scratched and scraped. He had a knife in a sheath, tied to his waist.

"Are you all right?" Mark asked.

"I'm good. I want to see my boys," the man answered

"I'll fetch food and bandages for you in the morning. You should rest tomorrow and leave at nightfall." Mark handed the man some bread. "Four men were here two days ago. They should be long gone now. I'll bring food at dawn, enough to hold you a couple of days. That's the best I can do."

"Thank you for keeping my boys safe," said the man, and hurried around the corner of the house.

****

The hinges squeaked as the root cellar door opened. The farmer always tapped first, so the boys stayed in their hiding places behind the big pickling crocks. When they heard their father's voice whisper, "Boys, you all right?" They rushed to embrace him.

"Pa, you made it," the younger boy said between sobs.

"Where's Ma" the oldest asked.

"She fell and hurt her leg. We think it broke 'cause she couldn't walk. I carried her for a time, but men were gaining on us. She made me leave her so I could catch up to care for you. She promised to find us when the fighting stops. Are you boys all right?"

"Yes," both boys whispered, as tears for their mother's sure capture made paths down their cheeks.

"We'll tell you all about our travels later. We was so worried you wouldn't find us. You should eat, Pa," the oldest boy said.

The boys made room for their father to sit between them.

"The farmer said he'd fetch food at dawn. We'll leave, but not until tomorrow night. I could use the rest.

I can't tell you how pleased I am to see you. We're safe here."

****

As promised, Mark packed a sack of food including a jar of peaches he knew the brave family would enjoy. At dawn, he tapped on the door and offered the sack, then walked to the barn to do chores like any other ordinary day at the farm.

He had helped another family reunite. The thought warmed his heart. He wasn't sure he could have let the boys leave on their own. If caught, it would have been a death sentence. Mark said a prayer for the hunted folks and wished them Godspeed.

The experience with the headhunters at his door filled Mark with apprehension. Had they been caught, his family could have been hurt, or worse killed by those men. When they held Jack at gunpoint to get in the house, fear hit home. A new plan must be created. They no longer could place an entire family in the root cellar together. He'd have to find another safe hiding place and separate the family to keep his family safe as well.

Chapter Twelve

In early September, while doing chores in the barn, Jack asked Mark, "Will the family go to the Harvest Festival this year?"

"Somebody needs to stay here in case anyone like those four bounty hunters come 'round again. I don't feel right leaving your ma and sisters home alone." Mark pitched hay into the milk cow's stall.

"I'll flip you for it," Jack said.

"Do you think you could handle the team of horses, get the supplies, and drop off the seed orders by yourself? You've never been to town alone before, son."

"Maybe it's time. I want to ask Billy's friend the blacksmith if he can forge some tools for my leatherwork, and I need more cowhides to tan. My next project is making belts and holsters." Jack drew a pretend pistol from his side. "If I learn to make them and my name gets around, I can make money. I can start a business. At least, that's my goal. Lydia said she'd make me a leather vest too."

Mark took a coin out of his pocket, flipped it into the air, and caught it. "That's a mighty large task. Are you sure you're ready?"

"I know, but I'll have the time this winter, and I might as well spend the time doing something I like. I'll never know if I don't try."

Mark flipped the coin high in the air again. "Do you have enough money for hides and salt?"

"I have five dollars, but I could always use more. Do you want to invest in my business? I'd be thankful. I'll pay you back when I make my first sales." Jack grinned as he patted his father's shoulder.

"I guess I could invest a few dollars. Would five dollars give you enough to buy all your supplies?" Mark slid the coin in his pocket.

"Five dollars would be great! And I'll give you back what I don't spend."

"All right, son, you can go to town this time, but promise me you'll be careful and return safely. I'll let your ma know I said you could go. But promise no fighting, no talking to strangers, and straight home the following day. You know she'll worry until you return."

"I promise, Pa, and I won't get in any trouble. I'll make sure to stop by the Parkers' and see my brothers and Elizabeth too."

"Don't push the horses too hard and remember to drop off the seed orders at the Hardware Store, mail Ma's letters, and oh, pick up a newspaper for me." Mark handed him some coins.

"I'll even bring home candy for Lydia and Johanna." Jack grinned.

****

Jack packed the wagon with crates and feed sacks so he could carry home the hides and heads he wanted from town. He also packed the letters he wrote to Abby Proctor who he hoped to dance with and talk to Saturday evening. Sarah gave him her letters to mail east, packed food for his trip, and a yellow cake with chocolate icing to put on the table as a contribution to the harvest picnic so he could join in.

Arriving in town, he headed to the Parker residence to see if Billy was there. Cain Gibbs the blacksmith was a friend of Billy's and Jack wanted an introduction.

Steven greeted him at the door and dragged him to the kitchen where the Parkers, Billy, and Elizabeth were talking.

"Can I steal Billy away for a half hour? I need his help with something." Jack addressed his question to Elizabeth.

"I don't mind, as long as he's back in time for the shooting contest and the picnic. Can Steven go along?" Elizabeth added.

"Sure," Billy said. "Come on, Steven."

"What do you need, Jack?" Billy inquired.

"Do you think your blacksmith friend Cain could forge some tools for me while I'm in town?"

****

When the wagon pulled to a stop at the blacksmith shop, Cain stepped away from the anvil. When he saw Billy, he said, "Haven't seen you since you came to town for a milk cow. How you doing?"

"Doing fine, Cain. This is my brother, Jack, and he needs work done if you have time."

Jack pulled out the sketches of the tools he needed made and showed Cain.

Cain looked at the designs for the five tools. "I can make them, but I won't have them done until Monday around noon."

"How much will you charge?" Jack put his hand in his pocket.

"They won't take long to make, and they don't

require much iron. For you, how about a dollar-fifty?"

Not knowing when he'd be in town again, Jack debated about staying the extra day so he could take the tools back with him. "Are you sure Monday is as soon as you could get them done?"

Billy offered, "How about if I get them for you on Monday and bring them along when we come to butcher the end of October. Would that work? We're staying until Monday anyways, so Elizabeth has more time with her family."

"Works for me. Thanks, Billy, and thank you too, Cain." Jack shook Cain's hand and paid him.

"Thanks for bringing me business, Billy. Don't be such a stranger." Cain ruffled the top of Steven's hair.

"Billy, I'll drop you at the Parkers' house, then I've got some errands. I'll see you later at the contest but I'm not shooting. Honestly, I forgot about it. I have my gun, but not the money for the entry fee."

"I could loan you the money if you want to shoot, Jack," Billy offered.

"No, that's all right. Thanks anyway." Jack shook his head.

"Okay, we'll see you later," Billy said, as Steven waved good-bye.

Jack stopped at Abby's house first to give her his letters. He rapped on the door. Nobody answered, so he set the letters tied with a string on the windowsill, beside the front door where someone would discover them.

At the Hardware Store, he dropped off the seed orders and crossed the street for the mail. He handed the clerk his mother's mail and received four letters. *Ma will be glad for news.* Two from Grandmother Clark, one from Grandmother Hewitt, and one for Mark from a name he didn't recognize. It looked like a women's handwriting.

The next stop—the Butcher Shop. He stepped to the counter and asked, "Will you have any cowhides I can buy tomorrow?"

"Cowhides tomorrow? No, son, tomorrow's Sunday and everyone's going to the picnic and dance tonight. Nobody's working tomorrow. They'll all be hungover or going to church. I have a mess of them I can sell you today if you want. They're from this morning and yesterday, so if'n you want ta tan 'em you got to get 'em done real soon."

"How many is a mess of them?"

"I can let you have at least fifteen. You want that many?"

"I'll take all you have, but since some are from yesterday and I'll miss the festival in order to get them home right away, how about I pay only one cent each today?"

"You drive a hard bargain, son, but it's a deal. I doubt anyone else will want them."

The man brought out the hides and Jack took the time to roll each one and slid them into feed sacks. He counted eighteen hides and paid the man eighteen cents. Then he went out back and picked through the waste pile until he found enough heads. *I better get these hides home and dealt with right away, or I'll have wasted my money and time.*

While loading the heads into the wagon he heard a man call out. "Why look at that. That boy's family is so poor they have to eat the cow's head. They can't even afford a piece of meat?"

Jack reared upright, looked into the eyes of the man who said the words, then recalled what his father said. "No fighting." He wanted to say something, the man wasn't that big, and Jack knew he could take him, but instead he lifted the last of the sacks into the wagon and drove to the Dry Goods Store.

"I'll take a newspaper," Jack said to the boy on the corner. He tucked it under his arm after reading the headline, *August 21, 1863, The Lawrence Massacre. The Worst Atrocity Committed by the Missouri Guerillas to Date.* Then he walked into the Dry Goods Store. Jack gathered the items on both Mrs. Frazer's and his mother's lists careful not to miss anything. He had the female clerk pick out fabric, buttons, and thread for the ladies while he selected rock candy, peppermint sticks, liquorish strings, and lemon drops enough to fill eight bags. He paid for each order separately and loaded the items into the wagon, careful to keep them as far away from the hides as possible.

Back in the store, he slung a fifty pound bag of salt against the counter, selected curved needles and four cones of heavy waxed thread for the business. Then he bought a tin of tobacco for Mark, flower scented perfume for Lydia, pretty stationary for his momma, and a storybook for Johanna, Steven, and Ethan. His momma must have forgotten to write down a pound bag of popping corn for the holiday, so he added it to his pile, then paid with his own money. Earlier, while he sorted through the waste pile at the slaughterhouse he set aside a set of horns he would use to make hair combs for the ladies. He'd also thrown six handfuls of rib bones in a sack to dry out and make wind chimes.

Glancing at the clock on Main Street, Jack saw he

had enough time to park the wagon, feed and water his horses, and find his brothers and Elizabeth before the contest.

"I must leave after the shoot," Jack said once he found the others. "I bought more hides at the Butcher Shop and have to get 'em home to tan. If you see Abigail, please tell her I'm sorry I couldn't stay. I left letters for her. Maybe you could bring hers home to me when you come next month?"

"I'll ask her for them when I see her." Billy bumped against Jack. "But she'll be disappointed."

"It can't be helped. I have a real opportunity if I can get these hides tanned."

****

The crowd seemed larger than usual in town and there were more shooters than Billy ever recalled. He stepped to the line when his name was called, sited in on the paper target, and hit dead center. He shattered the first two bottles, and the third wobbled and tipped over, but Billy didn't see any glass fly. *Maybe I hit the top rim enough to tip the bottle, but if someone else shatters all three, it won't matter.*

Waiting for the rest of the men to finish shooting seemed like hours.

Sure enough, one of the last few men to the line shattered all three. Billy was out of the running. To his surprise the sheriff declared a tie. Billy took the top of the bottle clean off and the sheriff counted it as a good hit. He asked both men to take one more shot at a distant bottle. Billy went first, aimed, drew in a breath and exhaled slowly. Drew in another breath and held it, aimed, and fired. Missed.

The second man checked the wind with a wet

95

finger and settled into his shot. Bang! The bottle shattered and the sheriff pronounced him the winner.

Billy walked back to his family, head held high. He was a good shot and he knew it. Winning wasn't in the cards this year, but he wouldn't let it ruin his day.

When he returned, Jack slapped him on the back, Elizabeth kissed him, and Steven hugged his leg.

"Next year," Elizabeth said.

"Not if I'm shooting," Jack remarked. Then Abby appeared working her way through the crowd toward him. "There's Abby. Billy, I'll tell Ma and Pa about your shooting. See you next month."

"Abby, I'm so glad you're here." Jack slipped a quick kiss on her cheek. "I missed you at your house. Did you find my letters?"

"Yes, I found them. I visited a friend this morning and didn't expect you'd get to town so early. Why didn't I see you in the shooting contest this time?" Abby asked, as she gave Jack a hug.

"I made the trip by myself this time and forgot to bring extra money for the entry fee. I bought some cowhides to tan, and I'm sorry, Abby. I won't be able to stay for the picnic and the dance. I must get the hides home right away. I hope you can forgive me."

"I understand. Do you have time to walk me home to get my letters?"

"Can we go right now?" Jack gazed into her lovely brown eyes.

Abby took his hand. "Sure, come on. When will I see you again?"

"I'm not certain, but I'll try to get back before Christmas if possible. You know I'd love to spend Christmas with you, Abby. I don't like having to leave today and miss the dance, but I wrote you all about my business plans. With the hides I bought today, I'm well on my way." Jack kissed her and gave her an enthusiastic hug that lifted her off her feet.

At her home, Abby quickly fetched the letters. Her pile was twice the size Jack left. She handed them to him and said, "Until we meet again."

Jack tucked the letters into his shirt, took her in his arms, and kissed her not once but three times, not wanting to leave. "Have a good time tonight. I'll be thinking of you all the way home. Knowing you'll be dancing with other men tonight doesn't make me happy, but if you can understand why I have to leave, I trust you won't fall in love with someone else because of one missed dance."

"You have nothing to worry about. I love you, Jack Clark. You're not getting rid of me that easily. I hope you can get back before the holidays, but if not, keep writing me. I read the letters we exchange over and over. It makes it seem like we're not so far apart."

"I'll keep writing and I'll write more often. I read one of your letters every day. I can hear your voice in my head as I read the words."

Jack gave her another loving hug and a sweet farewell kiss. "I must go." He kissed her on the forehead, whispered, "I love you" in her ear, turned, and took off for the wagon.

He rode until he could barely keep his eyes open. Trying to cover as much ground as possible, he hoped he wouldn't run into any trouble while on the road after hearing about the Lawrence Massacre by Missouri guerillas led by William Quantrill. They could still be in the area. When he stopped, he ate half the cake his momma made for the picnic and saved the rest for the next morning. His early return surprised the family.

Chapter Thirteen

Elizabeth was eager for the picnic to begin. She hadn't seen her girlfriends or heard any news since July. She spotted them as she took her dishes to the food tables. "Hey, Katie, Mary Jane, over here!"

The two girls ran to give Elizabeth a big hug as she hid her work roughened, red hands.

Katie whispered, "You look like you've gained a few pounds. Are you with child?"

"No, not yet, but we're trying," Elizabeth replied airily.

The girls giggled and Mary Jane said, "We saw Billy shoot. He's pretty good." Then whispered, "Too bad he's not that good in the bedroom or you'd be expecting by now. It's coming on six months since your wedding." A giggle escaped.

"Don't you worry. The next time you see me, I'll be with child. Billy wants a baby as much as I do. Enough about me. What have I missed?" Elizabeth put her arms around the waists of her friends and headed behind the church so they could talk in private.

Once out of sight and earshot of others, the girls were ready to speak candidly.

"So, tell me everything," Elizabeth pleaded.

Katie and Mary Jane took turns one upping the other with gossip and news. So and so is engaged; this boy and that classmate left to fight; the church social news and town dance events and so on until Elizabeth was caught up on everything she missed. But missing out made her feel even more isolated.

"Oh, and Quinn asked if we thought you'd be coming to the dance," Mary Jane said.

"Well, what did you tell him?" Elizabeth demanded.

"I told him last we knew you were coming." Mary Jane twisted a curl around her finger. "Why are you so interested? You're married."

"I'm not interested. I'm very happy with Billy," Elizabeth said, then immediately her thought turned to her last dance with Quinn. Being held in the arms of a man who knew how to dance well excited her. Of course she loved Billy, but his dancing couldn't compare to Quinn's. Often, in the middle of chores and farm work, her thoughts returned to the fun of being whirled about the floor by such an accomplished dancer.

"Oh my, an hour has passed. I must get back to Billy at the picnic." She rushed back to where he had spread the quilt when she left to put the food on the table, only to find a bare patch of grass and the picnic basket gone. People were milling around chatting, and ladies were already at the tables taking their empty bowls and platters. She had missed the picnic. She was not where she should have been by her husband's side. *But I had so much fun getting the gossip from my friends. Surely Billy knows how much I gave up when we got married. He has to! I work so hard and all I want now is a little fun.*

Glancing around the crowd, Billy and Steven were nowhere in sight. She walked home to find them sitting in the kitchen talking with her father.

"Where have you been, Elizabeth? I was worried about you." Billy looked at her with an expression on his face that she couldn't read. "When you didn't come back, Steven and I filled our plates and ate. We waited awhile and looked for you then figured you'd come back here."

"I got talking to Katie and Mary Jane, and we lost track of time."

"Did you eat at the picnic?" Billy asked.

"No, when I returned to the quilt, you were gone. I looked for you, but couldn't find you, so I came home."

"You missed some good food. Billy and I had seconds," Steven said.

"We could go back to the picnic for a while if you'd like, Steven," Elizabeth offered.

"I'm full up. Stuffed. I couldn't eat another bite." Steven rubbed his belly.

"Same here," Billy said.

Mr. Parker said, "Your ma has leftovers you can eat."

Elizabeth didn't feel much like eating.

"Billy said I can come to the dance for a while tonight. Won't that be fun?" Steven stood and danced a jig.

"Only for a little while, then you can come home and spend time with my parents before bedtime." Elizabeth seethed inside. *I wanted Billy to myself tonight. Now we'll have to leave the dance and take Steven back to the house.*

****

While Elizabeth gussied up for the dance, Billy and Steven hitched the wagon, headed to the Hardware

Store for supplies, and dropped off his seed order. Then they walked to the Dry Goods Store and picked out a new dress with ribbon the same color she could wear in her hair or on her hat to surprise Elizabeth for Christmas. The dress wouldn't be as fancy as the dress shop creations she was used to, but would be new and Billy hoped she would like it. While Steven filled a bag with candy, Billy selected a beginner reading book, a deck of cards, four new dime novels, paper tablets, ink, a tin of coca powder, and a pound bag of popping corn, all Christmas surprises.

He would be sure to give Elizabeth extra money so she could pick out Christmas surprises too.

He had heard bits and pieces about the Lawrence Massacre throughout the day. How Quantrill's men looted stores and burned buildings to the ground because Lawrence, Kansas was a stronghold for Jayhawkers and abolitionists. He bought a newspaper to read for himself, dropping it behind the seat. When they arrived, Elizabeth was already waiting at the door.

"I'm ready, let's go," Elizabeth said and grabbed her shawl.

"Steven and I need to wash up a little. You look beautiful, Elizabeth. Give us a minute, and we'll be right back."

Billy washed and shaved quickly, changed into a clean shirt, and combed his hair. Steven washed and changed his shirt, as well.

Running down the stairs, the little boy stopped short of the last step so he could look at himself in the mirror on the wall ahead of him. Steven said, "I look good, but Billy looks better."

As Billy came downstairs, Elizabeth glanced at the

handsome man she married gazing at her. The reasons she fell in love with him in the first place flooded her with feelings. *He is handsome, kind, takes my breath away when we kiss, and he has devoted his life to me. I am so lucky. It would be wonderful if we could live in town and not so far away from all the fun, but I guess that will never be. I'll have to get used to living on a farm out in the middle of nowhere.*

Tonight, she would show the town they were in love. She did love Billy and seeing him walk down the stairs reminded her of her first feelings for him. Something Mary Jane told her earlier weighed on her mind. Quinn had asked if Elizabeth would be attending the dance. No doubt he would be there tonight. Why did that matter? She was married, wanting a child with her husband. Why did his name, his question mean anything?

****

Walking toward the church, the music started to play while cheers and hoots and hollering rang out. Billy placed his arm around Elizabeth's waist. "There's a lot of men in town not from around these parts. Please stay close tonight and let me know if you leave to talk with friends. Let's stay in sight of each other. I can't protect you if I can't see you."

"All right, sweetheart. I promise not to let you out of my sight." Elizabeth smiled as she gazed at Billy, held Steven's hand tightly, and thought, *by next year at this time, I pray the war has ended. We'll have a child and walk through town to show off our baby. We'll have a family of our own. If Steven was back with the Hewitts, everything would be perfect.*

At the church, small fires were glowing, people

were dancing, and Elizabeth thought she recognized Katie on the dance floor with a young man. She was thankful Billy had not gone to fight so she could enjoy this evening with him. If, by chance, Quinn asked her to dance, she would say no. Just the same, she couldn't help herself, as she searched the crowd to see if he was present.

Making their way through the people to the refreshment table, she offered a cookie to Steven. He ate the small cookie in three bites. A slow song started to play.

"Can we dance," Steven asked Elizabeth.

"My goodness, yes." Elizabeth took his little hand and they stepped to the music together. Then she swept him into her arms and finished the song twirling them around as Billy happily watched.

When the song ended, she curtsied and said, "Thank you for the dance, Steven."

"Elizabeth is a good dancer," Steven said to his older brother. "Now I know why you picked her. Someday I'll find a girl like Elizabeth. Can I have another cookie before we go back to the house?"

"Of course you can. I'll fetch you one." Elizabeth walked to the refreshment table and, as she reached for a cookie, a man's hand touched hers.

"I hoped to see you tonight. Can I have a dance later?"

It was Quinn.

"No, I'm sorry, all my dances are taken. I'm married and want to spend the evening with my husband. We don't get to town often and when we do, we make it special by being together every moment."

"What's the matter? You danced with me before,

and I thought you rather enjoyed it."

"I said no. Now leave me alone." She turned to see Billy and Steven watching her.

Returning to them, she said, "Here you are, Steven. Enjoy your cookie. We'll dance one more tune, then it's time to take you back to the house."

****

Walking back after leaving Steven at the Parkers', Billy said, "Thanks for making tonight special for my little brother. He loves you, you know."

"He's becoming quite the young man," Elizabeth said. "He has a good big brother teaching him."

Dancing, holding hands, talking to friends, and enjoying the evening together, the music ended much too soon. The young couple walked back to the house pleasantly weary and woke up the next morning in each other's arms.

At the breakfast table, Billy said, "Cain is making some tools for Jack. Don't let me forget to stop for them. They won't be ready until noon. That gives us plenty of time to talk with your folks then get supplies. Make sure to get everything on our list. We might not come back to town before spring."

"You mean, we won't come to town for Christmas?"

"It all depends on the weather. I wouldn't plan on it. You know if the snow hits hard, we won't be able to travel the half day it takes to get here."

"He's right, Elizabeth," Mr. Parker agreed. "It would be too risky. There were a number of years we didn't get to town for the holidays when we lived on a farm. Isn't that right, Bertha?"

"Yes, don't worry. Whenever the next time we're

together is, we'll make it special," Elizabeth's mother said. "Plans don't always work out the way we want. Your safety comes first."

While Billy hitched the horses, Mr. Parker put a crate of Christmas surprises in the back of the wagon and said, "Hide these good or Elizabeth will find them." Then everyone went outside and said their good-byes as if it might be a long time before they saw each other again.

At the Dry Goods Store, Billy picked out pants, a wool shirt, and long johns to get him through the cold months, then did the same for Steven. "Here, Elizabeth." Billy handed her ample money to pay the bill. "I'll take Steven and we'll fetch Jack's tools and meet you back here to load the supplies. We'll be about twenty minutes, so you can take your time and shop."

****

Elizabeth browsed shelf-by-shelf selecting food and household items on her list. "What's the total?" she asked the clerk.

After paying, there was five dollars left over, so she chose yarn to crochet a new shawl, ribbons for her hair, a bar of scented soap, thread and buttons to fancy up an old dress, some lavender hand cream, and two yards each of two different fabrics to make a frilly skirt. As she laid the fabric on the counter, Billy and Steven walked in.

"Steven, why don't you pick out three cents worth of candy for yourself and the same to take to Johanna? Then we're all set." She paid the bill and helped load the wagon.

Chapter Fourteen

Jack, eager to get started on his hides, unloaded the wagon and took the supplies to the house along with the newspaper and the mail from his grandparents. After his chores were done, he got to work in the barn fleshing the hides. He knew how important it was to take the meat and unwanted fat and tallow off the hides as soon as possible so he could salt them to draw out the moisture.

He ate supper, did his evening chores, and stayed in the barn to work. Mark walked out to give him a hand.

"I have something for you, Mark." Jack reached in his pocket and pulled out the letter. "This came for you."

Mark glanced at the return address and stuck the letter in his pocket. *Katherine Weaver.*

"Aren't you going to read it?" Jack grabbed a hide and began fleshing.

"I suppose you figured the fancy writing was done by a woman or you wouldn't have saved it to give to me now," Mark said.

"Yeah, the handwriting was definitely a woman's, and if you want Ma to know, you'll tell her. Not my business, but I didn't want Ma's feelings hurt."

"You did the right thing, Jack. Thank you. I promise I'll never hurt your momma and especially not with another woman. I love your ma and our family too much. I'd do anything to keep us together."

"I know." Jack handed Mark the fleshed hide to throw on the pile and grabbed another and slung it onto the fleshing bench.

"You flesh 'em, I'll salt 'em for you." Mark shook out a hide from the pile, dug into the sack of salt, and rubbed a generous handful into the pliable skin.

The two men worked into the early hours of the morning and began again after chores the next day. They finished the last hide and minutes later heard Lydia and Johanna open the barn door to announce dinner was on the table.

Jack took the hide trimmings out beyond the clearing, then washed up.

"Ma, you should see the barn. Jack turned the whole thing into a foul-smelling, hide-curing workshop. It will take months before the barn smells better," Lydia said.

"It stinks!" Johanna added, pinching her noise.

Both men smelled a bit pungent, and Sarah had them wash a second time and change their shirts before sitting down at the table.

"Thanks for your help, Mark. I'd still be out there if you hadn't given me a hand." Jack reached for the bowl of mashed potatoes.

"You're welcome. I'm anxious to see what you're going to do with them." Mark passed the gravy to Jack.

"I'm starting a business." Jack took a bite of bread. "When he comes to butcher, Billy is bringing me tools his blacksmith friend Cain is making and I'm going into the leather business. I'll definitely need a seamstress. If people like my work, I'll have more orders than I can make by myself. You interested, Lydia?"

"Will you pay me?" A smile brightened Lydia's cheeks.

"Yup, but not until the item sells. I've given this a lot of thought. I'll give you fifteen cents on the dollar." Jack took a sip of milk. "Do you think that's fair?"

"Make it eighteen cents and you have a deal."

"All right, deal!" Jack held out his hand to shake.

Lydia stood, reached across the table, and they shook hands. "Deal," they agreed.

****

After dinner, Sarah brought out the mail from back East and read excerpts of the letter from her mother dated July 27, 1863.

Matthew got word to us that he is doing well. They have been in a few minor scrimmages and one major battle, but can't say where he is right now. He has advanced to serve as the general's personal correspondent and writes many of the dispatches sent between commands. Matthew's journalism background helped get him the position. I shared this news with his old boss, Mr. Reed, who is very pleased and promised not to mention the news to others. I trust he will keep his word.

I go daily to the Postal Office where casualty lists are posted to look for Matthew's name. I do not know what your father and I will do if he does not come home. I try not to dwell on what he must be seeing in his travels, but find myself in deep thought with Matthew on my mind every day.

Take care of yourselves. Father and I talk about each of you often and pray for your safety.

Sarah reached for the second letter and read word

for word.

August 14, 1863
Tidioute, Warren County, PA
Dearest Sarah,

Your sister Matilda met a gentleman who swept her off her feet. He rode into town in his tattered Union uniform needing medical attention, so the townspeople got him to Doc's office where Matilda is helping nurse him back to health. His name is Robert Martin. He was returning to his home in Busti, New York, just over the Pennsylvania line, but only made it as far as Tidioute. The young man is doing fine now and is working at the general store as a bookkeeper helping Mr. and Mrs. Anderson.

He notified his family of his condition and told them he would be staying in Tidioute until well enough to travel home for a visit. The other day he asked your father for Matilda's hand in marriage, but will not propose until closer to the end of the war. He is handsome, polite, and well liked in our community already. I believe he will make Matilda a good husband.

Emma and her husband Able are doing well. Their son Thomas turned one last week and enjoyed the cake I baked him. He proceeded to wipe a handful on his clothes, his face, and in his hair. Of course, I was more than glad to help bathe him.

We wish you were here with us but realize the miles and the war make it impossible at this time. I am still holding out hope that I will see you again before I leave this Earth.

Your father and I are well although aches and pains find us periodically. All in all, no major complaints. I guess getting old takes its toll on each of us sooner or later.

Tell the children we send our love, and if this is the last letter you receive for the year, enjoy your holiday, take care of each other, and know we think of you daily and send our love.

Sincerely,
Love, Mother

Opening Mother Hewitt's letter, Sarah read,
July 28, 1863
Tidioute, Warren County, PA
Dear Family,
I am happy for the union of Billy and Elizabeth. Thank you for writing and sharing all the details. I so wish we could be together without this distance between us, especially during these trying times for our country. I pray every day for the rebellion to end and that none of your family must go fight.

The weather in Tidioute is hotter than I remember in a number of years. My garden is producing faster than I can eat it all, and I'll have plenty of food in the pantry for the long winter months ahead.

I visited with your folks at the Fourth of July celebration. We caught up on news. They both looked well and were enjoying the nice day.

Sarah, your mother told me about Matthew going to fight. He is a brave lad and I pray every night that the Lord keeps him safe and returns him to us soon.

Please write and tell me your latest news and if any of your family has to leave to defend our country. I pray the fighting ends and our country becomes one again.

Take care of yourselves. Hug and kiss the children

for me.

    All my love, Mother Hewitt

    Sarah tucked the letters back in their envelopes and the children cleared the table and washed the dishes.

Chapter Fifteen

All the knives were sharp, and Sarah had bowls and crocks ready for the meat they would designate for brining, salting, smoking, and making into jerky and sausage. The butchering began before the Henry family arrived. Three head from the herd would feed the two families for the winter.

Elizabeth gagged when she saw the innards of an animal. She had no inkling what to do, so Sarah took Elizabeth under her wing and began explaining the process. Afraid to get her hands bloody, at first Elizabeth only poked at the meat. When Sarah insistently kept instructing on how this and that needed done, Elizabeth finally gave in and participated, all the while longing for the town life she once enjoyed.

Patiently, Sarah showed Elizabeth how to separate a hindquarter into roasts and how to cut steaks and trim fat and tallow which would later be rendered into oil for the lamps and soap making. They sliced some of the organs to pickle, and ground the scraps to stuff with seasoning into gut casings for sausage. Quite the experience for a town girl who was used to going to the butcher shop to buy fresh meat neatly wrapped.

Today, for the family's hard work, they would enjoy fresh steaks for supper. As the men finished cleaning off the tables in the barn, the ladies washed and began meal preparations. Lydia made two pumpkin pies, and Elizabeth scrubbed potatoes and set the table.

The men washed up on the porch and everyone enjoyed a grand feast.

****

When supper was done, Billy said, "I'm going to the grave for a few minutes."

Years earlier, Mark had carved a tombstone in memory of Billy's folks, a place he could go to think of them. Also the location where Billy had hidden most of the money his parents left him, a precaution in case the bank was robbed during these desperate times. If anything happened in the coming winter months, he'd have a little extra if he and Elizabeth needed medicine or something from Dead Flats. That is, if the weather let him make it to town.

Her chores completed, Lydia joined him. With all the conversations and children underfoot, she doubted she would be missed. She walked to the top of the knoll and stood beside Billy, who was at work digging for the strongbox buried at the foot of the symbolic grave.

Billy turned, and when he saw Lydia, returned to digging.

"Are you all right?" Lydia leaned against the old elm tree.

"Yeah, I'm fine." He let out a sigh and rested his arm on the shovel to glance at Lydia's father's tombstone. He'd seen the marker several times, but suddenly, the date of Samuel's death registered for the first time. Something clicked. *The date. It's the same date on my father's tombstone. How could this be?*

"Lydia, tell me again how your father died."

"He went hunting with Mark. You've heard the story several times."

"Yes, I know. But where were they hunting?"

"Up north somewhere. Why do you ask?"

"No reason, I guess." He resumed digging, opened the metal box, and removed twenty silver-dollar coins before returning it to the ground and tamping the earth so nobody would suspect anything was disturbed.

****

Billy had been awake all night thinking about the dates on the two tombstones—Samuel's and his father's. He'd put together many scenarios, but still needed an answer. He needed to know the truth. It couldn't be a coincidence that the date of death was the same on both markers. Helping Mark with chores the next morning, Billy asked, "Can we talk, Mark?" Then he shoved his hands in his pockets.

"Jack, can you handle the chores by yourself for a while?" Mark asked his son.

"Yeah, go ahead. I'll leave some work for you when you get back." Jack grabbed the milking stool and pail.

Once out of earshot, Billy flat out said, "I need to know the truth and you're the only one who can tell me. What did Samuel have to do with my father's death?"

Mark looked at Billy intently and said, "Why do you think Samuel has anything to do with your father?"

"I put the dates together last night. They both died on the same day. It doesn't seem possible that there isn't a connection. Both dead on the same day is a strange coincidence, don't you think?" Billy straightened his stance.

"I'm not sure what you're thinking, but I'll tell you the truth. Samuel is the man that saved your life the day your father was killed in the stage robbery. Samuel died shortly afterward from a gunshot wound. That's why he didn't tell the driver his name. He was hit bad and knew he probably wouldn't make it. Sarah is the only other person on this earth that knows that Samuel was present when the robbers attacked the stagecoach. She put all the pieces of the puzzle together herself. Samuel was a good man, and a good father to Jack and Lydia. We didn't tell them the truth at the time. Sarah didn't want them to think of their father as a killer."

"But if he hadn't killed those men, I might not be standing here today." Billy struggled to make sense of the startling information.

"Billy, we both know Samuel was a hero for saving you and the driver that day, but after Sarah learned the truth, she still thought it best to let the children continue to think his death was an accident. When Samuel lay dying in my arms, he begged me not to tell her he had killed the two men that robbed the stage. Knowing her strong faith, Samuel didn't want her to think of him as a killer. As he drew his last breaths, I swore to Samuel that I'd never tell Sarah the truth. I promised my best friend I'd take care of his family."

"I know the story," Billy added. "You stayed on to help with the crops and then you and Sarah fell in love." Billy shifted his stance.

"Yes, all that happened. And, yes, at first I lied to Sarah to keep my promise to Samuel. In fact I didn't tell her the truth about the reward money until after the barn burned and only then because she thought we didn't have money to rebuild. But I kept my promise to Samuel. I told her I was the one who killed the robbers, saved the boy and the driver's lives, and collected the reward money."

"Right after the barn fire is when you found me." Billy searched for the truth in Mark's eyes.

"Yes, if Sarah found out I wasn't the one who killed the robbers, my lies could have unraveled and she'd discover the truth that I wasn't the man who saved your life during the robbery."

Billy's hands hung limp at his sides. "You mean you took that risk for me knowing Sarah might learn the truth?"

"Yes, Billy. As Samuel lay dying, he told me about the young boy whose father was killed in the attempted robbery and about the unique birthmark on his neck. When I saw the mark on your neck as you sat tied to the peddler's wagon, helpless and in need of a friend, I knew you were the same boy Samuel described. I knew the sheriff gave you to Rusty and seeing the way he treated you, I knew I had to get you away from him. I don't know what I'd have done if you hadn't come with me to the farm that day. I couldn't let you go off on your own. I could never have forgiven myself if I didn't at least try to help you."

Billy straightened. "So you knew about me because Samuel told you before he died. You saved me that day, Mark. I never thought I'd ever get away from Rusty." Billy rubbed his wrists in memory.

"Yes, I rescued you. But not until you brought your brother home did Sarah put the final piece of the puzzle together and figured out that I saved you from Rusty, not from the stagecoach robbery. You said something about the man who saved you from the robbers and she figured I wasn't the man."

"Oh, Mark. I'm so sorry."

"No, you're not to blame. I should have told her

myself. I wanted to tell her several times, but it always came back to knowing I couldn't be the husband and father I wanted, if I couldn't keep a promise to a friend. If a man can't stand by his word, what does he have to stand by? I'll tell Sarah about our conversation. She'll be relieved to know you finally know the truth.

"Please let Jack and Lydia keep believing what we've told them. Sarah and I still think it's best for them to think their father's death was an accident."

"I agree. It's not my place to tell them. You're right, Mark. Samuel was a good man and I'm glad I met him. God works in mysterious ways. Isn't that what Ma says sometimes?" Billy stood, shaking his head slightly.

"Yes, Sarah says that a lot. And I believe her." Mark put his arm around Billy's shoulders as they started walking back to the barn. "Are you all right? That was a lot to find out about your past in one day."

Billy stopped and suddenly jerked himself from under Mark's arm. "No, I'm not all right. After all these years, why didn't you tell me the truth about Samuel? Didn't you and Sarah trust me enough to keep your secret? I'm a man now. I'm married, taking care of Steven, and responsible for my own place. And you still didn't trust me enough to tell me the truth."

"Billy, we never intended to deceive you. We just didn't want Lydia and Jack to know what happened to their father. I'm sorry. We do trust you. We should have told you."

"You're right. I should have known the truth." Billy turned and walked away heading for the house. His real father didn't tell him the truth about his mother's death and little brother living, and now Mark and Sarah hadn't told him the truth about Samuel being the hero of the stage robbery. Billy carried a heavy burden on his shoulders.

****

Midday, with the wagon packed with meat and jars of produce from Sarah's shelves, Jack lifted a wooden crate covered with empty feed sacks into the back of the wagon.

Taking Billy aside, Jack whispered, "These are presents for Christmas morning. You'll have to hide them until then. We want you all to remember we are thinking of you. Hopefully, we'll see you as soon as the weather breaks."

"Please, thank everyone for me." Billy gave Jack a hug. "Maybe the next time I see you, I'll have news, Uncle Jack."

Jack grinned and slapped Billy on the shoulder.

After everyone said their good-byes, Steven asked, "When will we come again, Billy?"

"Not for a while. Not until after the snow comes and goes, little brother," Billy said.

Sarah spoke up. "When the Frazers were here to pick up their new horse and supplies, we tentatively planned to get together the last Sunday in December for dinner, if the weather cooperates and it's safe to travel. Will you come join us? Please, do plan on coming. We'd love to have you with us. A visit will give everyone something to look forward to over these long winter months. You're welcome to stay as long as you can."

"No, don't count on us," Billy said still reeling from his conversation with Mark earlier.

"Then I need another hug and kiss from everyone. That's a long time to go without hugs and kisses."

Steven climbed out of the wagon and made his rounds again.

"If we have a light winter, Jack or I will try to stop by," Mark added.

"Suit yourself. Oh, that reminds me," Billy mumbled. "I thought I'd try my hand at trapping this winter. I know you and Jack will probably string a trap line, but could I borrow four traps if you wouldn't miss them?"

Mark patted his tense shoulder. "Sure. Happy to lend them."

Jack spoke up, "I'll get 'em. I'm going to tan some of our furs this year instead of sell them in town." Returning quickly, he tossed the traps into the back of the wagon.

"Come on, Steven, time to get going."

Flicking the reins, Billy didn't look back as the Hewitt family waved.

****

This winter the family would be apart for the first time. Mark said a silent prayer as he watched the wagon pull away. *I pray Billy can forgive me for not telling him about Samuel. I hope for Sarah's sake, he will reconsider and come in December. I also pray that no illnesses or harm comes to our families, and that we have harvested enough food to feed both ourselves and the animals. Hopefully, when spring arrives the war will be over, and the threat of going to fight is a non-issue.*

Chapter Sixteen

The Long Winter

As Christmas approached, Steven became excited. He and Billy worked together on a surprise for Elizabeth in the lean-to they had enlarged to a small barn to accommodate the horses and milk cow.

"Elizabeth, I gotta hurry with these dishes. Billy needs my help in the barn," Steven excitedly told Elizabeth.

"The outside chores are done. What are you working on?" Elizabeth asked.

"I can't tell, or it won't be a surprise," the young boy answered eagerly.

"Surprise for what?"

"A surprise for you for Christmas." Steven immediately cupped his hand over his mouth. "I can't say anything else." He ran out.

"I let it slip that we're making a surprise for Elizabeth," Steven blurted out when he saw Billy.

When Billy looked up from the project, Steven looked at his feet. "I didn't tell her what we were making, only that I had to hurry to help."

"Don't worry, little brother. I'm sure she's making you a surprise too. As long as she doesn't know what we're planning, it will still be a surprise."

Billy had boiled the cow ribs Jack gave him, and

now dried they turned an ivory color. Sliding his hands over the smooth bones, today Billy would help Steven drill the holes and hang them off a sturdy forked branch that would let the bones dance and intone in the wind.

"I hope she likes it," Steven said as they tied the last rib in place with slender strips of rawhide.

"You made this for her, Steven, so I'm sure she'll like it. Let's try it out."

Steven held the branch in the air and tilted it back and forth as if the wind made the bones dance. The subtle clacking of the bones sounded like a musical instrument. "Where can I hide it, Billy?"

"Why don't you put your surprise in the back of the wagon? We won't be going anywhere. Elizabeth would never look there."

"That's a great idea!" Billy slid the chimes under a tarp and covered them with feed sacks.

****

That evening, Elizabeth asked, "What's this about you boys making surprises for Christmas?"

"It's a tradition Steven and I learned from the Hewitts. We always made gifts for each other. On Christmas morning we'd exchange and surprise one another. Mark and Sarah made sure we each received a store bought gift too, but the handmade ones were the most special. I won't tell you, so don't ask what we're making. And don't feel you have to make anything for us. I'm sure you bought gifts in town with the money I gave you."

Smiling weakly, Elizabeth said, "Well, if I want to get my handmade gifts finished in time, I must get busy." She shifted uneasily in her chair. While in town, she had not thought to buy anything for Billy or Steven or anyone else for that matter. *Christmas is only three weeks away and buying gifts never crossed my mind. What was I thinking? I knew it would be our last trip to town before the holiday. Now what am I supposed to do?*

Wait…yarn. I bought yarn to make myself a shawl. I've started, but could take it apart and knit them each a scarf. I hope I can knit fast enough in so little time. I must keep them hidden or they won't be a surprise. Elizabeth vowed to work late into the evening and get up early if necessary to get the presents finished.

That evening after Billy was in bed, she started her projects. She'd make Steven's first. As she sat knitting, she thought of other surprises she could make, such as an apron for Steven to wear when he helped her bake, which he loved to do. A brand new pair of store-bought gloves for Billy would have been a thoughtful gift. His were wearing thin. She didn't have the right goods to make new ones, but she resolved to at least mend the holes in the old ones. While in town last she had been selfish buying things only for herself and not anyone else. But she quickly soothed her conscience by rationalizing, *It's not my fault. I'm deprived of so many things. I deserved to pamper myself a little.*

By the middle of the second week, after spending every minute she could spare, Elizabeth gave in to the fact that she would never get the scarves finished if she didn't have more hours to work on them. "Why don't you and Steven set the traps and see how you fare?"

"Steven, you want to go along and carry the traps? Snow fell last night so fresh tracks will be easy to spot. We might catch something," Billy said.

Already grabbing his coat and tugging on his boots,

a grin covered Steven's face. "Sure, Billy, let's go."

Billy put another log on the fire and said, "We'll be gone a couple hours. You sure you'll be all right here alone, sweetheart?"

"I'll be fine. Go ahead, and I'll have a hearty meal ready when you get home. If you take your gun along maybe you'll get a rabbit," Elizabeth encouraged.

Grabbing his gun and making sure Steven was bundled warmly, the two brothers left and Elizabeth knitted feverishly.

After a while, she took a break to make a venison stew with potatoes and carrots and to mix a batch of corn muffins. Returning to her knitting, she figured a few more inches and Steven's scarf would be finished. She would start Billy's tomorrow as soon as they headed out to check the traps.

The boys checked the traps for five days, giving Elizabeth time to work on Billy's scarf. A blustery snowstorm blew in, so the brothers went out one final time to pull the traps. They had a large fox and a beautiful mink to show for their efforts. These furs would be sold come spring for a good price.

During that week, Elizabeth had time to finish both scarves and make the apron for Steven. The fancy fabric she purchased to make herself a skirt, she knew Billy wouldn't wear made into a shirt. Again her conscience had a momentary tweak of humiliation that she hadn't considered buying gifts when she had the chance and the money. But, true to form, she discarded the thought.

****

Christmas Eve, Billy set a small sumac tree in the corner of the sitting room. After supper, he popped the corn. Elizabeth threaded needles and Steven enjoyed eating as many kernels as he strung, before hanging the garlands on the tree branches. Elizabeth showed Steven how to cut folded paper into snowflakes and they made many small designs to hang on the tree.

Opening the family Bible, Billy read the Christmas story from the books of Luke and Matthew. Afterward, Steven placed his sock on the fireplace hearth, kissed and hugged his brother and Elizabeth, then climbed the ladder to go to bed.

Elizabeth brewed mint tea, and she and Billy enjoyed steaming mugs by the fire while swapping memories of Christmases past.

****

At the Hewitt farm, after decorating the tree with popped corn strands and putting out socks, Lydia read the stories of the nativity while little Johanna yawned and rubbed her eyes.

Mark carried her to bed and whispered, "Sweet dreams."

As the fire crackled, Jack said, "How about you let me beat you in a game of checkers, Mark?"

"Sure. You're on."

Lydia and Sarah made a batch of peanut brittle and mixed bread dough to let proof overnight for sweet rolls on Christmas morning.

Christmas day was extra special for Johanna. She received new books, candy from the store, and homemade peanut brittle. Jack had hand carved her a whistle and attached a pink satin ribbon. He explained, "Johanna, always wear this, always. If any strangers come by, blow your whistle while running to the house."

Nodding, she blew as hard as she could to make sure it worked.

The family sang Christmas carols led by Lydia, played games, and spent a loving day together. Soon the calendar would turn to 1864, but the fighting between the states still raged with no end in sight.

****

At the Henry farm, when Steven climbed down the ladder from the loft, Billy and Elizabeth were at the kitchen table watching the fresh snow float past the window and cover the already white ground.

Steven's eyes brightened when he saw his bulging stocking. A peppermint stick peeked out the top.

He couldn't wait to give Elizabeth her surprise. He had brought the present in the house wrapped in a feed sack and slid the sack under her chair when she wasn't looking along with the box holding her dress from Billy.

Billy brought in the crate from the Hewitts and the box from the Parkers. Everyone had surprises too open, but when Elizabeth opened the dress box Billy gave her, she jumped onto his lap and gave him a kiss. "I love it, Billy," she said, then ran to the bedroom to try it on.

"I'm glad you like it," Billy managed to say before the bedroom door closed.

Elizabeth, still in her new dress, returned and twirled around, then reached for Steven's gift to open.

Steven, sitting on a blanket on the floor, scooted closer to Elizabeth's chair.

When Elizabeth reached in and took the chimes out of the feed sack she was delighted and made them sing. "I love the soft music they make. Where do you think we should hang the wind chimes?"

Steven grinned and rushed to her side. "I'm glad you like it. We can hang them by the kitchen window, and they can sing to us when we do the dishes," Steven suggested.

"Great idea," Billy agreed. "We can hang them as soon as we finish with our presents."

Steven and Billy opened their gift from Elizabeth and made a fuss over the warm scarves and Steven's fancy apron.

Billy looked around at all the presents. Elizabeth had not bought Steven any store gifts, and she had not helped Steven make him a homemade gift either. *I know I gave her plenty of money. I wonder what she spent the money on? I'm glad I picked out gifts in town for Steven. And I'm glad Elizabeth liked her new dress. Come to think of it, she didn't give me a store bought gift either.*

"Can we make a chocolate cake with white icing this afternoon, so I can wear my new apron?" Steven asked.

"Sure, we can celebrate baby Jesus' birthday with a cake," Elizabeth said.

Chapter Seventeen

The last Sunday in December 1863

As Sarah sat up in bed, she nudged Mark. "You awake?"

"I am now." Mark rolled over and gazed at Sarah as he pulled the covers around his neck against the morning chill.

"I'm so excited that the Frazers might be joining us for dinner tomorrow. Lydia and I have been cooking for days. I can't wait to see them all. I bet Ethan has grown. I know Johanna will be happy when he's here."

"I wouldn't get my hopes up, sweetheart. If Seth doesn't feel safe making the trip, they won't come. Their trip is at least four hours. They may need to clear limbs off the path from the last storm and the creek is probably frozen in places. I know Seth will take everything into consideration before they head out." Mark got out of bed and pulled on his shirt. "The weather conditions for me to consider making the journey would be green grass and sunshine."

"Oh, Mark. I promise you a feast tomorrow, and I'm counting on sharing our meal with our friends," Sarah said. "I need to get the bread in the oven, bake the pumpkin and custard pies, and add a few more finishing touches. Do you think Billy will change his mind? It'd be wonderful to have everyone together."

"We probably won't be seeing Billy's family. He said he wouldn't be coming, and I believe he meant it. He was pretty upset that we didn't tell him about Samuel. I'll make it a point to ride out and check on them once the weather breaks."

****

Before dawn the next morning, at the Frazers', Emily said, "It didn't snow last night, and the sky is clear. What do you think, Seth? Can we make the trip today? Seeing our friends would be a wonderful relief from the drudgery of winter."

Seth took a sip of tea from a steaming mug. "I know how much you want to go, Em. I see you're bringing all manner of things for an overnight stay. The weather looks like it will hold, so I'll hitch the horses and we'll be on our way. With extra feed the animals will be fine. Best you pack a few extra clothes," he said looking at the carpetbag by the door. "We could be with the Hewitts more than overnight if the weather changes."

Their wagon, pulled by two willing horses, made good progress despite the snow. After a bright dawn, the sun peeked in and out of the clouds, casting purple hues on the ground. The family sang songs to pass the hours of travel. Three-year-old Ethan stood behind the wagon seat where his parents sat when suddenly, one of the wagon's wheels hit a rock hidden under the snow. Although the wagon lurched a little, the horses kept going. They were about to cross the creek that marked halfway to the Hewitt farm when without warning, the wagon suddenly tilted to one side and Seth and Emily almost slid off the seat. Ethan grabbed for his mother and somehow managed to hold on.

Pulling the horses to a halt, Seth jumped down and assessed the damage. "It's the wheel. The spokes are busted, and the rim is cracked. We can't go any farther.

"We better head back. I don't like the looks of the weather. It's beginning to cloud over, and the wind is getting colder. Could be a rogue storm coming. We'll be better off at home than continuing on to Mark and Sarah's place. If it does storm, we'll be able to feed the animals. I'll unhitch the horses so you and Ethan can ride one, and I'll take the other. Hopefully we can make it home before the winds get too bad and the temperature drops."

He gave Emily a leg up onto the older horse and draped her in blankets, then set Ethan in front of his mother and wrapped him in blankets as well. "Hold on to the horse's mane, Em, you'll feel safer."

Seth pulled the flap tight across the back of the covered wagon and the disappointed family started retracing their tracks toward home.

****

Midday at the Hewitt homestead, Mark announced, "I'm hungry, I think we should go ahead and eat. By the looks of things, the Frazers must have decided not to come, and we know Billy isn't, so I guess it's only us."

Sarah said, "Looks like you're right, dear. Surely the Frazers would be here by now if they could make the trip. We'll be eating leftovers for a few days, but I doubt anyone will complain."

"I sure won't," Jack said as he took his seat at the table laden with food.

Lydia said, "It's too bad they couldn't come. Sure is sad they'll be missing all this good food."

Sarah placed Johanna in her chair and offered the dinner prayer. The family dug into sumptuous roast venison, and steaming bowls of mashed potatoes, canned carrots and peas, freshly made noodles, bread, and gravy. But the conversation always returned to the Frazers. "What if they started and something happened to them?" Sarah asked more than once, each time with increased concern.

Digging into the flaky crust of a slice of custard pie, Mark finally said, "All right, tomorrow morning, weather permitting, Jack and I will ride out and look for any indication they were headed our way. If we don't see anything, we'll be back before dark, and you can stop worrying."

"Thank you, Mark. I'll rest easier tonight, knowing you're going to check on them."

****

After riding steadily, bodies huddled against the bitter cold and whipping winds, Seth made the decision to leave the road and take a direct route home. Holding the lead of the other horse, he turned toward the windswept plain in the direction of the farm. Following the new course, the family would need to cross the meandering creek twice, but Seth figured they'd get home sooner. Pulling his scarf tighter, he called to his wife, "Em, are you and the boy all right?"

"We're fine," a muffled voice from under the mound of blankets said.

Approaching the first crossing, they stopped while Seth surveyed the situation. "Hang tight to Ethan, Em. You may have to nudge your horse to get him to go in the water. You'll be fine. I'll be right behind you."

Emily did as Seth advised and crossed the creek

safely.

Seth started to follow when, suddenly, his horse lost its footing. Stumbling, the creature went down in the icy water, pinning Seth beneath its massive weight. Struggling to get his leg out from under the thrashing animal, he finally pulled free as the horse got its footing, and limped to the other side. Seth staggered out of the water, soaking wet and shivering violently from the dousing.

Emily quickly slid off her horse, helped Ethan down, and rushed to help Seth.

"I need to get out of these wet clothes right away, Em." Seth shook uncontrollably as he hung his soaked coat on a tree limb.

The carpetbag tied to his saddle was thankfully not wet enough to soak the clothes inside. Emily quickly helped him into a dry shirt and pants, then dug frantically through the bag once, and then a second time.

"I can't believe it," Emily moaned.

"What are you looking for?"

"I didn't pack extra stockings. How could I be so foolish?"

Seth took off his boots and drained the water from them and wrung out his stockings before putting them back on. Slowly getting to his feet he asked, "Are you and Ethan all right?"

"We're fine," Emily said. "Let me build a fire to get you warmed up."

"I get sticks," Ethan offered.

"No, a fire would slow us down," Seth insisted. "We need to get home as quickly as we can. This wind is serious and we can't risk being outside a moment longer than necessary. Let's keep going. I can't wait to crawl into bed and get warm."

Seth walked toward the horse and said softly, "That was quite the spill. Are you all right, girl?" He reached for the reins and a spot of blood in the snow caught his eye. The horse favored one leg. A rock had cut into the flesh near her hoof, but the leg didn't appear broken. "This mishap could have been worse, but I better not ride her. My weight could do her more harm."

Seth draped a skirt Emily had packed around his shoulders and an apron around his waist as extra barriers against the cold, then struggled into the damp wool coat.

"I'll walk and you ride with Ethan," Emily insisted.

"No, I'll walk the horse. Besides, if I keep moving, I'll stay warmer." Seth helped Emily and Ethan back on their horse, and the trio set out in the blowing snow toward the farm.

The wind kicked up even more and the air turned bitterly cold. Seth had to stop several times to keep his bearings. The material of his sodden coat became frozen and encased him in a hard shell that further hampered his every movement. He suspected his poor feet were taking a beating rubbing against the hard, frozen leather of his boots.

A howling vortex of wind encircled them. Seth held tight to both leads to ensure they stayed together. The horses suddenly panicked and pulled in different directions, turning Seth in circles. Disoriented and now unsure which way to head in the swirling snow, he squinted his eyes looking for a familiar landmark. *The second crossing of the creek should be straight ahead. At least that's the direction I thought we were heading before that last onslaught.*

As Emily leaned down to brush snow off her husband's shoulders in a momentary lull, she asked, "How are you holding up?"

Seth blew into his gloves to warm his numb hands. "I'm all right. Don't worry, dear. We must be close to home, but I'm not sure which direction to head. If I make the wrong choice, we could be out here for hours."

"I trust you, Seth. We'll get home," Emily said, pulling the blankets tighter around her son.

The family trudged on, finally reaching the creek. Seth was in misery. Every step was agony. He dreaded the thought of wading through the cold water again, but eased the horses into the creek and braved the crossing. On the other side, he emptied his boots trying to hide the bloody flesh on his stone cold white feet from Emily.

Following the creek to their property line, Seth knew the farmhouse was only a few miles away. With his energy fading and his scarf frozen to his face, his family staggered into their farmyard. Emily rushed Ethan to bed, piling on quilts to warm him and started fires in the cook stove to heat water for tea and in the fireplace to warm the farmhouse.

Seth returned from the barn after settling the horses. As Emily took the pail of milk he handed her, he winced.

"What is it Seth?" she asked.

He glanced at his feet.

She tugged off his boots and peeled off his stockings to reveal bloody blisters on his heels. His toes and feet were white and hard—"Frostbite!" she cried.

Wrapping him in a quilt, she quickly checked his hands, ears, face, and chin. They were pink and cold, but not frozen.

"I'm sorry I insisted we go, Seth." she said as she poured the water she'd heated for tea into the dishpan to clean and warm his feet.

****

"Mark, you know how concerned I am the Frazers didn't come yesterday. Thank you for offering to ride to look for them. Emily wanted this gathering as badly as I did. Maybe one of them is ill. That's the only reason I can think of that would keep them home." Sarah warmed Mark's coffee.

"Don't worry, dear. The weather is fine today. Jack and I'll head west toward the Frazers' and make sure nothing happened to them. If everything is all right, we'll be home by supper time."

A few hours into the ride, Mark said, "We're almost half way, Jack, and we haven't seen anything yet. We'll go as far as the next creek crossing. It's up ahead around the bend. If we don't see them by then, I think it's safe to assume they stayed home yesterday." Mark nudged Ruby on.

Standing on the bank of the creek looking across to the other side, Mark and Jack were about to turn back when Jack saw something in the distance. "That looks like the Frazers' wagon. We better check it out."

The horses splashed into the creek and out the other side. As they got closer, the wagon appeared to lean to one side. A few wheel spokes were broken.

Mark lifted the canvas flap not knowing what to expect inside. Peering in, he found only a cloth covered basket which he tied to his saddlebag. "It was wicked cold yesterday. They must have rode the horses home instead of coming on. We better follow the road to their place and make sure they got there safely." Mark mounted Ruby and led the way.

****

Arriving at the Frazers', a dim light flickered through the window. "Jack, take the horses to the barn. I'll check on them." Mark headed to the house and knocked on the door, calling out, "It's Mark and Jack Hewitt."

Opening the door, Emily embraced Mark. "Oh, Mark. I'm so happy to see you! I've been so scared. Seth has frostbite. He talked nonsense all night in his sleep. He sweat through his clothes, so I kept cold compresses on his head until the fever finally broke this morning. Ethan has had a slight fever as well, but thankfully not as bad."

"Frostbite? How bad is it?"

"His hands and face are getting color back. I think they were nipped. But his feet have the most damage. I washed and soaked them for a while, then wrapped them with clean bandages. Seth said we should wait and see what they look like today. He finally fell asleep so I haven't disturbed him. Have you had any experience with frostbite?"

"Yes, I had a friend in a similar situation once. You probably shouldn't have soaked them, but I'll take a look when he wakes up. I'm sure he's exhausted. If he can sleep, rest is the best thing. Don't worry, Emily, Jack and I aren't going anywhere until I know you're fine and can manage on your own."

Jack walked in carrying a pail of milk in one hand, a half dozen eggs cradled in his jacket pocket, and the basket Mark found in the wagon. "I've fed and watered the stock, so the chores are done for now. Is there anything else I can do for you, Mrs. Frazer?"

"No, Jack. Thanks. I hadn't given any thought to the chores." She brushed away a tear and said, "You must be hungry. Thank you for bringing my basket from the wagon. Can I fix you something?"

"Mother sent along food and I'm sure there's enough for everyone. You sit and talk with Father while I get things ready." Jack brought in his saddlebags and began preparations.

Ethan crawled up on his mother's lap.

Emily gently pressed her lips to his forehead. "You're cooler now, son. Are you feeling better?"

"I good, Mama. Why Mr. Hewitt and Jack here?"

"We're here to make sure you're all right, Ethan. We missed you yesterday and worried something might have happened. But something did happen, didn't it?" Mark reached over and brushed Ethan's cheek.

Ethan smiled. "Yup. Wagon broke. I ride the horsie."

Emily shared the events of their thwarted journey as they gratefully ate Sarah's food.

Afterward, Jack played games with Ethan and read him a story before putting him to bed for a nap.

"Will you be here when I wake up, Jack?" Ethan asked.

"Yes, Ethan, I promise." Jack tousled his hair, and tucked the covers around his neck.

****

Seth awoke and carefully unwrapped the bandages. He saw bluish-white, waxy-looking skin with lots of blisters on his feet, but nothing dark gray or black.

"Em, can you come. I need your help."

"What's wrong?" a deep voice answered.

He looked. Behind Emily stood Mark.

"Mark, what are you doing here?"

"When you didn't show yesterday and the weather turned so beastly cold, Sarah worried something might have happened. To ease her mind, Jack and I rode out this morning and when we saw the damaged wagon, we figured we better come check on you. And I'm glad we did." Looking at Seth's feet he said, "You're not going anywhere on those for a while, my friend. From what Emily shared, you're one lucky man. I checked out your horse and she'll be fine. How are you feeling?"

"Sore and bruised, but not broken. You're right, Mark, I am fortunate, indeed. It could have been much worse. That wheel could have collapsed while we were crossing the creek. And I don't want to imagine what would have happened if my leg broke while pinned under the horse."

Emily rewrapped Seth's feet in clean bandages while the men talked.

Afterward, Mark called to Jack, "Come help me carry Seth to the kitchen. And, Emily, please bring some pillows to elevate his feet to help reduce the swelling."

****

Mark sent Jack home the next day and stayed until he was sure Emily and Seth could manage on their own. Seth still wasn't one hundred percent, and there was damage, but no joint or muscle weakness. Mark fashioned a pair of crutches so he could help with the chores, but he wouldn't fully recover for quite a while.

On the morning he was set to leave, Mark found

Seth alone in the barn. "I'll come back once the snow melts. You should be in good shape by then, and we can get your wagon. No one regularly uses that road and, unless someone has another wheel with them, the wagon won't be going anywhere."

Seth chuckled as he leaned against the stall for balance. "No need to make an extra trip. Emily and I can get the wagon. I have a spare wheel in the barn. If you could pick up our seed order and this list of provisions for us in the spring, that would be a great help." Seth took a list and money out of his pocket and gave them to Mark.

"Sure, no problem. I'll have these for you by the first week of May." Mark cinched the saddle on his horse. "You know, you're lucky, Seth. I don't think you should worry about fighting in the war. When the doctor sees the damage to your feet, you won't be drafted. Remember, once you have frostbite, it's easy to get again, so be careful from now on."

Seth shook Mark's hand. "Thanks for all your help, Mark. I hate to think how we would have managed without you." Waving his crutch, he grinned. "You really think they'll turn me away because of my feet?"

"I sure do," Mark said.

"Well then, maybe this pain is worth every minute. You might want to give frostbite a try yourself."

Mark laughed. "I think I'll keep my feet just the way they are, thank you."

Chapter Eighteen

January 1864

Mark walked through the door and Sarah rushed to greet him.

"It's so good to have you home again, sweetheart." Standing on her tiptoes, she wrapped her arms around Mark's neck and whispered, "I'll never suggest a gathering during the winter months again."

Mark enfolded her in his arms. "What happened was no one's fault. Blame Mother Nature if you want to blame someone, but don't take it out on yourself. Emily feels badly too and sends her love, but their troubles weren't her doing either."

Sarah helped him out of his coat, took his arm, and led him to the kitchen. "I was glad you sent Jack home when you did. I was about to ride out to look for you myself." She poured them each a steaming cup of coffee.

As Mark sipped, sharing a humorous story about Seth using his crutches for the first time, Sarah enjoyed his soft smiles and reassuring presence. He was her strength and protection and she was grateful for him and his love.

Mark went on, "Jack, the Frazers also send you their thanks."

"I didn't do that much," Jack said. "I'm glad

they're all right. I enjoyed seeing Ethan. He's growing like a weed.

"And speaking of growing," Jack said, "my new business venture has kept Lydia and me really busy. When our regular chores are done, we work on belts and holsters. We might not meet our goal of thirty by the Fourth of July, but we're working hard, and the ones we've finished are well crafted. I'll go get a few from the barn so you can judge for yourself. Lydia's doing a great job of stitching. Tell Pa about it, Lydia," Jack called.

"Ma helped me with different ideas for the stitching," Lydia said. "I'm proud of our work, but you tell us if there's something we could improve on. Jack is putting in a lot of time, so they must sell. They just have to. He really wants the money so he can ask Abby to marry him." Immediately covering her mouth, she said, "Oh, maybe I wasn't to tell you that. Don't tell Jack…"

Jack barreled in. "It sure is c-cold out there. Here. What do you think?" he said as he handed Mark two different style holsters attached to belts.

"You've been busy," Mark said as he gave the handiwork close inspection.

He tried a belt on for size. "I'd buy this one with a matching holster. It fits just right. How much you figure you'll charge?"

"I'm not sure. I think I'll ask some storeowners in town to get a better idea. I want them to sell, so I can't be too high, but I don't want to give them away either." Jack strapped on the remaining belt and cinched it tight. "I'm making a few different sizes."

Mark slipped off the belt. "Your workmanship is

improving. Keep up the good work. I'm sure they'll sell. Mr. Hovis at the Hardware Store is the person you want to talk to."

****

Mid-February, after celebrating his eighteenth birthday with the family, Jack took advantage of a patch of nice weather and rode out to see Billy and his family. After exchanging pleasantries, Jack took Billy outside to talk while he brushed down his horse. "What's the matter between you and the folks?"

"Why do you ask?" Billy's brow raised slightly.

"Pa wanted to come then sent me at the last minute. Is there something wrong between you two?"

"It's not your concern," Billy replied.

"I don't need to know the details. I know Pa loves you. He'd do anything for you. And you're my brother. You can count on me too." Jack hung the horse brush back on its hook. "If you want to talk, I'm here."

"Don't worry, Jack We'll work things out when I come to help with the fields this spring." Billy put his arm around his brother's shoulders. "It sure is good to see you. Steven is glad you're here too."

"Before we go inside, I want to show you the belts and holsters Lydia and I made." He dug one of each out of his saddlebag and handed it to his brother.

"These look as good as you'd buy at the store," Billy said as he tried them on.

"Well, I hope so. I put a lot of time and work into making them. If Mr. Hovis won't take them, I'm not sure what I'll do."

"He'll sell them all right." Billy handed them to Jack who put them back in his saddlebag.

"Is there anything you want to tell me?" Jack

grinned, puffed out his belly, and held it with both hands. "Ma and Lydia are dying to know if Elizabeth is expecting."

"No, not yet, but we aren't giving up." Billy winked. "If things haven't changed by the next time we get to town, Elizabeth will see Doc Glasgow to make sure everything is all right." Billy poked Jack in the gut, grinned, and shook his head. He wouldn't admit it to Jack, but he too wondered why there was no sign of a baby yet.

****

After supper, Jack said, "Come on, Steven. Show me how smart you've gotten this winter. Billy and Elizabeth tell me you've been working on your letters and numbers."

The six-year-old's face turned into a big smile. "I can count to twenty-eight. And I can write words like bat, cat, fat, and hat. I can do adds and take-a-ways if I use the number pyramid Billy made me."

Jack and Steven sat at the kitchen table and worked on numbers and words until Steven's bedtime. "Oh, I forgot to ask. What did you name your little pony, Steven? Lydia wants to know."

"I named him Cloud."

"I like that name. Ma and Lydia will too."

Jack looked out the window. The sky was clear and the moon was bright. "I'm going to take my wares to town tomorrow," Jack shared, "so I'll need an early start to get back by nightfall. If you would save me a plate of supper, please, Elizabeth, I'd appreciate it. I'll be back tomorrow night for sure." Jack said his good nights and climbed the ladder to the loft.

****

Up before dawn, Jack cut a thick piece of bread and spread it generously with butter and jam before he headed out. The weather cooperated and temperatures stayed above freezing so travel was easy. He arrived mid-morning and went directly to the harness maker's shop, introduced himself to the owner, Ezra Gray, and asked, "Mr. Gray, sir, would you be willing to give me your opinion on my workmanship and what you think I should charge for these belts and holsters?"

Looking at them with a critical eye, the harness maker said, "Your craftsmanship is very good, young fella. How long have you been working with leather?"

"My pa taught me the tooling, and I learned to tan the hides on my own. I'm sure there are tricks and tips I don't know yet, and I'm willing to learn."

Ezra reached in a cupboard and returned with a book. "Here, Jack, you can borrow this. It's the one I read when I got started."

Reading the title, *A Step-by-Step Guide to Tanning Hides*, Jack beamed

"Thank you. Thank you, sir. This will be really helpful. The soonest I can get this back to you is April when we come in to pick up our seed order. Will that be soon enough?"

"That's fine. As for your work, I like that you offer two holster styles." Mr. Gray slid a holster off the belt for closer inspection. "Some men like the open-toed style, and others like closed. Some like the full cover flaps that protect the cylinders, and some don't. Making both increases appeal to more people. The slits on the back are the right length to fit all belts.

"It looks like you gave this a lot of thought. I'd ask six to ten dollars for the belts and maybe a little more for the holsters because they're more of a specialty item. The fancier the better."

Jack shook Mr. Gray's hand. "Thanks for loaning me the book and for all your advice, sir. My pa might be the one who returns the book in April, but I'll make sure you get it back. You've been a big help."

"Stop by anytime, Jack. Let me know how you make out with sales. I can see you're going at this seriously. You can make good money if your craftsmanship stays consistent or even improves."

"I'll work on that," Jack said and left with a grin.

Stopping by the livery, Jack bought a scoop of oats for Buttons then walked to the gunsmith's shop run by Silas Ebersmith. After introducing himself, Jack asked, "Mr. Ebersmith, you see a number of men come in wearing pretty fancy belts and holsters. Would you look at mine and give me your opinion on what I should charge?"

The gunsmith tried on a set and slid a gun in the holster to check the fit. "They aren't as fancy as some, but nicer than others. I'd say you could get eight for the belts and possibly twelve dollars for the holsters."

"Thanks for your honesty, sir. You've helped me narrow down the price. Would you be willing to take some on consignment?"

"It's not that I'm not interested, Jack, but I think they'd get more eyes on them at the Hardware Store. Have you tried there?" the gunsmith asked.

"No, I'm heading there next." Jack gathered the six belts and four holsters.

"Come back if Mr. Hovis turns you down. We can work out something."

"Thanks," Jack said and headed to the Hardware

Store. Setting the belts and holsters on the counter, he waited for the owner to finish with the customer ahead of him.

Mr. Hovis looked over. Jack took a breath and reached out his hand. "Hello, I'm Jack Clark. I made these belts and holsters and wondered if you'd consider taking them on consignment."

Mr. Hovis checked out the goods. "Well, what are you charging for each?"

Taking the amounts from the harness maker and gunsmith into consideration, Jack recalled a conversation he'd had with his father about pricing his work on the higher side. If he charged too little to start, he'd never be able to raise his asking price. If he started high, he could always come down a bit if they didn't sell. Straightening and looking Mr. Hovis in the eye, he said, "That depends on how much you'd want for selling them."

Taking a minute to re-examine Jack's work, Mr. Hovis called two men from the back of the store and, after a discussion, announced, "I'll take seventy-five cents for a belt and two-fifty for a set. I know you need to make profit too."

"How about seventy-five cents for a belt and two dollars a set?" Jack quickly countered. "They'll be priced according to the amount of work in them. I figure ten to twelve for the belts and twelve to eighteen for the holster," Jack answered.

"Are these all you have, or will there be more?"

"I'll have more to sell in April and again in July." Jack stood tall and thrust out his chest.

"All right, son. You have a deal. I'll write these up and see how they sell between now and April. Write your prices on these tags and we'll get them on the shelf."

Jack mentally calculated Mr. Hovis' commission, Lydia's wage for stitching, his time, and the money he had invested for skins, then priced the items even higher than he originally planned. *I'll either get what I'm asking or I won't. I can always take them to a bigger town.*

One of the men from the back picked up a belt and rubbing his fingers over the tooled design said, "I'll buy this one for my son."

"Give your money to Jack," Hovis said. "It wasn't on the shelf long enough to require a commission."

Jack walked out with a receipt and money in his pocket. *I hope they all sell by April. I made a good deal. Pa will be proud of me.*

He crossed the street to the Postal Office where two letters awaited. His mother would be pleased. He also bought a newspaper for his father and stuffed everything in his saddlebag. The weather had turned colder, and a few snowflakes started to fall. *I should head back to Billy's, but I rode all this way. I really want to share my good news.* Jack mounted his horse, pulled his hat low, and nudged his horse toward Abby's house.

While hitching Buttons out front, Abby ran out the door and called, "Jack Clark, what are you doing here?"

He took off his hat. "Abby. I'm so glad you're home."

A gust of wind lifted his hair. "I brought you letters, and I have great news. Mr. Hovis is willing to sell my leather goods."

"Come in so we can talk." She pulled on his sleeve.

Jack dug his letters out of his saddlebag and handed them to Abby as they hurried into the house.

"I had to see you. I can't stay long. How are you and your folks?"

Abby led him to the parlor.

Mrs. Proctor peered around the corner and when she saw Jack offered, "Can I fix you something to eat?"

"That would be great." Jack took a seat on the sofa beside Abby and they caught up on news they'd shared in their letters.

"Happy belated birthday, Jack," Abby said. "I know I'll turn eighteen this year too, but as I'm sure you read in my letter, my parents don't want us to marry until the war is over."

"I know, but that could be awhile." Jack sighed. "Don't get me wrong. Waiting will give me time to earn more money and buy a parcel of land. I'm hoping by next fall to have saved enough and then I can start building our place."

"Not too far out of town, I hope. You'll need to come in often to sell your wares."

"No, not too far away. We'll have to see what's available. Just talking about our dreams makes them seem possible."

Mrs. Proctor called them into the kitchen where Jack dug into the bowl of soup Mrs. Proctor placed before him. Conversation turned to the next time they would be together.

"Pa's coming for the seed in April. He can bring my letters then. I might not be back until July."

"I'm so thankful to see you today. July is only five months away. We can pray the war is ended by then. You know you have my whole heart." Under the table,

Abby reached for his hand and gave it a squeeze. "I can't wait for our dreams to happen. If things go well, we'll have a lifetime together."

He gave her hand a quick squeeze in return. "Thank you for your hospitality, Mrs. Proctor. The soup was delicious. I hate to leave so soon, but I'm staying with my brother for a few days and need to get back."

As Jack put on his coat, Abby pulled him aside and they held each other close. She whispered in his ear, "I'll look forward to July and have a whole stack of letters for you. Oh, I didn't give you my letters for today." She ran upstairs and returned quickly. "I told you all about Christmas, wished you happy birthday on your birthday, and, well, you'll need to read them to learn the rest."

Jack tilted her head and gently kissed her. Then again, and again, and finally said, "I better go. I could do this all day."

Abby smiled as she reached for the door handle and couldn't help herself. She spun back around and kissed Jack once and twice more before turning the knob and letting him pass.

"Be careful," Mrs. Proctor called from the kitchen.

"See you in five months," Jack said once more.

Abby waved good-bye as she closed the door against the chill.

Jack counted as the town clock chimed once and headed out of town.

****

A few hours later, the wind calmed, and the sun peeked out of the clouds as he watched for the signpost pointing the way to Billy's farm. "Hang on, Buttons. Soon you'll be in the barn."

Chapter Nineteen

The sun had set by the time Jack made it back to Billy's place. He took care of Buttons and walked into the house as the clock chimed half past the hour. He looked at the clock…six-thirty. He had been in the saddle a long time.

"Well, did Mr. Hovis take your leather goods?" Billy asked when Jack was inside and warm.

"He sure did!"

"Good for you. I bet he'll take more too."

I told him I'd bring him items in April and again in July. He seemed pleased."

"I'm happy for you. This means you have a lot of work ahead, and I know you'll do well with your new business."

Elizabeth set a steaming bowl of beef stew and two slices of bread in front of him.

Jack needed no urging to dig into the hearty meal. He hadn't had much to eat all day. "Thanks, Elizabeth. This sure tastes good."

"Is Buttons all right?" Billy stood and poured Jack another cup of tea. "That was a long trip this time of year."

"She's sore and she's plain tuckered out. I rubbed her down, fed her, and gave her water. She'll recover, but it looks like I'll be staying a few days to give her a rest."

"Did you get to see Abby?" Elizabeth inquired.

"Yes, we had a short visit and exchanged letters. I'm anxious to read about her Christmas and New Year's social events. She mentioned the dance this year was especially nice. She joined the church choir and a needle point group that she really likes."

Suddenly silent, Elizabeth got up and headed to the bedroom. Jack looked at Billy who shrugged his shoulders.

****

The following morning Jack was up early. He fed Buttons, along with the other horses and cows, and had started milking Buttercup when Billy walked into the barn.

"To be honest, I was so excited to tell you about Mr. Hovis taking my belts and holsters and wanting more, that I forgot to tell you I made my first sale. I also stopped to talk to the owner of the harness shop. He liked my workmanship and loaned me a book on tanning hides. The gunsmith also said I had done a nice job and mine looked as good as most he's seen."

"I'm really proud of you, Jack. Ma and Pa will be too." Billy picked up the bucket of milk and headed for the door.

Jack dug in his saddlebags and pulled out the book and the newspaper, grabbed the egg basket, and followed Billy to the house.

Putting the newspaper on the table he read the bold headline, *"Reaction to Lincoln's Emancipation Proclamation Stuns the Country."*

He picked up the newspaper again and read the article in silence.

"This isn't at all what Lincoln's first draft said was

supposed to happen. There is no gradual emancipation of all slaves, and where is the compensation for the slaveholders? This says the proclamation only applies to the Confederate states currently in rebellion, and there is no compensation."

"You're right, Jack. These words mean nothing to slaves in our part of the country," Billy said. "They'll keep on having to run away to find freedom."

Elizabeth added, "I know there are people in town who help slaves escape, but my pa says it's not our affair so we always stayed out of those circles. If we lived in town, we'd know the news daily, and we could have gone to the Christmas dance."

Jack looked at Billy and shrugged.

****

For the next few days, Jack helped Billy with small projects, entertained Steven, and in the evenings read the book about tanning hides alternating with Abby's letters. When a morning bright with sunshine promised to hold the temperature above freezing, he said, "It's time for me to take off for home and share my news with the family." He spun Steven around on his heels. "You be good and keep working on your letters and numbers. I'll tell Ma and Lydia how good you're getting. Johanna asks about you all the time. And I'll be sure to tell Pa how tall you've grown. They'll be glad to see you when the snow thaws."

Jack reached out and shook Billy's hand.

Steven gave Jack a hug. "I'm glad you came. Tell everyone I love them."

"I'm glad I came to visit too, and I'll tell them." Jack picked up his saddlebags and a sack of food Elizabeth had fixed.

"I'll see you again when you come help with the planting. I hope you'll have good news to share with the family then." Jack shook Billy's hand again.

"You mean when I'm an uncle, right Jack?" Steven grinned then turned and looked at Elizabeth.

"Yes, we'll both be uncles." Jack winked at both Billy and Elizabeth. "He doesn't miss much does he?"

Billy let out a long sigh. "No, he doesn't miss a thing."

"I explained what an uncle's responsibilities are and Steven can't wait," Elizabeth added. "Seems like we're all waiting."

"That'll make Ma and Pa grandparents," Jack said as he tousled Steven's hair.

****

Back at the Hewitt homestead, Jack handed Sarah the mail and Mark the newspaper. After telling all of Billy's family news and about Steven's growth and accomplishments he said, "As you know, I took my belts and holsters along to see if Mr. Hovis at the Hardware Store would sell them for me. I needed to find out if starting a business was a good idea."

"What'd he say?" Mark asked, glancing up from the newspaper.

"He said he'd take them and he wants more. He's asking a fair amount for his shelf space and I even sold a belt." Jack went on to explain his conversations with the harness maker and gunsmith. "They were both very helpful," Jack said and showed everyone the book he borrowed.

"Congratulations." Mark put aside the newspaper and shook Jack's hand. "I know how much this means to you. Hearing others tell you your workmanship is good enough to sell means a lot."

"Lydia, I can pay you now for the stitching you did. The way I figured it, you've earned two dollars and sixteen cents." Jack handed her the carefully counted coins.

Lydia's face lit with a smile as she tucked the money safely into her apron pocket.

"What are you saving your money for, Lydia?" her mother asked.

"I think I'll save for a sewing machine and someday own a dress shop."

"Then we'll each have a business." Jack turned to his pa and handed him a five dollar gold piece. "Thank you for all your trust and advice. I want to pay you back now with money from my first sale." Jack closed his money pouch and tucked it in his pocket.

"I'm proud of both of you," Mark said. "You took on this additional responsibility and you're seeing it through with success. Two business owners in the family. How about that."

"Then who will work the farm and take care of me when I get old?" Sarah asked.

Everyone started laughing, then Jack's thoughts drifted to the money he would earn and the life he could provide for Abby when they married.

Chapter Twenty

Spring Thaw

As April began with a stretch of warm days promising spring, the Henrys headed to town.

"Look, Billy, the doctor's shade is open. He must be in. Please drop me off now. I can't wait another minute to find out why we can't make a baby."

In Doc Glasgow's parlor, one of Elizabeth's former classmates glanced up from her chair.

"Elizabeth! I heard you got married. I haven't seen you in quite some time." The friend rose to give Elizabeth an embrace. "Are you ill?"

"Nothing Doc can't fix." Elizabeth opened her arms to hug her friend and couldn't help but see she was with child.

"When are you expecting?" Elizabeth inquired. "You must be so excited."

"I have another two months, but I check in with Doc regularly to make sure everything is all right."

Doc Glasgow stepped into the room. "Have a seat, Elizabeth. I'll be with you next," he said as he motioned for the expectant mother to enter his examination room.

Oh, how desperately Elizabeth wished she could trade places with her old classmate.

When her friend left, Doc Glasgow called her to the other room.

After a thorough exam, Doc said, "Elizabeth, you're in good health. There's no reason you can't have a baby." Thinking out loud in a muffled voice as he turned away from Elizabeth, he muttered, "Unless...."

Elizabeth wasn't sure what he said and then heard him say, "Just be patient."

****

Billy and Steven left the wagon in front of the Dry Goods Store and soon carried out the items on Elizabeth's list, plus a few extras supplies Billy was sure she must have forgotten. Steven held tightly to his two-cent bag of candy as Billy lifted him onto the wagon seat. "Let's stop in and see my friend Cain at his blacksmith shop before we go to the Parkers' house."

At the shop, Billy shook Cain's hand. "I wanted to drop by to see how you're doing. After a long winter it's good to see you again, my friend. I was afraid maybe the war caught up with you."

"Nobody has come calling my name yet, Billy. I'm still here and doing well, but I doubt we'll be waiting long. Have you heard any news lately?"

Billy shook his head.

"Ulysses S. Grant was named General-in-Chief of the Union Armies recently. The Union troops in Kansas are well organized along the eastern border now, and the guerrilla raids have practically ceased. Quantrill and his troops aren't such a threat anymore, but people still shouldn't let down their guard.

"There's fighting near the Mississippi River in Tennessee, where there was a massacre at one of the forts. Sounds like they're getting closer. Lincoln signed the Emancipation Proclamation, but it didn't do much good around here. It only helps the eastern slaves."

Cain wiped his brow.

"I heard about Lincoln, but Grant becoming general is news to me," Billy said. "I bet you're right and we get called up this year. I thought for sure we'd be on the fighting lines by now. I guess after Lincoln gave the deserters amnesty, there must have been enough men to meet their quota. Then, when congress signed the Conscription Act, calling for the enlistment of all able-bodied males between twenty and forty-five years of age for a three-year terms, it looks like they mustered enough men to fight without us. Well, at least for the time being."

"That's all right with me." Cain threw wood into the forge. "Stand back, Steven," he said as he pumped the bellows.

"Oh, I know all about hot fires, Mr. Cain. Elizabeth yells at me all the time to stay away from the stove."

"It was good seeing you, Cain, but we better get going. We still have to stop at the Hardware Store for our seed and meet my wife at her parents' place. We're staying the night and then heading home. By the way, how's the Missus and your boy?"

"Good seeing you too." Cain gave him another firm handshake. "They're both good. My son is growing fast and likes to visit the shop. He's a little too young for the heat around here, but it won't be long. Have safe travels and I'll see you next time you're in town." Cain turned back to his work as Billy and Steven crossed the street to the Hardware Store. They loaded their bags of seed into the wagon and headed to the Parker home.

****

At the Parkers', Elizabeth shared her good news

with her mother, but stopped abruptly when the brothers walked in the door.

"Is everything all right?" Billy directed the question to Elizabeth.

"As far as Doc can tell, everything is good. He said I was in good health and we should keep trying, that we hadn't been married a year, and that if it's meant to be, it will be," Elizabeth answered.

Billy gave her a kiss on the cheek. "I'm glad all your worries were for nothing."

"Uncle. Uncle Steven." Steven jumped in circles clapping his hands.

"It better not take too much time. I want a baby. Something of my own to take care of," Elizabeth mused aloud.

****

In the morning, Elizabeth kissed Billy gently on the cheek to see if he was asleep. When he stirred she said, "I didn't get a wink of sleep and the way you tossed and turned all night, I know you didn't either. I'm so glad Doc said I was healthy and that there is no reason why we can't have a baby."

Holding her close, Billy tilted Elizabeth's head to kiss away her happy tears. "I know you want a baby and how much a child means to you. We will have children, many children. But I'll love you regardless of whether we have any or not. You, me, and Steven are already a family, and nothing will ever change that. We must be patient."

Elizabeth wrapped her arms around Billy as tears rolled down her cheeks. "I hope the next time we come to town it'll be for a checkup for our baby."

Mrs. Parker called out, "Breakfast is ready." The

smell of bacon and biscuits wafted up the stairs.

"Why don't you leave Steven here while you run to town," Elizabeth's mother offered. "I'm going to do some baking after the breakfast dishes are done."

Steven's eyes widened. "It's all right. You go without me," he said.

The happy couple strolled to the bank greeting people along the way then stopped to pay the doctor for Elizabeth's visit. She had been so eager to see Doc, she forgot to ask Billy for money to pay yesterday.

Elizabeth started to introduce Billy when Billy said, "Good to see you again, Doc. We've already met. I fetched you when Ma, Mrs. Hewitt, had Johanna on the way home from the Fall Festival four years ago."

"Yes, I remember that," Doc said. "You look like you're in good health, son."

"Never better. I'm glad Elizabeth's in good health too. We'll keep trying to have a baby and, yes, we'll be patient."

Billy paid the man and they walked back to the Parkers' house.

With the wagon loaded, the family headed toward home. A happy Steven held a tin of freshly baked biscuits, Billy held renewed hope, and Elizabeth held a steely determination to have a baby as soon as possible now that Doc said there wasn't anything standing in their way.

Chapter Twenty-One

"Well, Sarah, two calves were born this week and there will be plenty more in the months ahead. Our dreams of turning the farm into a ranch have finally become reality. It took us four years, but I'd say we now have the ranch we always longed for. The herd has grown to a healthy thirty-four head of cattle. We'll brand them this year before we drive them to town."

Lydia pulled a paper from the drawer. "I made sketches of different designs we can use for our branding iron. This is my favorite. Lydia held up a sketch on paper showing a capital C with the bottom curve extending through three vertical lines creating two H's. CHH. The letters represent Clark, Hewitt, and Henry."

"That one's my favorite too." Jack took his morning plate to the sink. "We'll be driving cattle to town this fall for sure, and not only a few cows. Billy will help us. We'll have our hands full."

"Selling half the herd will give use money for winter supplies and next year's seed with some left. Finally, a profit for all our hard work. Speaking of hard work, I'm going out to check the fields today to make sure they're ready to plow," Mark said, finishing his coffee. A flash of movement toward the barn caught his attention.

"Jack, the bull busted out of his pen again. Get

your roping arm ready. Let's go." Mark left his coat on the hook. "The winds have finally been blowing in from the south, so after we get that bull penned up, I'm sure we can start on the fields."

****

Jack and Mark toiled weeks of long days working the ground in preparation for the planting season. Sarah and the girls helped pick rocks.

Coming back from the fields one night, Jack said, "Pa, when you go to town and check on Billy's family, could you do a few things for me while you're there?"

"Sure, Jack, what do you need?"

"Lydia and I have belts and holsters ready. Could you take them to Mr. Hovis at the Hardware and collect any money I made from the ones that sold? Also would you be willing to return Mr. Gray's book on tanning hides? I'll give you money to buy hides from the butcher and supplies from the Dry Goods Store. I'll take all the hides the butcher has. Ask what he wants for them and, if he wants more than three cents a hide, offer him three and see if he'll take it. If I have to pay more, all right, but no higher than five cents each. That's my limit."

"Are you sure about that price? To continue your business you need the hides, but can you afford to pay five cents and still make a good profit?"

"Well, if I pay a higher price for the hides, then the price of the holsters and belts must go higher and I'm not sure they'll sell."

"All right, Jack, I'll haggle for you. Hope for the best. Anything else?"

"Would you mind stopping by Abby's house to drop off my letters? Tell her I miss her and that I'll try

161

to get to town in July."

"Sure I will, son. And I'll bring her letters back. I know how much she means to you."

"I'm going to ask her to marry me once the war is over. Her folks won't let us marry until then. At least that's what her letters say. They think she's safer in town and besides, I don't have land or a house started yet. I'm hoping to earn enough from my leatherwork to buy land next fall."

"I know it's hard, but it's smarter to wait. I'm sure when the time comes, Billy will help you build your home and you know you can count on me. If that's your goal, we'll make it happen." Mark reached out and shook Jack's hand, appreciating how responsible he had become.

Sitting around the supper table that evening, Mark announced, "I'm leaving for town tomorrow. Make your lists if you want anything."

After dinner, everyone sat at the table and wrote out their wishes and needs.

"Peppermint stick," Johanna added.

"Don't worry, Johanna. Pa will bring you a peppermint stick." Mark picked her up and twirled her around.

****

With lists and money in his pocket, Mark headed out, arriving in Dead Flats after spending a night at the old oak campsite. He'd planned to stop at the Henrys' then changed his mind. It might be better to wait until Billy came home. That way, he and Sarah could talk to him together. Pulling the wagon to a halt at the Hardware Store, he went inside and looked for Jack's wares on the shelf. Not seeing them anywhere, he asked the man at the counter, "Hello. Is Mr. Hovis in?"

"I'm Hovis. How can I help you?" the owner asked as he appeared from around the corner.

"I'm Jack Clark's stepfather, Mark Hewitt." The men shook hands. "He left belts and holsters for you to sell."

"Yes, they weren't on the shelf long and they all sold, I hope you have more with you."

"They're in the wagon. I'll fetch them while you figure up his receipt."

Mark returned with ten belts and seven holsters priced and ready to sell.

Mr. Hovis handed Mark a copy of a ledger page and money. Each sale was detailed with the selling price minus his commission. "I'll write a receipt for these new items while you shop. Your boy said he'd have more again in July. Is that still his plan?"

"Yes, he'll be in for the church festival and will bring his handiwork for you. He has other pieces as well. Would you be interested in hunting bags or coin pouches?"

"Sure, if the quality of the workmanship is the same, they should sell." Mr. Hovis opened his ledger and began writing.

Mark said, "I'm also here to get my seed, Seth Frazer's order, and a piece of angle iron to make a branding stick, oh, and fence rails if you have any."

Mr. Hovis called a man in from the back of the store to help load. Mark picked up the receipt of Jack's items and paid, then was off to the Postal Office with three letters from Sarah to mail. Two awaited in return. With a newspaper tucked under his arm, he walked on to the Dry Goods Store to pick up the provisions on

Sarah's and Emily's lists, and he didn't forget the peppermint stick for Johanna. He put one in Ethan's bag too.

He saved the Butcher Shop for next to last. The man behind the meat counter asked, "What can I get for you, sir?"

"Do you have any hides I could buy?" Mark dug in his pocket for his coin pouch.

"Well, I believe I could let you have some today. How many you want?"

"They're for my son, Jack. You may remember him. He bought from you before. He'll take all you have."

"All of them?"

"Yup, how many would that be?"

"I have a few left from yesterday, you want them too?"

"It depends on the price. What ya asking?"

The man called to a worker and asked, "How many hides do we have out back?"

"Don't know exactly, but I'd say at least fifteen," the butcher answered.

"How much?" Mark jingled his coin pouch.

"How about three cents each? I usually get five," the man said.

Mark replied, "How about two cents each and you're rid of all of them, and I need the heads too. You know my son will use them and they won't go to waste."

"All right. I remember your boy coming in a few times. Two cents each. Thirty cents total."

Mark counted out the coins and paid.

"Go 'round back and I'll have a guy meet you there

with sacks and rope to tie them together."

With the hides and heads loaded, the next stop was Abby Proctor's house. He knocked on the door, letters in hand.

Abby answered and when she saw what Mark held in his hands welcomed him into the house.

"Nice to see you, Abby. I'm dropping off letters for Jack. He wanted to come, but one of us had to stay at the farm. Jack agreed I could come if I dropped these off for you and picked up any you may have to send him."

"I'll be right back, Mr. Hewitt." Abby ran upstairs and was back in a flash.

"Please tell Jack I enjoyed his last letters, that I miss him, and that I hope he can come in July," Abby said rapidly.

"I'll tell him and, yes, that's the plan. He'll come in July, of course depending on the war and if there's fighting in these parts. If his brother and I are called up to fight, the plan is he'll stay with the family."

"Let's pray it never comes to that," Abby said.

"Yes, I pray every day the war ends." Mark reached for the door. "I better get going."

"Good seeing you again, Mr. Hewitt," Abby said.

He was about to leave town when he glanced down and there was the book Billy had borrowed from Mr. Gray. He pulled the wagon to a halt in front of the harness shop.

Inside, Mr. Gray was working on a bridle and Mark held up the book wrapped in paper with a note from Jack sticking out.

"You must be Jack's father," Mr. Gray said.

The storeowner set aside his work and Mark said,

"I'm Mark Hewitt. Thank you for letting my son, Jack, borrow your book on tanning. I hope he hasn't rubbed the ink off the pages. He must have read it three or four times front to back. He said to thank you and that he's anxious to try some of the new information he read about. I picked up hides today, so I know what we'll be doing tomorrow when I get home."

"He's a talented young man, Mr. Hewitt. How did he make out selling what he showed me?"

"Mr. Hovis at the Hardware Store sold everything he left previously. I dropped off several items today and Hovis wants more come July."

"You can be proud of him. I've never seen someone his age so serious about making this a thriving business. I'm sure he'll make out well. Have him stop in and see me when he's in town."

"I'll tell him, Mr. Gray, and thanks again for all your help and encouragement."

As a last minute decision, Mark made a quick stop to see if the sheriff was in his office. He pulled up, the door swung open, and the sheriff motioned for him to come in.

Mark took his hat off as the sheriff held out a cup of coffee as an offering.

"Have a seat," the sheriff said, standing to shake Mark's hand.

"I can't stay long. I stopped to see if you'd heard or seen anything with the Hewitt or Henry names regarding the draft. I can't imagine getting through this entire war without getting called to serve."

"Well, a matter of fact I have. If they need a large group to hold our boarder between Kansas and Missouri, you'll both most likely make the short list."

"I figured as much. Any idea when that might be?"

"Nope, it all depends on how aggressive the fighting gets and how far west they come. We had trouble with Quantrill last fall, but nothing out of him recently. We'll probably have more slave movement this year though. The Senate started drafting an amendment to abolish slavery and involuntary servitude, but the amendment still has to pass the House and be signed into law. And who knows when that will happen."

Mark looked around cautiously, then said, "We had four bounty hunters give us a hard time when you sent the two boys ahead of their father last fall, but we handled it with no violence. They got away fine. I suspect you'll be sending more soon."

"Yah, if you don't mind, I will. It works well sending them to Billy's farm first, then on to you, if they want to head west."

"I'll give Billy a heads-up next time I see him. Well, I better get going." Mark finished his coffee, put on his hat, and reached for the door.

"I'll get word to Billy and he can let you know when we need you to fight. You'll report to Fort Riley and get your orders there," Sherriff Sloan said, shook Mark's hand, and closed the door behind him.

With the wagon lumbering down the road, Mark looked forward to reaching the old oak campsite to settle his thoughts on the war issue.

Building a fire, he reached in his coat for a scrap of paper to use to start a fire and from his inside coat pocket pulled out an envelope. He had forgotten all about Katherine's letter that arrived months ago. He mused, *Should I open it?* He poured a steaming cup of coffee and slipped the envelope back into his pocket.

He turned his thought back to the war. *I'm not looking forward to telling this to Sarah and Billy. Having to fight was inevitable. After three years, I should count myself lucky that Jack has grown up enough to handle the farm. I pray we get the crops harvested before we leave so we won't lose the herd. If we lose the herd, we're back to starting over. I'm too old to start over.*

Chapter Twenty-Two

Jack hung his hat on a hook inside the farmhouse and took an appreciative whiff of supper. "Sure smells good! Once Billy and his family arrive with his plow, we'll finish in no time. There's about twelve more acres that need tilling, and the garden and pumpkin patch should be turned over."

"They could arrive any day now. We'd better start baking extra bread and pies and plan on some of Billy's favorite meals," Sarah suggested to Lydia.

"How about some of my favorites," Jack said.

"You always get your favorites," Lydia countered. "And remember, Elizabeth doesn't like to cook like Ma does. I guess she's still learning."

"That's for sure. You won't recognize Billy and poor little Steven when they get here. They've wasted away to nothing." Jack grinned and sat down as Johanna placed forks and knives in the right spots on the table.

Walking in from the porch, Mark caught the tail end of the conversation. "Who's wasting away to nothing?"

"Oh, your son is teasing me," Sarah said. "I hope you're hungry, dear. We're having one of Jack's favorite meals tonight."

"I'm surprised the Frasers haven't come for their supplies yet," Mark said, lifting Johanna into her chair at the table. "I hope they didn't have a problem getting the wheel on the wagon. I told Seth I'd come help, but he thought he and Emily could handle it."

Sarah set the food on the table. "Well, then we might have lots of company if they all come at the same time."

****

Two days later, the Frazers drove in mid-morning. The women walked to the house to catch up while the men loaded the supplies in the wagon.

"Please stay for dinner. It's no problem at all," Sarah insisted.

"If you're sure it's no bother, and you'll let me help," Emily agreed.

Sarah called out the door, "Seth, you're staying for dinner. We'll have it ready in an hour. You can eat and then be on your way."

Seth yelled back, "That's fine," then went on to explain to the men, "I need to get back tonight. I have a cow that might drop a calf soon, and I need to get back in case it's rough going."

With the barn full of hides in different stages of the tanning process, and various leather projects underway, Jack showed Seth his work while he recounted the story of selling his wares.

Afterward, Mark offered, "How are you doing for chickens? We have an abundance. If you could use six or seven, we can spare them."

"I can't turn away an offer like that." Seth shook Mark's hand. "We'll take them, won't we, Ethan."

"Come on, Ethan, you can help me catch them," Jack said. "There must be something around that we can put them in." The boys took off, and in no time had a crate loaded in the back of the Frazers' wagon covered with a feed sack to quiet the hens inside.

Lydia stepped out on the porch and called out, "Time to eat, everyone!"

Sarah gave a quick word of thanks in prayer, then the group sat around the table. They covered everything from the kinds of pies that the Frazers didn't get to enjoy back in December to the fields that were tilled so far. And of course, the latest news about Generals Grant's and Sherman's appointments in the Union Armies and the amendment to the US Constitution abolishing slavery and involuntary servitude being passed by the Senate. When the meal was over, Mark gave Seth a recent newspaper to take home.

Saying good-bye in a spontaneous gesture of affection, Emily gave Sarah a hug and kiss on the cheek.

"Come visit again real soon. It's been lovely to have another woman to talk with," Sarah said, returning the kiss.

Seeing his mother show affection, Ethan took Johanna's hand and gave her a hug and a kiss on the cheek.

"Come visit again," Johanna said and kissed his cheek.

Lydia and Jack were the only ones to see this exchange. They smiled as Jack picked up Ethan and placed him on the wagon seat.

As the Frazers drove away, Jack and Lydia headed to the barn to work on their leather projects.

"I miss them already," Sarah said, linking her arm with Mark's. "I wish they lived closer so we could visit more often." Sarah and Mark walked back to the house,

Johanna in his arms.

****

At the end of the following week, Billy, Elizabeth, and Steven arrived. The neighbor boy agreed to tend to their animals, so they could stay as long as necessary. When they crossed the creek onto the Hewitt property, the weather was bright and sunny, and the cows were enjoying the lush pasturage.

After pleasantries, Mark said, "Jack, why don't you show everyone what you and Lydia have been working on in the barn? Billy, your ma and I would like to talk to you, if you could give us a minute."

"Sure, Pa," Jack said. "Come on, Elizabeth. You can give us your opinion about the coin pouches we made, and tell us if you think they're fancy enough for the women in town."

Closing the door behind them, Mark said, "Billy, your ma and I feel terrible about the way we left things the last time you were here. Please, let us explain."

"No, Pa, I've given our last conversation a lot of thought the past few months. At first, I was hot about your secret when I found out. Now I understand your reason for Jack and Lydia not knowing about Samuel's death. It's not for me to say if your decision is right or wrong. If I hadn't seen the dates on the tombstones were the same, I'd never know either.

"You're the one who wanted me to stop at the cemetery in Marysville to see my father's grave. You knew then there was a chance I would connect the two dates, yet you encouraged me to stop, because you knew I had things to get off my chest. I'm glad I figured out the truth. If you don't want Jack and Lydia to know, it's not up to me to tell them." Billy hugged his ma. "I know you're trying to protect them, but what Samuel did was heroic. If you told them the truth now, I believe they would be understanding. But then they'd realize that you lied to them when it happened."

"You're right, Billy, Samuel was a true hero. I kept my promise to him until Sarah figured out what actually happened."

A tear escaped and coursed down Sarah's cheek as a sob shook her body.

Mark put his arm around her shoulders and kissed her forehead. Billy went to his mother to comfort her and his pa, then said, "I will never tell. They'll never hear about any of this from me."

"Thank you, Billy," Sarah said as she drew him in for a warm embrace.

Billy kissed her cheek and said, "Come on, let's go see what Jack and Lydia have been working on. I bet you're proud of them. I was impressed when Jack showed me his wares before he took them to town."

****

By the time the threesome walked in, Johanna and Steven had found Muzzy and Momma Kitty. The two were sitting on the spring wagon, each holding a purring cat on their lap.

Elizabeth was engaged in giving suggestions to Jack on fashioning a design on a coin pouch. When Elizabeth finished speaking, Mark said, "All right, men, let's get the plows hitched to the horses so we can get going after the noon meal."

"Many hands make light work," Jack and Billy said in unison.

Lydia took Steven and Johanna to check for eggs in the chicken coop.

Walking back to the farmhouse to start preparing the dinner meal, Sarah put her arm around Elizabeth's waist and said softly, "Are you with child yet, dear?"

Elizabeth hung her head as she shook it slightly.

Sarah gave her a gentle squeeze.

Shortly, Johanna ran into the house carrying a half-dozen eggs in her little apron. "Here, Ma! Cook," she said.

Sarah added another dozen from the morning basket and put them on the stove to boil while Lydia made a creamy white sauce from butter, flour, and milk.

"Elizabeth, would you please slice two loaves of bread and brown them in butter on the griddle?" Sarah then made a pan of corn muffins to go with the dish she called creamed eggs. Once the eggs were cooked and shelled, she sliced them into the creamy sauce, added a few spices, and called the men in to eat before they headed out to the fields.

Elizabeth said, "I was skeptical about the combination of eggs in cream sauce spooned on top of grilled bread, but it's really delicious. I've never had eggs fixed like this before. I watched how you made them so I can make them at home."

"Good," Steven said. "I like these eggs and we can eat them for every meal. Right, Elizabeth?"

Elizabeth kept eating.

"Right, Billy?" Steven asked.

"Yup, every meal, little brother," Billy agreed as he thought, *Elizabeth's poor cooking and lack of mothering toward Steven concerns me. She doesn't seem to take an interest in anything we do on the farm, and sometimes, I have to remind her when our clothes need washed. Sarah or Lydia would never let this happen. I wonder if this is how Elizabeth would treat her own child.*

Chapter Twenty-Three

After saying the morning meal prayer, Sarah said, "Thank you all for your hard work."

Steven said, "Pass the sausage, please."

"Well, it took us three weeks, but the fields are planted, the garden is in, and Jack and Billy even got the pumpkin patch done," Mark said. "Now pray for a good growing season and that the war doesn't call us away before we get the crops harvested."

"I finished bending the branding iron into Lydia's design and we can start marking the cattle as soon as we're done eating," Jack said as he passed the platter of fried eggs. "The Clark, Hewitt, and Henry brand will look good on those cows."

"Here's how I see us working this," Mark offered. "We'll build a fire outside the corral, separate the herd into three groups starting with some in the corral, some in the barn, and the new calves tied to the hitching post. Separating them will take time, but the time will make the branding go a lot faster. We should be able to get them all done today."

"That sounds good to me," Jack said.

"Me too," Billy agreed.

Steven said, "And me too."

"All right." Mark nodded. "But you're going to have to do exactly what I tell you, Steven, or you'll be staying in the house with your ma and Johanna because everyone else will have a job to do."

"I'll be good. I'll help." Steven took a bite of sausage.

****

Mark and Billy gathered the grazing cattle and got them separated. Jack built a fire and Steven helped carry wood to the fire pit so Lydia and Elizabeth could keep the fire going to heat the branding iron and then pass it through the fence to the men.

Billy and Jack roped the cattle and held them while Mark put the iron to them. The odor of scorched hair and flesh turned Elizabeth's stomach on the first few, but she got used to it.

By noon, they completed the cows held in the corral. The group took a quick break to eat then branded the calves. The weather cooperated and the well-organized team worked until the last cow bore the CHH mark.

"That pot of venison stew smells great, Ma. Oh, and fresh rolls and two pies for dessert. Hurry up, everyone, I'm hungry," Steven announced. "I miss living here. Elizabeth doesn't make many pies."

Scraping the last piece of pie crust onto his fork, Billy announced, "I have planting of my own to finish. We'll be heading home tomorrow, so that means an early night for us."

****

The following morning, around the breakfast table, Mark finally mentioned, "When I was in town, I stopped by the sheriff's office to see what Sheriff Sloan knew about our area being called to fight. He figures if the fighting gets much closer to Kansas, Billy and I will get called up to fight and must report to Fort Riley."

Elizabeth spoke. "If Billy has to go fight, I plan to go to town and live with my parents. My father will take care of me and I feel being in town would be safer than coming here."

"Elizabeth! You never told me this." Billy raised his voice then lowered it again. "I guess we never discussed it. I always thought you and Steven would stay with my family. I'm sure you'd be safe, and I know Ma is expecting you to stay."

Sarah glanced at Elizabeth and then at Billy. "You're certainly welcome here, Elizabeth. I hope you know that, dear. But if you'll feel better living with your parents in case something might happen to them, then that's where you should be."

"Well, I guess you're right, Mother, if she wants to stay in town to take care of her parents," Billy conceded.

"What about me?" Steven looked at Billy, and then at his ma and pa.

Mark said in a strong tone, "Steven, you'll come stay with your family and help Jack with the farm."

"Good, I hoped you'd say that. I'll help you, Jack." Steven grinned.

Elizabeth wiped her mouth and put the napkin on the table. "I'm glad you want to stay with your family, Steven. You wouldn't be happy in town."

"The sheriff said he'd get word to you first, Billy. You'll have to pack your house items of value the best you can and bring your animals here. We've talked about this possibility now for three years, but I'm afraid this is our year. There's no telling how long we'll be gone. An empty house can be tempting to travelers passing through. Clean out the root cellar and divide the food between here and town. Pack a bedroll, food, and utensils for yourself, and all your firearms and ammo." Mark slammed his hand on the table. "I don't like talking about war plans any more than anyone else, but we need a plan in place."

Billy shoved himself away from the table and stood. "You're right, Pa. We'll start preparing. Steven, grab your things. Come on, Elizabeth, we must get going."

"You want a few baby chicks to take with you?" Mark asked.

"If you can spare four or five, that'd be great." Billy put his hand on Steven's shoulder. "Throw your bag in the wagon then help Pa with the chickens."

As Lydia and Elizabeth headed out to the wagon, Billy said, "Ma, I apologize if Elizabeth hurt your feelings. I'm not sure why she'd rather go to Dead Flats."

"Don't worry about that, Billy. If she feels she needs to stay in town to take care of her parents, I can see her reasoning. Don't give it another thought. You know if you have to go fight, we'll take good care of Steven." Sarah gave him a kiss on his forehead and a pat on his back. "I don't think the family will be going to Dead Flats in July, so I don't know when I'll see you again. Jack will want to take his wares to sell, but there's no reason everyone needs to go."

Mark called, "You two all right in there?"

"Yes, we're coming." Sarah slipped her arm around Billy.

Steven and Johanna were sitting in the back of the wagon with the chickens while Jack, Lydia, and Elizabeth chatted.

"Steven," Billy called. "You better say your good-byes and give everyone a hug and a kiss. Hard telling when you'll see them again."

Jack helped the two youngsters off the wagon and Steven started making his rounds. Elizabeth did the same.

"Plan on stopping by next month on your way to the Fourth of July Festival, Jack," Billy suggested. "Why don't you come a few days early and we can practice our shooting for this year's contest, maybe even make a friendly bet."

"Okay, you're on," Jack accepted.

"Good luck with your garden this year, Elizabeth," Sarah said. "I'm sure Steven will help with the weeding."

"Make sure you take care of Cloud and brush him regularly," Lydia reminded Steven.

"Cloud's a good horse. Smart too. Billy and I go for rides. I always take good care of Cloud," the young boy responded.

Hugs, kisses, and good-byes said, Billy turned the wagon and headed toward home.

Chapter Twenty-Four

Crossing the creek and traveling a few miles down the road, the chickens quieted. In the warmth of the morning sun, Steven curled up on a blanket and said, "I'm tired. Wake me when we get to the turn-off."

Once Billy was sure Steven was asleep and wouldn't overhear the conversation, he said, "Your announcement at breakfast was quite a surprise, Elizabeth. We never discussed what would happen if I had to leave for war. You behaved as though everything was settled when you told my family your decision to stay with your folks when obviously I was as surprised as they were. You embarrassed me in front of my family. Ma covered for you and hid her feeling of disappointment, but I know she was hurt.

"You made it sound as though your pa could protect you better than my family."

"I'd feel safer living in town with my parents," Elizabeth replied, looking away.

"I don't think it's because of your parents, Elizabeth, or because you'll feel safer."

"Of course that's the reason. If anything does happen to them, I'll be there to help." Elizabeth inched away from Billy on the seat.

"No, if you live with your parents, you won't be expected to do anything. I think you want your parents to pamper and take care of you."

"You're wrong. Besides, the Hewitt family has enough mouths to feed. I don't see why they'd complain about one less."

"That's not the point. You're my wife now. The Good Book says a man is to love his wife as himself, and let the wife put her trust in God and accept the authority of her husband. In the past, we've always talked over decisions that affect both of us. Not discussing your decision with me was disrespectful. I don't think that's how your mother treats your father. And what would you do if your father is called up to fight?"

"Well, if he does have to leave, that's all the more reason I should be there with my mother."

"And who would care for you then?" Billy raised his voice and quickly quieted. "You have no family in Dead Flats other than your parents."

"We could go live with my mother's sister and her husband in Missouri."

"And how would you get there safely, not knowing where the fighting is taking place?"

"I don't know! I don't know! But I don't want to stay with your family on the farm." Elizabeth crossed her arms and huffed.

"What have they ever been to you but kind and supportive?" Billy's voice rose again.

"There would be too many of us living there. If something happened, where would I run? Town is a day and a half ride from the ranch, and I couldn't make it on my own. I can't hitch up a wagon or even saddle a horse myself." Elizabeth straightened, sitting rigid on the wagon seat.

"Jack would be there to protect you. Ma and Lydia

know how to use a gun. Would you feel safer if I taught you how to use one too?"

"No. I couldn't shoot anyone. I'm not a murderer. I don't have killing in my heart."

"Even if they were trying to kill you?" Billy ripped his hat off his head and slammed it beside him on the wagon seat.

"I couldn't! I just couldn't!" Elizabeth argued.

"Then it's a good thing we don't have a baby right now. I fear you both would die," Billy countered.

"What do you mean? I'd never harm our child."

"Being willing to fight for your family is taking care of it. How would you take care of our baby if you're not willing to fight? As it is, you don't even take care of Steven well. You say you want a baby, but your motherly feelings and behavior toward Steven don't show that you'd be a good mother. You rarely take any interest in what he does other than tell him what not to do. And you barely show him any affection."

Elizabeth raised her voice. "Billy Henry, yes, I do!"

"I'm being honest, Elizabeth. I don't see your affection and am sure he doesn't feel your love the way a child desires."

"Well, you spend more time with him than you do with me."

"So, is that why we're having this discussion? I don't spend enough time with you?" Billy held the reins in one hand and turned Elizabeth's face to look directly into his eyes with the other. He said, "My brother is only six years old. He needs us. He needs both of us, like our own child would at his age."

Elizabeth became silent and turned away. They

rode several miles before she addressed Billy, "I am going to stay with my parents when you leave. I've given it much thought. I hoped you wouldn't be called up, but now that it looks inevitable, I must tell you I couldn't survive living with your family. I'd have to live on their schedule and do as they asked every minute of every day. I'm not cut out for farming the way they are. It's all right when it's only us on our farm. We live closer to town and at least I get to see my parents and friends from time to time. I miss the life I had before we were married, Billy. There was always something fun and interesting going on. Now life seems like work, work, work."

Steven stirred in the back of the wagon, and Billy said softly, "I wish you had shared your feelings with me before now, Elizabeth. Truly, I didn't know you were so unhappy. Apparently, Steven and I aren't enough to make you love this new life we're building. Since you spoke your mind, so will I. I'm glad you're not with child right now for many reasons. If you still want a baby when I return, we can discuss it then."

"What do you mean for many reasons? You know I love you and want a child," Elizabeth protested, her eyes welling with tears.

"We will talk about children when I return," Billy said with finality. As he raised the reins, the horses picked up the pace and the wagon lunged forward.

Steven awoke and popped up making urgent motions for Billy to pull over.

Once he returned to the wagon, Elizabeth said, wiping tears from her eyes, "We're almost home, Steven. What would you like for your midday meal?"

"How about some creamed eggs," Steven

suggested.

"Great idea, brother," Billy agreed. "We should have enough eggs and milk." He reached back and tousled the little boy's hair then touched Elizabeth gently on the shoulder as the wagon rolled into the farmyard.

****

A few weeks later, Jack arrived at Billy's farm in time for supper. Elizabeth had made a large pot of chicken and dumplings. The house was tidy, and freshly washed clothes danced on the line in the yard. He grabbed a bowl and fork before claiming a spot at the table. "Billy, are you ready to lose to your little brother in this year's shooting contest? That rifle prize is already mine. I've been practicing, and even Pa said I was good enough to win this time."

"We'll see about that. Tomorrow morning we'll have a contest of our own," Billy said.

After eating, the men went to the barn to brush the horses and catch up on family doings. Jack led off, "Pa gave me a note to give to the bank president asking for all but a fourth of our savings. He thought you might want to do the same in case you have to leave unexpectedly to fight. You'd have money to give to Elizabeth and with the fighting coming this way, Pa's worried money won't be safe in the bank."

"That's not a bad idea. I'll do the same. I can give Elizabeth money and send the rest home with you to put in our hiding place under the old elm tree."

"Happy to help. I hope you know that if you do leave to fight, the whole family will be praying for your safe return," Jack said.

"Thanks, Jack. That'll give me courage and

strength. Please let Ma know I'll watch out for Pa, and we'll come home safe together."

Jack said, "Together. That reminds me. Lydia wanted to come along so we could give Elizabeth her surprise, but said if we waited, it might be awhile. We want her to have the money pouch she helped us create. We made several with her design." Jack reached in his saddlebag and pulled out a prettily wrapped package, and handed the box to Billy.

"No, you give it to Elizabeth, Jack. You and Lydia made the gift."

"Okay, I'll surprise her tomorrow. Hope she likes it."

****

Bang! Bang! Bang! Cans flew in the air. After competing, Jack said, "We may have tied today, brother, but I won't let you win tomorrow." Jack helped Billy with projects around the farm, and then the three brothers saddled their horses to ride out and check on the fields. Steven was almost tall enough to throw the saddle on Cloud. Once Billy got the saddle on, Steven tightened the cinch and they were ready to leave.

"We'll be back in an hour," Billy called to Elizabeth as she hung fresh wash on the line.

The brothers rode slowly through a three-acre grazing plot of clover and grasses where a cow and her calf were roaming. Billy explained, "Steven and I planted four acres this year. Two in corn, one in oats, and one in wheat."

"You sure were busy," Jack commented.

"I was a big help this year, wasn't I, Billy," Steven said.

"You sure were, little brother. I couldn't have done

it without you." Billy dropped back putting Steven in front so he could talk to his brother. "I know you'll take good care of Steven when I leave, Jack. He'll help with chores and anything else you need him to do."

"What about Elizabeth? Has she changed her mind about staying in town?" Jack asked.

"Nope," Billy said. "She insists that's where she's going, so I'm not arguing with her about it."

"Ma wanted me to extend the invitation again to come stay at the farm with us. I'll ask her at supper tonight. Then I can tell Ma I tried." Jack sat tall in his saddle.

"You can extend it, but I'm pretty sure I know what her answer will be."

After a tour of the fields, the brothers headed back to the house, brushed the horses, did the chores, and went in for supper.

"Smells good, Elizabeth, and you made rolls too." Steven smiled.

Elizabeth set the food on the table, Billy said the prayer, and everyone dug in with gusto.

Jack wiped gravy from his chin, then said, "Ma asked me to extend the offer again for you to stay with us, Elizabeth."

"That was nice of her, but please let her know Billy and I discussed it, and I will be going to town." Elizabeth set her fork on her plate, got up, and asked, "Would anyone else like more milk? I made an apple cake for dessert."

While Elizabeth plated the cake, Jack fetched the surprise and put the package at her place.

Eyes wide and a smile on her face when she saw the gift, Elizabeth asked, "Where did this come from?"

187

"It's from Lydia and me," Jack said. "Go ahead and open it."

Untying the bow to save for her hair, the coin pouch was revealed. "Thank you, Jack, and thank Lydia too. You used my design. I'm so pleased."

"Yes," Jack said, "and we liked your design so much we made several to sell in town."

"I love it. I simply love it." Elizabeth clenched it to her heart.

Billy added, "And I'll give you money tomorrow after I go to the bank."

Chapter Twenty-Five

Everyone was up early to head to Dead Flats. "Can I ride with Jack?" Steven asked, fingers crossed.

"I don't mind," Jack said.

"Sure. You two head out now and we'll catch up." Billy wasn't looking forward to the half-day ride with Elizabeth. The couple rode in silence the first hour or so.

"Billy, I think we need to discuss..." Then suddenly, two neighbor boys walking along the road interrupted the conversation.

Billy slowed the wagon and asked, "Hey, Peter. Where ya headed?"

"We're going to town, Mr. Henry. Ma needs supplies and we want to see some of the doings," Peter said. "Don't fret. My older brother is doing your chores."

"Hop in." Billy motioned. "You can ride with us and get there quicker. You spendin' the night?"

"No, we must get back tonight. Pa don't like us gone too long," the younger boy said.

"Well, you're in luck. My brother Jack in the wagon up ahead is coming back this way tonight. You can hitch a ride with him."

The boys hopped in the wagon and, to Billy's relief, began talking about farming, crops, cattle, and the new pen they built to raise hogs.

"How's your family doing?" Billy turned and looked at Peter.

The brothers went silent. Then Peter said, "Ma, Pa, and the rest are well, but my oldest brother Gus was called to fight and our family's worried 'cause we haven't heard from him since he left. That's part of the reason Pa sent us to town, so we can check the Postal Office for a letter and see if his name is on the posted list for wounded or worse."

"I'll pray for a letter," Elizabeth said.

"Thank you, ma'am," the boys said. They talked constantly for the remainder of the trip.

As the wagon crossed the bridge into Dead Flats, the activity in the church grove ahead was sparse. Where before there were strings of wagons pulled in along the stream and dotted among the trees, now there was only a scattering. Only a few horses were tied in front of the saloon and the streets were almost empty of people.

Jack pulled up in front of the Hardware Store and Billy followed.

"Where is everyone? Are you sure this is the right day?" Steven asked.

"Yes, this is the right day. I'm not sure where everyone is," Jack said.

Jumping out of the wagon, Billy introduced Peter and his brother to Jack. "These boys are my neighbors and would like to hitch a ride back home tonight. Can they leave with you after the shooting contest?"

"Sure, I'd enjoy the company. When I'm done here, I'll pull the wagon over by those trees. Meet me there after the shooting contest." Jack shook their hands.

"Thanks a lot! We'll be there," the boys said and went on their way.

"I'll meet up with you at the contest. We might have a good chance to win. It doesn't look like many people made the trip this year," Jack said, as he reached into the back of the wagon and pulled out two sacks of his wares. He was anxious to see if anything his father dropped off in April remained on the shelf.

"Good morning, Mr. Hovis. I brought you more leather items to sell."

"I wondered if you'd make the trip. I'm glad you did. I only have one belt left on the shelf and your pa said you had different items you were working on. Well, let's see them."

Jack slung the two sacks on the counter and Mr. Hovis was pleased with everything as he inspected each item and wrote up a consignment receipt.

"Thank you again for putting my work on your shelf space," Jack said when Mr. Hovis paid him for the sold items. "I sure was surprised when we rode in today. Where is everyone? It hardly feels like a day of celebration."

"Oh, you haven't heard, I guess. The town cancelled everything except the shooting contest and the church picnic this year. Most of the men are fighting and large gatherings stir up trouble with folks passing through and the town folk."

"So no parade and no dance tonight?" Jack inquired.

"That's right. It's not good for business, but that's the town council's decision for the safety of all."

"Mr. Hovis, I'm not sure when I'll get back again, so will you hold the money from the new items until I return?"

"Sure I will, Jack. It'll be waiting for you, and I'll take more items whenever you can get them to me."

Jack picked up supplies and medicine for his ma, first. Then, at the Postal Office he received one letter and mailed his mother's letters telling his grandparents the planting went well, about the new calves born this year, and the branding event with Billy's family. On his way out, he looked at the list of wounded and death notices posted on the door and didn't recognize any of the names, then drove the wagon to the Butcher Shop.

As Jack walked in, the bell on the door rang and the owner stepped out to ask, "How can I help you?"

"I'm hoping you have hides I can buy. You have any today?"

"You're in luck, my boy. We butchered this morning, and I'm sure there are some from yesterday and the day before. I'd say there are twelve good hides and a couple smaller. I won't even make you haggle on the price today. You can have them all for a quarter."

Jack reached in his pocket and pulled out a quarter, plopped it on the counter, and said, "Sold. That's with the heads too, right?"

"Yup, heads too." The owner called to the help in the back room to wrap the hides and to help Jack load the wagon.

With that task completed, Jack headed to the sheriff's office. Billy was at the front of the line for the shooting contest about to sign the book and pay his entry fee. Jack called his name and waved to let him know he was there.

Billy waved back, took his turn paying, and went to talk to Jack. "How did you make out with your wares?

Get any hides this trip?"

"I sold all but one belt. Mr. Hovis likes my new items and, yes, I picked up hides. As soon as I win the rifle and see Abby, I must start for home. Did you hear there's no dance tonight?"

"Yeah, Elizabeth is upset about it."

"How about I wait for you, then we can take care of our other business? When we're finished, we can get Steven and Elizabeth to watch the contest," Billy suggested.

"You'll have to get 'em, I'm going to find Abby and give her my letters." Jack reached the front of the line, signed, and paid his fee. Then the brothers walked to the bank, withdrew all but a quarter of their money as planned, and went their separate ways.

****

Happily, Jack found Abby at home. He twirled her in his arms and the young couple exchanged letters while sitting on the back steps catching up. "I heard there's no dance tonight," Jack said.

"That's all right. I usually spend my time talking with friends and watching others dance. It's not the same without you."

"Well, I thought we could have our own dance. May I have the pleasure, Abby?" Jack stood, twirled her around again, and drew her close.

"What song would you like me to hum, Jack?" Abby inquired.

"Something long and slow." Jack pressed his cheek against hers.

Abby softly hummed a tune and their bodies swayed back and forth. At the end of the song, Abby said, "I could dance like this all night."

"I could hold you like this forever," Jack said. Taking her face in his hands he kissed her sweetly and then kissed her breathless before returning to their seats on the steps. "I can't wait for this war to end. Then people can get on with their lives. Pretty soon I'll have enough money saved to buy us a piece of land and start building. My leather items are selling well. And with what I dropped off and what I plan to make with the hides I picked up today, I figure by next fall, if the war's over, we could get married."

Abby buried her head in his shoulder. "I want that more than anything, Jack Clark. I pray for us every night."

The town clock chimed, Jack's signal to get to the shooting contest. "I'm going to win the rifle this year. Are you coming to watch?"

"Yes, I'll let Ma know where I'm going and we can walk together," she said kissing him soundly for good luck.

By the time Jack and Abby arrived, the sheriff had already given his speech and the first shooters were ready to fire. The couple located Billy in the crowd.

Billy's number was announced, and he took his first shot from the firing line, hitting the paper target dead center. When he looked to where his family stood, Elizabeth wasn't with them. He searched the crowd as he reloaded—no Elizabeth.

Taking aim on the first bottle at one hundred yards, Billy told himself, "Focus." The bottle shattered. He searched the crowd again and spotted her with friends. He let out a sigh of relief and shot the second target. The bottle shattered. Reloading for the third shot, he looked again to where Elizabeth had been and saw

Quinn standing beside her. Billy raised the gun and made himself focus. The shot veered to the left and completely missed the third bottle. Glancing to where Elizabeth was, Billy noticed she was gone. He looked where his family stood, and there she was, clapping with the others as if she had never left.

Billy made his way through the crowd to his family. Jack slapped him on the back and said, "You didn't have to make it this easy for me, brother."

"If you win today, you won fair and square," Billy replied. He took Elizabeth's hand and led her away from the noise and the crowd.

"Did you watch me shoot, sweetheart?" Billy asked.

"Why, yes, of course. I'm sorry you missed the third bottle," Elizabeth said in a low voice.

"I watched you, too," Billy said. "As soon as I left your side, you were talking to your girlfriends and then with Quinn. I know you enjoy talking to your friends, but with everything happening in the area right now, I'd feel better if we traveled back with Jack. Maybe I could talk him into staying for the picnic. What do you think?"

"I think you worry too much. I'd like to spend the night and leave in the morning as we planned."

"All right, Elizabeth. I know you don't get to see your parents as often as you'd like. We'll stay." Billy nodded.

The sheriff called the next number. Jack's number.

Billy and Elizabeth made their way back through the crowd to Steven and Abby as Jack hit the bullseye on the first target. Then, bottles one, two, and three fell in order. Nobody else had a clean score so far, but there were still more shooters to try their luck.

Afterward, Jack admitted, "My stomach did a flip flop when I realized I have a chance to win!"

"I wish the whole family could have been here to see you shoot." Billy gave his brother a hug.

"If you win, everyone but me will have won a rifle." Steven stomped his foot.

"You must wait your turn," Jack said. "I can remember my father shooting in the contest when I was too young to enter."

"All in due time," Abby said and took Steven's hand.

Finally, the last contestant shot and missed two bottles. Jack had won. The sheriff called him to collect his rifle and four boxes of ammo.

Proudly, Jack held the gun high in the air and thanked the sheriff and the other contestants.

Sherriff Sloan said, "Your pa will be proud of you, Jack."

The crowd dispersed to the church grove for the picnic. Jack said his good-byes to his family, and Abby walked him to the wagon where the two Morgan brothers were waiting. "Throw your stuff in the back and hop in, boys. We'll be leaving in a minute."

Jack kissed Abby behind the tree and said, "Oh, Abby. I don't know when I'll get back again. Please keep safe. I worry that the town could be overrun with fighting and you might be hurt."

"And I worry some renegade soldiers might find your farm and burn it to the ground because they can," Abby countered. "I'll keep safe for you if you keep safe for me."

"It's a deal. I don't know what I'd do without you

in my life, Abby. I can't wait for the day when we can always be together." Jack drew her close and held her tight.

"Is that a promise, Jack Clark? I love you."

"I promise, Abby," Jack said, returning her kiss. "I love you, too. I better get going. I need to get these hides home as soon as possible."

Jack climbed onto the wagon seat, waved, and blew Abby a kiss.

As the wagon pulled away, Abby returned the gestures and called out, "I love you, Jack."

****

"Can I go back for seconds," Steven asked, as the trio sat together on a quilt spread in the same spot the family usually sat. Elizabeth's parents didn't join them this year.

"Yes, Steven, I'm ready for more. Can we get anything for you, Elizabeth?" Billy offered.

"No, you two go, I'm not quite ready for seconds yet," Elizabeth said.

Mary Jane, one of Elizabeth's friends, walked over to chat with Elizabeth while the brothers were in line. The gals talked until the brothers returned and Mary Jane excused herself.

"I think I'm ready for seconds now," Elizabeth said. As she stepped in line, her friend Katie appeared.

Observing this, Billy said, "Elizabeth sure has a lot of friends in this town, but I guess in all fairness, if I still lived in Kansas City where I went to school, I'd have more friends I'd talk with at events too."

Katie returned with Elizabeth to say hello to Billy and Steven.

Billy offered, "Stay and talk, if you'd like, Katie.

Come on, Steven. We'll go get dessert. We'll be back in a few minutes, ladies."

Katie and Elizabeth chatted until the brothers returned with plates piled high with cake and a slice of pie.

"I better get going," Katie said.

"Walk with me to the sweets table, Katie," Elizabeth said.

When Billy looked up, Quinn was in line behind Elizabeth. A surge of emotion rose in his chest. *Am I jealous*? *Or is Quinn just another good friend?* He knew not to say something he'd regret.

He would ask Elizabeth about her relationship with Quinn later. Maybe he was concerned for no reason. At least he hoped that was the case.

Elizabeth returned and they joked and laughed until the church ladies started to clean up. "I'll go get our dishes," Billy said. "Steven, you can stay and help Elizabeth fold the quilt. I'll be right back."

Billy was about to reach for the crock of baked beans Mrs. Parker fixed for the picnic when Quinn stepped in front of him and said, "I see there are a few beans left. I'll finish them up. I always enjoyed Mrs. Parker's cooking. Tell her that for me, will you." He scraped the sides of the crock, put the last spoonful on his plate, and walked away.

Again, Billy pulsed with a surge of confused emotions. *What was with Quinn? Is he taunting me? I'll relay Quinn's message to Mrs. Parker and see what she has to say before I ask Elizabeth.*

Billy put the crock in the basket. "Come on, Elizabeth." He took her hand and the threesome headed back to the Parker residence.

****

"We're getting close to the path we take to get home, Jack," Peter Morgan said. "We really appreciate the ride. Our folks will be surprised to see us home so soon."

"I was glad for the company. Now I'll have to start talking to myself to stay awake," Jack joked.

"Right here is good, Jack. Thanks again for the ride. Maybe we'll see you again in town sometime," Peter said.

As the wagon slowed to a stop, Jack said, "I'll look forward to it."

The boys got their things from the wagon and hurried on their way.

Jack continued for a while before getting out for a stretch and to eat some biscuits Elizabeth packed. He inspected his new rifle, enjoying the thrill of winning such a prize, and then continued home. He wanted to get the hides home as soon as possible so he only stopped to rest a few hours to give the horses a break. Wearily pulling into the yard in the early morning, he carried Sarah's supplies to the house, then began unloading the hides at the barn.

Mark went out to give a hand. When all the hides were unrolled and hanging over the rafters, Jack pulled his prize out from under the wagon seat. "You can have your rifle back now, Pa. Maybe pass it on to Lydia. I won my own. And I won mine fair and square. Billy missed the last target completely, and nobody else shot a perfect score."

"Congratulations, Jack! I'm proud of you. That's a nice piece of wood on that stock. Let's go show everyone. You look dead tired. I'll start on these hides while you catch a little shuteye. Don't worry; I'll wake you in a couple hours."

****

That evening at the Parkers', Billy paced around the room waiting for the right time to speak to Mrs. Parker about Quinn. He wanted to speak to his mother-in-law alone.

"I think I'll turn in early tonight," Elizabeth announced.

Billy leaned in to kiss her goodnight, but Elizabeth turned and went up the stairs. He thought, *Perfect. Now I can hopefully find out the truth about Quinn and his relationship with Elizabeth.*

Billy caught Bertha Parker in the kitchen and said as casually as possible, "I bumped into Quinn at the picnic and he said to tell you how much he enjoyed your beans. Can you tell me how long he and Elizabeth have been good friends or was there more to their relationship at one time? He talked as though he'd spent a lot of time at your house."

"Oh, you must mean Quinn Harris. Elizabeth and Quinn had a falling out."

"Well, what happened?" Billy inquired.

"I believe there was an incident that involved a cat. Even though the cat wasn't Elizabeth's pet, the way the cat died affected her greatly."

"So I take it Quinn had something to do with the cat's death?"

"Well, he always denied his involvement, but sadly, Elizabeth wouldn't forgive him."

Billy cocked his head. "Do you remember when this happened? Was it about the same time I started to see Elizabeth?"

"Why, yes," Mrs. Parker admitted. "Come to think of it, I believe you're right."

"Thank you, Mrs. Parker. Every time we come to town Quinn is extremely attentive to Elizabeth and even though she's now married, she doesn't seem to mind his behavior. Maybe Quinn wishes Elizabeth had waited for him to return from war instead of marrying me."

"Well, he is a hero. He was wounded fighting for his country," Mrs. Parker said.

"I, too, will be fighting for my country when needed. I hope that doesn't mean I must come home wounded just to be considered a hero." Once said, Billy wished he could take it back, but nonetheless he was sure Mrs. Parker had gotten his point.

"I'm going to say goodnight to Elizabeth before turning in. I hope you have a good journey home tomorrow and keep my daughter safe. Give the Hewitts our best the next time you see them. Would you be a dear and take care of all the lamps before you go to bed?" Mrs. Parker left the room.

"Goodnight," Billy said and proceeded to blow out the lanterns. He was not looking forward to the ride home. He wouldn't mention his conversation with his mother-in-law and did not wish to discuss Elizabeth's concerns about a baby. What occupied him now were worries about going to war and what the future would hold for him and Elizabeth. He had a sinking feeling in his heart that Elizabeth might harbor other reasons for wanting to stay in town if he was away.

Chapter Twenty-Six

"One more day and we'll have all the hay cut and stacked to dry. Then we can start gathering the cattle in the corral for the drive," Jack said as he finished hitching up the horses. "How many head are we selling, Pa?"

"We'll butcher three for the winter and sell ten. You can help me get them as far as Billy's, then he can help me get them to Dead Flats while you come back and look after the family. Should the war take a turn for the worst and I'm called up, I'm trusting you to handle the farm and protect the family on your own, Jack. Don't stay away for more than a few hours when you go hunting. Everyone will be depending on you, son."

"I'll take care of them. Don't worry, Pa. Ma and Lydia are stronger than you think," Jack responded as he led the horses out of the barn to work in the fields.

****

"Hurry, Lydia. If you finish that piece, I can add it to the items to sell." Jack packed feed sacks with completed items plus his letters for Abby for Mark to deliver. Sarah packed the men a substantial meal to eat along the way.

"Open the corral gate, Lydia," Jack called.

The cattle poured out anxious to stretch their legs. Jack started hooting and hollering to keep the ten head of cattle moving toward the Henry farm.

With only a few strays to keep in line, Jack and Mark arrived at Billy's midafternoon and herded the cattle into Billy's small corral. Steven ran out. "Boy, am I glad to see you."

"Come on in. I'll warm up leftovers," Elizabeth offered.

"Thanks, Elizabeth. I'll grab jerky and a few biscuits and head back home." Jack gave his letters and wares to Mark. "I know you'll get a fair price for the cattle, Father. I'll see you back home soon," Jack said, and rode off, not wanting to leave the family alone too long.

****

Bright and early the next day, a crisp fall breeze blew across the plains. Billy and Steven loaded the wagon, Elizabeth grabbed the supply list and tucked it in her pocket, and they began the trek with cattle in front of the wagon and Mark on horseback rounding up the stragglers.

In Dead Flats, Mark haggled a good price for the cattle, but when he reached the bank to deposit the money, he found it had been robbed about a month before. All their savings were gone. Thank goodness he and Billy had withdrawn the major share of their accounts earlier. He pocketed the profits from the cattle sale and headed to the Hardware to drop off Jack's wares and get his profits. With space in his saddlebags, Mark picked up a few winter supplies for Sarah plus some extras: fabric, yarn, and crochet thread to keep the women's hands busy, a ladies magazine, two new novels, and a picture book. He didn't forget sweets for the young ones. He would save the candy to give them if he had to leave for war.

On the way to the Postal Office Mark picked up a newspaper and dropped off two letters from Sarah for folks back East. She'd written about selling the cattle, the condition of the crops, and that everyone was healthy, and war hadn't come close to Dead Flats yet. There was one letter waiting for Sarah that he tucked into the inside pocket of his coat.

Abby's letters were his last delivery. When he knocked on the door, Mrs. Proctor answered. "I'm sorry, Mr. Hewitt, Abby isn't home. I'll give her these letters when she returns."

"Thank you, ma'am," Mark said, and headed to the sheriff's office to catch up on news.

Sheriff Sloan sat writing at his desk when Mark entered. The sheriff looked up and said, "Good to see you. What brings you to town?"

"Billy and I brought cattle in. I heard the bank was robbed. Anyone hurt?"

"No, they did it at night. Picked the lock on the door and blew the safe. Got clean away." The sheriff offered coffee from the pot sitting on the potbelly stove.

Mark accepted and asked, taking a sip of good, strong coffee, "Any chance you'll get the money back?"

"It doesn't look like it. I took a posse out, but we never found any sign of them and don't even know how many of them there where," the sheriff said.

"What's the latest on the fighting? Are they close to Kansas?"

"A troop of soldiers were through the other day. Looks like the Rebels may be heading our way. A Confederate general named Sterling Price is gathering an army. They'll start from Arkansas then will probably march through Missouri. If they aren't defeated somewhere along the way, they may get to Kansas." Sloan shook his head. "I hoped the fighting would never come this close to home, but now it's only a matter of time. We have possibly a month or a few weeks. I'd get prepared and be ready to head directly to Fort Riley on short notice. Your orders will await you there."

"You'll get word to us?"

"Yes, I'll get word to Billy. He'll then spread the message to you and the Frazers."

"I'll let Billy know. Do you think there's any chance that David Parker will be called up?" Mark asked.

"No, Parker paid his commutation of three hundred dollars to escape the draft and avoid the war two years ago, but don't mention that to anyone, not even Billy."

"I won't. But it's good to know. Elizabeth will be living with them while Billy is gone."

"I'll keep watch on her when I can."

"Thanks for everything, Sheriff Sloan. I better get going. Take care. Depending on the way things go, it could be a while before we have a chance to spend time together again." Mark left to connect with Billy at Elizabeth's parents' home.

Steven was outside watching ants building a mound when Mark rode up. "I thought you were going home, Pa."

"I am, son. But I need to talk to Billy first. Run and fetch him for me, will you, please."

"Be right back." Steven darted for the door and returned with Billy.

"Steven, you go play. Pa and I need to talk." Billy

turned so his back was to the house as he asked, "What's up, Pa?"

"I talked to the sheriff and he told me we should be prepared to leave. It could be weeks or possibly a month, but I wanted to let you know so you could start getting things together. If you were planning on going to the bank for money, there is none. The bank was robbed."

"Mrs. Parker told us about the bank," Billy said, "but I don't think she knows how close the fighting could be."

"I wouldn't want to panic her, and I'm not saying to leave and go home right now, but this will probably be your last time in town for quite a while. Do you need money for supplies?"

"No, Pa. I brought money with me, and we're good on supplies. I'll bring all our animals and items from the root cellar to your place when Steven and I come. Elizabeth still insists on staying with her folks."

"I wouldn't worry about her. She'll be fine here, and the sheriff said he'd watch out for her."

"Thanks. That makes me feel better. It looks like I'll be seeing you soon. Tell Ma and everyone I send my love." Billy stood back and let Mark mount his horse.

Steven ran over. "You leaving now, Pa?"

"Yup, you be a good boy, and I'll see you soon." Mark tipped his hat and waved good-bye.

****

The next morning, the Henry family got an early start. Billy commented as they rode, "It could be any day when I get word to fight. We should get our things in order, Elizabeth, so it won't take us long to get you to town."

"You mean you don't mind if I stay with my parents now?" Elizabeth gasped.

"No. If that's where you feel safe, that's where you should be. I'm not upset. I still don't understand, but that's all right. I'm sure your father can take care of you."

"I'm so relieved you changed your mind. Please tell me you had a change of heart about us having a baby now too?" Elizabeth clasped her hands together.

"No, I haven't," Billy said, looking away. "We'll decide that after I return."

"We don't need a baby now," Steven said. "Elizabeth's neighbor's dog had puppies last week. He'll give me one. They're real cute. Can I have a puppy? Pleeease."

"We'll see," Billy said, before Elizabeth could respond.

Chapter Twenty-Seven

All the way home, Mark's thoughts were about protecting Sarah and his family since he knew he might be leaving soon to fight.

At home, Sarah rushed out to greet Mark. "I'm glad you're back. I worry when you're gone."

Mark leaned in and kissed her on the cheek. I'm fine. I'll come in when I finish in the barn. He put the extras he bought in his hiding spot in the tack room as Jack walked in to help with his horse. "Here's your money and receipt from Mr. Hovis, Jack. I'm proud of you, son. You and Lydia are doing well with your leather business." They fed and watered Ruby and walked together into the house where everyone was gathered. Mark announced, "Jack, help me sharpen the knives, and, Sarah, please get the crocks and cutting boards out. We're going to start butchering tomorrow."

"Is there something wrong, Mark? I sense an urgency in your voice I haven't heard since the barn burned in the storm five years ago," Sarah said as she sat by his side.

"I talked to the sheriff. He strongly suggested we get things in order in case I must leave." Mark took Sarah's hands in his. "No one knows when, but the sheriff suspects strongly that the fighting will eventually reach Kansas soil. We must be as prepared as possible." With those words, Mark enfolded Sarah in an embrace, feeling her breast against his chest; he ran his fingers down her back. He breathed in the scent of her hair savoring the smell for days ahead when they'd be apart. These times were precarious and nothing was sure except that dark clouds were gathering.

Even though Sarah had everything organized and everyone knew their jobs, the butchering took all day and into the evening to complete. A weary Mark announced, "We can finish grinding the meat for sausage tomorrow. Jack and I will smoke two front shoulders and you gals will have to can what's left over. With the extra mouths to feed, thank goodness the garden produced a fine crop this year. I don't want you worrying about food. You'll have enough on your mind."

Everyone was in the house when Mark said, "Oh, I almost forgot, Sarah, there's a letter from your mother in my coat pocket."

"I'll get it," Johanna offered. She ran to the coat and pulled a letter from the pocket. Then reached deeper and pulled out a second letter. "Look, two, Ma," she said and handed them to her mother.

The first one was from her mother. The handwriting on the second envelope was also feminine.

Mark was dumbfounded at first, then it dawned on him. *The letter from Kathrine!*

Jack glanced at Mark. Mark caught his gaze and motioned to the door with his eyes.

"Come on, Johanna and Lydia, let's go to the barn. You can help me with the hides. Ma will tell us the news later."

The letter was addressed to Mark. Sarah stared at him, bewildered. She offered him the letter, but he drew back.

Mark said, "As you can see, I didn't open it. I forgot all about it. We can read it together if you'd like. I have nothing to hide from you, Sarah."

"It's from Katherine. I've seen the handwriting before." Sarah turned the enveloped over and opened it.

"Whatever the letter says, it isn't important. I love you. And I love our family. Nothing in that letter will change the feelings in my heart."

Sarah unfolded the letter, noted the date—July 1863—and read aloud.

July 1863
Heather Forks, Missouri
Dear Mark,
I am writing to say I am sorry, and I hope there are no hard feelings.

My father passed away about a month ago, and my mother finally told me the truth. My father hired those thugs to beat you up when you were here last in Heather Forks. I thought you would like to know your suspicions of Father were right. Please don't harbor any ill feeling toward him. In his eyes he did what he had to do. I realize now our love was never meant to be, especially when you expressed your feelings for Sarah.

After you left, I started seeing Cliff Adams. You remember Cliff. We were married and have a little girl. She is almost three. We named her Beatrice May Adams.

I am sorry to say that Cliff got called up to fight, and I hated watching him ride out. I do not condone the war, and I pray daily for his safe return.

The war has taken so much from so many, but it

has caused quite a demand for hardware supplies and business is good. Mother helps in the store sometimes, but mostly she stays at home enjoying her granddaughter.

I hope this letter finds your family out of harm's reach of war. I also pray if you must go fight, that you come home safe to your family. I know how much they mean to you.

Sincerely,
Katherine Adams

"My, you have been carrying that envelope around a while," Sarah said. "The last time I heard her name was six years ago, when you told her about me and that your life together was over."

Mark grinned. "I hope you can see a letter from Katherine didn't mean anything to me. You're the only woman in my life and that's the way it will always be."

"I think Katherine wanted to resolve some issues from your past when the two of you were close." Sarah folded the letter and put it back in the envelope.

"Yes, I believe she is happy with the way everything turned out." Taking the letter from Sarah, he dropped it in the cook stove. "That's the last we'll hear from Katherine Adams." He took Sarah in his arms, held her close, and then tilted her chin with his finger to raise her lips to his.

They kissed and then kissed again until Sarah was on her tiptoes with her arms around Mark's neck. He was reluctant to let go.

Finally, Sarah said, "Jack knew about this letter, didn't he?"

"Yes," Mark admitted. "Jack is the one who picked

it up in town."

"Shall we go show him the letter didn't have any effect?" Sarah took Mark's hand and they walked arm-in-arm to the barn.

****

Three weeks after the Henry family returned from town, Peter, one of the neighbor boys, rapped on Billy's door bright and early one morning. Out of breath and in an urgent voice, the young boy said, "The sheriff came early this morning and said to spread the word. You need to get to Fort Riley as soon as possible."

"Thanks for letting us know, Peter. We just sat down to eat. Come, join us," Billy offered.

"I'd like to, but Pa said to get right back so I can see him before he leaves. He's going to town to pick up my cousin, and then they'll head to Fort Riley together."

"Hear that, Elizabeth? Mr. Morgan is going to town. I'm sure if we ask, he'll get you there safely. You're packed and ready to go, right? Grab your bags so you can go with Peter."

"I packed some things, but I wouldn't say I'm ready to leave." Elizabeth stood then froze in place not knowing what to do next.

"Steven, help Elizabeth finish packing. Peter can help me catch the chickens then he must leave. You have ten minutes, hurry!"

Grabbing things here and there and stuffing them into her bags, Elizabeth said, "Steven, get my hair things off the bureau and put them in the bag. Then please locate my other shoes and my shawl. They're by the door, I think."

Billy returned and called, "Come on, Elizabeth.

You and Peter have to get going."

Elizabeth walked out of the bedroom dragging her two carpetbags. "I thought I'd have more time. I'm sure I'm forgetting things."

"You'll be fine, Elizabeth," Billy reassured her. He took her in his arms and kissed her, then kissed her again. "I love you, Elizabeth. Keep safe and I'll return as soon as possible."

Steven gave Elizabeth a kiss on the cheek and said, "I'll miss you, Elizabeth. Take good care of your family."

Billy helped Elizabeth up onto the horse behind Peter and, handing up her belongings, said, "Squeeze the bags between you and Peter and hold on."

"I love you, Billy Henry. Be careful and come home to me. I'll pray for you every day," Elizabeth said.

"I love you, too," Billy said, as the horse left the yard.

Steven shouted, "Good-bye, good-bye!"

Billy and Steven loaded the wagon and lifted the chickens into the back. Then they tied on buttercup, the beef cow and her calf, and Cloud and Lucky to follow behind. He recalled what Mark said about leaving the house empty of valuables and ran back in to check each room one more time. In the bedroom, a necklace lay on the floor by the night table. He noticed Elizabeth had been wearing it lately. He tucked the necklace into his coat pocket. Everything else of value was already loaded.

The brothers arrived at the Hewitts' by midday. Jack immediately rode to tell Seth and Emily the news. Meanwhile, Billy, Steven, and Mark tended to the animals and unloaded the goods from the wagon into the root cellar.

****

With Buttons giving it his all, Jack arrived at the Frazers', saw a light in the barn, and called out, "Its Jack, Jack Clark, I have news of the war."

Seth ran out from the barn. "What about the war?"

"You're being called up along with Billy and Father. They are waiting for you at our farm and sent me to help you load your wagon and fetch the livestock. You need to get to Fort Riley as soon as possible." Jack jumped down from Buttons and walked her around to cool her off.

"Even with your help, it will take a lot of time." Seth ran in the house to tell his family. "Emily, start packing inside, Jack and I will pack up the root cellar and get the animals and feed ready to travel in the morning." Seth paced back and forth. "Well, it happened. I knew fighting would hit Kansas one day. And today's as good as any, I guess. Let's get working. Ethan, you help your ma pack your things. No telling if they'll send me home on account of my feet or make me fight. We'll prepare for the worst."

It was after midnight when Seth said, "I'm tired. We better get some sleep. Don't worry, that rooster wakes me every morning at the crack of dawn. We'll finish loading the wagon and get on our way tomorrow. Jack you can bunk with Ethan tonight."

The loaded wagon groaned under the weight of valuables, food, and grain for the livestock. The wagon rolled out of the yard midmorning and arrived at the Hewitts' before the evening meal.

"Emily," Sarah called out, running to embrace her

friend.

"Oh, Sarah, this is awful, just awful."

"We'll be all right. Everything will be fine." Sarah and Emily walked arm in arm to the house, and as the men took care of the livestock the three youngest ran off to play.

"We're going to feast tonight, Emily," Sarah said. "Our men need a good meal and a good night's rest. They'll leave first thing in the morning, but tonight we'll celebrate friendship and family."

With adults crowded around the table, Lydia volunteered, "I'll sit with the three youngsters on the floor in the sitting room." After supper she took them upstairs, said prayers, and tucked them into bed. In the kitchen stories were being told and laughter filled the air. Lydia joined in and the conversations went on for hours.

Finally, Mark suggested, "We better get some sleep. It will be at least a full two, possibly three-day ride to Fort Riley, so we should get on the road early."

Saying goodnight, everyone quietly dispersed. The Frazers slept in Lydia's room.

Sarah and Mark shared tender touches, soft kisses, and loving memories ending with Mark's arms wrapped around Sarah as they drifted off to sleep. Not a good-bye, more like, *until I see you again.*

Billy stepped outside and walked up to the tombstone of his parents under the old elm tree. "I'm afraid," he confessed. "Please, Lord, give me strength and courage to fight and let me come home safe and in one piece to my family."

Billy walked back in the house and put a log on the fire to take the chill out of the damp fall air. He and his brother and sister slept on the floor in the sitting room as the fire in the hearth crackled and shadows of the flame danced on the wall.

****

With horses saddled, bedrolls tied on with small keepsake quilts folded inside with each of the families' names embroidered by Sarah and Lydia, and saddlebags full of food enough to last for days, the men walked the horses out of the barn and tied them to the rail. Both families waited to say their good-byes.

Emily kissed Seth and held him close. "I love you, sweetheart. Take care of yourself and come home to us."

Seth wiped a tear from her cheek with his thumb and said, "I love you, too, Emily." Then turning his attention to Ethan, said, "Always remember, I love you, son. Promise you'll take care of your mother and get along with everyone."

Ethan hugged tight to his pa's leg, Emily kissed the top of Ethan's head, and Seth put his arms around them both. He picked Ethan up and held him in one arm and drew Emily close with the other. Then in a low voice he said, "I love you both with all my heart. You have brought joy to my life and made me whole again. I'll come home even if I have to crawl all the way. You will be on my mind and in my heart every minute. Keep praying. I will return. I promise."

Mark and Billy were also saying their last good-byes. First in line was Sarah, then Jack holding Steven's hand, and last, Lydia holding Johanna. Mark went down the line first, hugging and kissing everyone, saying a few words to each loved one, and drying tears. Billy was next. He especially took note of Lydia. She had braided her hair back and pinned it up. She wasn't a little girl anymore. He had already told each of them how much he would love and miss them last night. Today, he'd say good-bye with a smile and hope this was the way his family would remember him.

"Well, we better get on our way. We can't be the last ones there," Mark said with an attempt at humor to lighten the mood.

The threesome mounted their horses and prepared to ride out. Billy suddenly remembered the necklace he had put in his coat pocket, the one Elizabeth left behind that he never saw her wear until after their last trip to town. He handed the necklace to Lydia and said, "Please keep this safe until I get home. I found it on the floor at the farm."

Lydia looked at the gold chain with a heart and two blue stones in the middle. "I'll keep it safe. Do you mind, can I wear it?"

"Sure you can and think of me." Billy settled into the saddle, waved, and hurried to catch up with Mark and Seth.

Chapter Twenty-Eight

"Mark Hewitt, Seth Frazer, and William Henry reporting for duty," Mark called up to the sentry posted above the massive wooden gate in the guard tower at Fort Riley. As the big door swung open, the three men rode inside to the courtyard and dismounted.

With rifle drawn, a burly uniformed soldier approached them. "Your papers, please."

"We don't have any papers," Mark answered. "We're all from west of Dead Flats. Sheriff John Sloan sent word for us to report as soon as possible. It's a few days from here, but we rode straight through the night."

The soldier relaxed, lowered his gun, and pointed to a large limestone building. "Report to the sergeant, second door from the left."

"Thanks," Mark said, but the soldier with no time for small talk had already turned and walked away.

The three men took a good look around. They saw several buildings that looked the same inside the fort, a corral with horses, and the interior walkway that surrounded the front of the fort.

"This fort is bigger than I expected," Billy said. "The buildings are really sturdy." An enticing scent of savory beef wafted across the compound and he could see the smoke rising where the meat cooked beside a large tent. "I hope they save some for us. I'm hungry, and I could sure use a wash."

"I'm with you, Billy. That does smell good, and we don't." Seth patted his horse's neck. "I'm sure you're hungry too, girl, aren't you?"

"Come on, men, let's find out where we're bunking and see about food for us and the horses." Mark led the way to the Officer's Headquarters and requested to see the sergeant.

"Your names?" a meticulously uniformed and groomed sergeant ordered.

The three men stood a little straighter and each said his name as the sergeant wrote them down.

"And where are you from?" The sergeant's voice grew louder.

The men straightened even more and Mark said for all of them, "We're from west of Dead Flats, sir."

The sergeant added this town to his list. "We're waiting for more men to arrive tonight. You'll bunk in C Building. Report to the corporal, then get a hot meal in you and some sleep. You'll move out tomorrow to meet up with other troops.

"Yes, sir," the men said in unison.

"Sir, may I inquire if my friend Cain Gibbs is on your list yet?"

"I assume he'd be coming from near Dead Flats, too," the sergeant said.

"Yes, sir," Billy replied.

"No, I don't see his name, son. He might be one of the lucky ones this time and not chosen, or he's not arrived yet," the sergeant said.

"Thank you for checking, sir." Billy nodded.

Outside, Mark asked a passing soldier for directions to C Building Bunkhouse. There they reported to the corporal, a thin man with a stern face who looked like he had seen hard times. He logged them in and instructed them to each grab a bunk.

As the threesome looked around, there were four rows of wooden double bunks stretching the length of the room. Many had bedrolls and blankets on them already claimed. Men were stirring about talking in small groups. Lamps hung on wall brackets chest high with windows higher on the walls to let in light and fresh air.

Stomach growling, Mark spoke up, "We haven't eaten since this morning, sir. Would it be possible to get something to eat and bed down our horses? We'll be riding them to where we're fighting, won't we, sir?"

"Yes. Your horse is your responsibility at all times. Once you pick up your rations, ammo, and get squared away with a bunk, you can take them to the stable and bed them down. Then head to the mess tent and get food. Do any of you have any health issues that I should note?" the corporal said as he looked over his papers.

Mark nudged Seth in the ribs.

Seth spoke up, "I did have bad frostbite on my feet last winter, but they healed pretty well."

"Frostbite, you say? That puts you at risk," the corporal stated as he made notes.

"Yes, sir. That is my understanding too." Seth shifted his stance.

"Well, we do need men at Fort Leavenworth for processing paperwork. Can you read?"

"Yes, sir, I can read and do numbers."

"Excellent. Report to me in the morning after chow," the corporal said. "You'll report to Fort Leavenworth. Hopefully, no fighting, but your job is just as important to the government."

With an audible sigh of relief, Seth said, "Thank you, sir."

"That will be all, men," the corporal said.

"Well, let's hurry and get our bed rolls, claim our bunks and rations, and take care of the horses. I'm starving," Billy said.

They returned to C Building Bunkhouse almost an hour later with their saddles and gear to find more men in the large bunkroom. Billy looked around to find Cain but didn't see him. Then he struck up a conversation with a young man his age.

"I'm JJ Stanton. JJ stands for John Junior."

"My name is Billy Henry."

"I'm ready to head to the mess tent for supper, if you can call it that. I hope we get some of that beef tonight," JJ said reaching out his hand in welcome.

"How long you been here?" Billy's large hand clasped JJ's smaller one.

"It's my second day. They say we're leaving tomorrow."

"That's what they told us, too," Billy responded. "Did you find out who our commanding officer is, JJ?"

"Nope, they'll tell us tomorrow morning, I guess. You don't ask and they don't tell you. You'll learn real fast how to say 'yes, sir,' and 'no, sir.' "

Billy had a sudden memory of life with the peddler Rusty when JJ said those words, but this time he wasn't the captive. Now he stood proud to fight to unite the country and free the slaves.

"I come from west of Dead Flats. Ever hear of that town?" Billy said, changing the subject.

"I heard of it, but never been there. I live on a farm outside Rock Creek. You ever hear of Rock Creek?" the young man asked.

"Nope." Billy shook his head. "Can't say that I have."

JJ's face muscles tightened. "I must be honest with you. I'm not scared or nothing. Well, maybe a little scared. But other than hunting, I've never been away from home by myself. You mind if I get in line for supper with you and ride with you tomorrow if we're in the same regiment?"

"Don't mind at all, but you can shoot, can't you?" Billy smiled.

"Yeah, I can shoot. I've put many a squirrel, rabbit, and deer on the table, but I've never killed nobody," JJ was quick to point out.

"Me either," Billy said, "but I won't hesitate to fire if it's them or me. I have a family back home who needs me to return in one piece."

"Then, here's to returning in one piece," JJ said with a whoop. "But, Billy, can I ask you a favor if something does happen to me?"

"Sure, I guess so, but nothing's going to happen. What do you want?"

"I got this letter in my pocket I wrote my ma the day I got here, telling her all about Fort Riley and how much I love and miss her. If anything happens, would you make sure she gets it?" Not wanting to court trouble, JJ pulled out the letter and quickly tucked it back into his shirt pocket.

"You can give that to your mother yourself when you see her next," Billy replied, looking away. "But I promise I'll send her the letter if need be."

JJ's face brightened. "Thanks, that means a lot."

After supper, with their stomachs barely full from

only a spoonful of baked beans, a thin slice of beef, mushy mixed vegetables, and a piece of bread, the men returned to the C Building Bunkhouse. Billy looked around for Cain again, but still no sign of him. Everyone attempted to heed the orders to get some shuteye but worrying about the unknown insured a restless night. The bugle's revelry before dawn had the men stumbling over each other to gather their belongings in order to get their horses ready.

The men quickly savored a hot bowl of grits or oatmeal, threw back a cup of coffee and two muffins, not knowing when they'd eat again. Cinching up their horses' saddles, Mark and Billy said good-bye to their dear friend. "Take care of yourself, Seth. If you get home first, please care for our families." Mark slapped him on the back. Billy reached out and shook his hand.

"You, too," Seth said. "I'll be praying we all get home soon and in one piece," he said winking at JJ and Billy. "I better find the corporal. Be safe. I'll see you back home when all this is over."

Billy said, "Yes, see you back home."

"Stay safe," Mark added, and Seth waved, mounted, and rode off without looking back.

With horses in tow, a sergeant called for Building C to fall into formation. "You're here on Governor Carney's orders and we leave today for Olathe where you will meet up with cavalry troops and proceed to the fighting from there. You are the Kansas State Militia, called up to keep General Price's Confederate campaign from reaching the Kansas border. You make up the Army of the Border, and don't you forget it. You are Union Yankees through and through. You'll ride two-by-two. Keep the talking to a minimum and you'll report to Major General George Dietzler when you arrive at Olathe. He is in charge of the Kansas Militia Division under Major General Samuel Curtis. I trust everyone picked up their rations, blankets, and ammo. Our best chance at victory is to follow your commander's orders. Good luck, men." The sergeant saluted the men, then ordered, "Mount up."

JJ fell in behind Mark and Billy riding beside an old man with the smell of whiskey on his breath already. On the road to Olathe, Mark, Billy, and JJ talked about family, hunting stories, their farms, and what they were missing back home. At a steady pace, it took the troops a day and a half of travel over rugged roads before the troops reached Olathe. Upon arrival, the men learned other Kansas State Militia troops assembled at Atchison, Paola, Mound City, Fort Scott, and Wyandotte.

"I'm starting to get the feeling General Price's troops are a force to be reckoned with," Mark admitted.

"If we don't stop them, they could march into Kansas and God only knows how far they could get if they cut us down at the border. We must stop them. Our families are depending on us, and I want to return home to our family and farm still alive and standing," Billy said.

JJ nodded in agreement and said, "We're here to fight and give it our all."

General Dietzler addressed his men. "The militia will now ride with cavalry troops to assist when needed in the pursuit of General Price, the Confederate officer who led an expedition north through Missouri gathering supplies and weapons for the southern army. His wagon train is reported to consist of five hundred wagons that should be slowing him down. Price's campaign through Missouri was to win the state for the Confederacy, hoping it might affect the outcome of President Lincoln's chances of re-election in November. Price also recruited soldiers along the way who sympathized with the southern cause. We can't let them into Kansas. We must defend our border!"

Chapter Twenty-Nine

Meanwhile, Sarah and the family were dealing with an issue of their own.

Early one morning, as Jack drew water from the well for the animals, he heard a faint voice calling from the corner of the barn, "Please, will you help us?" Looking up he saw a black woman staggering toward him and out of breath.

Jack rushed to the woman and she collapsed in his arms. "Ma, come quick," Jack yelled.

Sarah, fixing breakfast, rushed outside to find Jack holding a woman, and a young boy running toward his mother in ragged clothes. "Get her inside," Sarah said, and scooped the young child into her arms and rushed him to his mother's side.

"Please help us," the woman said again.

"We'll help you," Sarah said, "is someone chasing you?"

"No, the sheriff from town said he'd send them north, and we come west. My husband is bad off, sweat'n hot. He can't walk no more," the woman panted.

"Where is he?" Jack asked.

"I left him by the creek with our bag. Then I saw the planted fields and knew there were people close. I left my son with him, but he must have followed me. I told him to stay with his pa, but he followed all this way. Please help us."

"We'll help. You rest and quiet your son." Sarah patted her shoulder. "What's wrong with your husband?"

"Master whipped him. Tore him up something awful. Ordered him to kill a white man who stole some food from the root cellar. The man was old, not from around our parts. My husband's no killer. Didn't want the white man's blood on his hands."

"Jack, take the wagon and go get him. Lydia, you go with Jack." Sarah took the woman's hand. "What's his name?"

"Malcom, his name is Malcom," the woman answered.

"Steven, fetch water," Sarah ordered, and the children scattered.

"What can I do, Sarah?" Emily asked.

"Gather blankets, take them to the barn and fix a stall in the back for Malcom to rest when he gets here. That would help." Sarah gave the wife a sip of cool water and offered some to the little boy. "How old are you, sweetheart?"

"He's four," the woman said.

"My daughter Johanna is four. Do you mind if they sit together? She'll help comfort him."

"Thank you, ma'am. My son's name is Luke, from the Bible."

Johanna, Ethan, and Steven rushed over to meet Luke and soon the children were playing together making a circle on the floor with their feet touching, and rolling a ball of yarn back and forth.

Sarah tore rags to use as bandages and grabbed a cloth and a bucket of water. Through the window she saw Jack drive the wagon into the yard. "Children, you stay and play. We'll be right outside."

The wagon pulled into the barn, and the wife ran to her husband's side. She and Lydia helped Malcom off the wagon to where Emily fashioned a clean space for him to rest.

"Oh, Malcom, these good people are gonna help us."

Malcom whispered breathlessly, "I'm all right," before he collapsed to the barn floor.

"Lydia, fetch a ladle of vinegar from the root cellar and take it to the house. Jack, put the wagon away." Sarah lit a lamp for more light as the wife helped her husband remove his blood-stained shirt. That's when Sarah saw the deep slashes and welts crisscrossing the man's chest, back, arms, and legs. She gasped and Emily froze in place. Neither woman had ever seen such abuse.

"Master hung him by his wrists in a tree, his feet dangled off the ground. He swung him around as his sons took turns whipping him. Said Malcom was an example. Said no one else better disobey him again." The wife broke into tears. "Left him there into the night till I cut him down and we run off.

"Sent dogs after us, but we followed a creek and lost them by gettin' out in a thick briar patch. I filled my apron with water and washed away our tracks on the bank so's they couldn't follow us. Been running ever since, getting to Kansas for freedom," the wife explained.

"I'm sorry, I never asked your name. Mine is Sarah and this is my good friend Emily."

"My name is Penny." She wiped a tear from her

cheek. "Master said I was only worth a penny when I was born and that's what he calls me."

"It's all right, Penny. You're safe here," Sarah said. "You can stay until Malcom is able to travel. I better go make poultices. Penny, use this cloth and water to clean the wounds the best you can." Sarah poured the water from the pail into a crock and headed to the house with Emily to give the couple time together.

****

While Emily heated water to make tea for Penny, Sarah selected herbs and spices, put them in cloth pouches tied with string, and simmered them in vinegar. *The last time I had to make poultices was when Richard died over his land dispute.* She thought of her brother, counting back the years. *My, ten years have passed already since my brother passed.*

"Lydia, dear, why don't you read the children a story? And Jack and Steven, you may as well finish the chores. We'll have our morning meal after we see to Malcom's wounds."

I know Mark may have done things differently. He never liked to get too personal with our guests, but I feel it's best if little Luke sleeps in the house. Jack and Steven can show him how to hide under the floorboards if necessary. I'll keep the husband in the barn and the wife in the root cellar. Yes, separating them is the safest way. If we do have trouble, it's less likely they'll all be found. Sarah sighed. *Mark, I wish you were here, and I pray you and Billy are safe wherever you are. Come home safe to us, and Seth too.*

****

Tending to Malcom took time. Emily took Penny tea and assisted. Sarah packed the worst gashes with the poultices and soaked the rags in the vinegar before wrapping his arms and legs. Penny wanted to stay with him, but Sarah insisted she go to the root cellar and showed her how to hide behind the large crocks in case she heard loud or strange voices. "I'm trying to keep you safe. I'll fetch you food and when I do, I'll knock on the door and leave it outside. I will always knock so you know it's me. If the handle turns and you haven't heard a knock first, hide quick. Malcom will rest now and you should too. I'll check on him from time to time. Don't worry about Luke. He'll be safe in the house with the other children. We have a place to hide him, too. This evening, after you eat your meal, you can go to the barn to see Malcom while the boys are doing their chores. Jack will come for you, and Lydia will bring Luke to the barn to see you. But afterward, for safety, it's best for everyone to hide in separate places."

It was now mid-morning when the group finally ate. Cooking for three more mouths was no bother. Jack took Malcom his food and fed him, then Sarah knocked on the door and left Penny her food.

After two days, Malcom's fever still hadn't broken. "What will Penny do if her husband doesn't survive?" Sarah said to Emily, as they sat at the table drinking a cup of tea before bed. "She can't travel with Luke by herself."

"We must pray Malcom pulls through." Emily said a silent prayer then asked, "This isn't the first time you've sheltered salves is it?"

"No, we have helped several families on their way to freedom," Sarah said.

"Aren't you afraid you'll get caught?" Emily's eyes widened. "I've heard what they've done to abolitionists who help them."

Sarah said, "It's a risk our family is willing to take. I'm sorry if you're uncomfortable with them staying."

"I admit, I am a little worried, but hearing what they did to Malcom and seeing how brave Penny is and how much they all love each other, it would be hard to turn them away. I don't know what Seth and I would have done if they showed up at our door."

"I think you would have let your heart be the judge and welcomed them as we did." Sarah put her hand on Emily's arm and smiled. "Come on. Time to turn in for the night."

Before Sarah pulled the quilt her mother and the church ladies gave her before she left Pennsylvania up around her neck, she traced the word, Mother, embroidered on the block her mother made. She did this every night before saying a silent prayer for Mark, Billy, Matthew, and Seth to come home safely and for strength and courage to carry on.

Three more days passed. Malcom's fever finally broke and he said to Sarah, "Thank you, missus. You took good care of me and my family. Now we gonna move on. We leave in the morning."

"Could you wait a day or so? I'd like to give you food to take with you, and I need time to bake bread and biscuits."

Malcom and Penny discussed their plans to leave. Penny explained to Sarah, "Malcom agreed to stay two days. He worries about the weather and how long it will take to get across the border into Nebraska."

"We've found it's better for you to travel by night and sleep most of the day. Malcom is still healing and three more days would do his body good. He'd be stronger by then. At least ask him to wait until after supper to leave. You'll have a few hours of daylight to travel and then take it slow. You don't want his wounds reopening." Sarah reached for Penny's hands and drew them to her heart. "Now you can start over and have a good life."

Penny said, "Yes, a new life."

Sarah, Emily, and Lydia baked and prepared food to last the family five days. Jack and Steven picked vegetables from the garden and packed everything in three feed sacks. Even Luke had a sack to carry.

The evening of the second day, Sarah invited Malcom and Penny to eat with them in the house. The family was together again as everyone enjoyed the meal and fellowship.

"We're going to miss you," Sarah said as Lydia cleared the table.

"I wish you all the best," Emily said and embraced Penny. "You're a brave woman."

"We best get going. Thank you for your kindness. We will never forget you," Malcom said to everyone.

Jack picked up Luke and tossed him in the air. Luke giggled and Jack let him down slowly until his feet touched the floor. "Yes, we'll miss you all."

Johanna gave Luke a hug followed by Ethan and Steven. "Good friend," Johanna said and scooted up the ladder to the loft. When she returned, she said to Luke. "Pretty rock for you." Then pressed the treasure into her new friend's small hand.

Sarah motioned to the three sacks inside the door. "May this food give you strength and God's speed on your journey," she said as the family departed.

Chapter Thirty

While Billy and JJ huddled with men from their regiment around a crackling fire, Mark compared war to hunting. "You always must anticipate the animals' actions and keep one step ahead. General Dietzler has to watch General Price's Confederate troops to help plan the Union's next attack."

Orders came down the following day for Dietzler to move his troops north in anticipation of Price's next assault. Mark, Billy, and JJ saddled up as the bugle rang out calling the hundreds of men to move out.

On October 14th, the border militia met with additional troops at Shawnee, Kansas. Blankets and additional rations were distributed. Stretching for miles along the horizon, Billy could see hundreds of tents and clusters of men dotting the fields, campfires blazing to take the chill off the damp night.

Warming his hands, JJ said, "I sure hope this fighting doesn't last long. I need to get back home and help my pa get the crops in. I know Ma is worried sick already."

"Yeah, my brother has to deal with the farm by himself, too. And I miss my wife something awful. Do you have a girlfriend, JJ?" Billy nudged him.

"Nope, there's not many girls around Rock Creek my age. Besides, I don't get into town that often. My folks are old and need my help. I'm mostly on the farm." JJ shrugged.

"That doesn't mean you couldn't find a nice gal. Then you could both live with your folks and help with the farm." Billy grinned.

"Well, I suppose so," JJ said as he dug out a pan to heat up beans and rice. "That would work. Ma would probably like another female around to talk to. But I don't know where I'd look for a gal."

"Maybe on your way home, a war hero like you might meet someone, JJ. My wife and I wrote letters back and forth to get to know each other before we finally got married. Gosh I miss Elizabeth. Hey, maybe you could do that. Meet a gal and write letters to each other," Billy suggested, putting wood on the fire.

"I never wrote a letter to a girl before, Billy. What would I say?"

"Just tell her what you do, what your farm is like, and everyday things. Tell her about your folks and ask her about her life and what she likes to do. Maybe you could share your hopes for the future. You know, stuff like that. It's not hard. You already wrote a letter to your ma."

"Yeah, well that letter to my ma is different. I wrote it in case anything happens to me. But I guess I could write to a gal. I'd have to find one first."

"So, find one, someone you'd like to get to know better. You do want to get married and have a family someday, don't you, JJ?"

"Yes, it'd be nice to have a wife and a family, but—"

"But what? No more buts or you'll never find a wife. Elizabeth is waiting for me. She wants to start a family as soon as I get home, and I think now I'm ready."

****

A few days later, word filtered down through the ranks that General Dietzler was to advance with General Blunt into Independence, the next likely stronghold for Price's invasion of Missouri. Dietzler balked, not wanting to leave the Kansas border vulnerable. So Blunt's cavalry headed out alone.

It wasn't until some of Blunt's men returned for medical treatment that Billy saw the toll of war firsthand. Stretcher after stretcher was unloaded from wagons carrying the wounded; men with missing body parts, gaping gunshot wounds, and looks of horror on their bloodied faces. Billy learned there had been two separate battles in Independence. In the first, Price's army drove Blunt's men out of the city. The second had resulted in Major General Alfred Pleasonton's Union Cavalry chasing Price's army west to Byram's Ford.

After hearing about Independence, Dietzler agreed to move his troops east to the Blue River, five miles southeast of Kansas City. Mark, Billy, and JJ were on the march again.

The talk around camp about the bloody battles in Independence had Billy's stomach in knots. After another sleepless night, he admitted to Mark, "Looks like the Confederates are coming our way. It's likely we'll have to fight."

"Yep, I'm fairly sure we will be in the thick of it soon. Make sure you stay close and stay calm. Remember, we'll be watching out for each other." Mark took a heaping spoonful of beans and washed them down with a swig of strong coffee.

****

On October 23rd, hoping to catch Price off guard, Dietzler ordered his men to form a line and take a firm stand on the Blue River east of Westport. Even as the Union troops stood ready, Price moved south and outflanked the offensive by successfully crossing downriver.

Dietzler's men fell back to Westport to hold the northern border, while Blunt and his men were directed to construct defensive lines along the east and west. The Union soldiers, even the most courageous among them, prayed they were ready for Price's next move.

****

In the early morning hours, shots rang out.

"Remember, stay close," Mark said as he nudged Ruby forward under the bugler's call to advance.

Billy and JJ did as Mark instructed, their hearts racing, nearly paralyzed with fear. The shots became louder and rained in volleys around them. With not much cover around, the men steeled themselves, mustering up the courage to fight, hold the line, and die if necessary.

The faces of his loved-ones filled Mark's head as he thought. *Price and his men must be stopped and stopped now.* The line charged forward then were pushed back by the aggressive opposition. Each side would catch their breath and charge forward again and again, gaining and losing ground with each surge. With soldiers continually dropping around them and medics rushing into the action to drag them to safety, the brutal battle raged for hours. Exhausted and drenched with sweat, Mark held Ruby's reins tightly, coaxing her on despite knowing she too, was close to exhaustion. Leaning over in his saddle, trying to catch his breath, he caught a glimpse of Billy and JJ nearby.

The threesome surged ahead into battle again. The blast from guns, the smoke of the powder, horses' bodies clashing, and screams from the wounded punctuated the chaos around them on the battlefield. Mark heard a sudden shout. The voice was his own. Looking down, a stain rapidly spread on his right pant leg. His foot warmed as his boot filled with blood. He grabbed his leg and called out, "Billy, I'm hit!"

Billy raced to his side and cried out for JJ to fall back and stand guard.

Ripping the sleeve off his shirt, Billy wound the bandage tightly around Mark's leg to staunch the flow.

"It burns." Mark gasped. He grabbed at his shaking leg to steady it while Billy managed to wrap the wound and tie a knot.

Mark grimaced as he turned Ruby back toward the fighting.

"Hold up, Father. You're not going back in," Billy insisted. "Keep pressure on your leg and head back to one of the medical stations. Don't worry, JJ and I'll find you when the battle is over."

Mark nodded and reluctantly turned Ruby back toward camp.

"Come on, Billy," JJ shouted. "Remember, we're both getting home in one piece."

"Yes." Billy grinned. "In one piece."

Then suddenly, a loud cheer went up. Billy saw more Kansas militia reinforcements join the fight, giving the Union soldiers on the front line a renewed surge of courage and energy to finish the battle. The Union army outnumbered the Confederates and pushed hard until the enemy turned tail and headed south.

Judy Sharer

****

When the shooting gradually fell away and the smoke cleared, hundreds of dead and wounded soldiers from both sides littered the battlefield. Billy heard soldiers call out for help as their lives slipped away. Hardened men pleaded for their mothers; others cried for the Lord to take them home. Some begged for water and others, using their guns as a crutch, limped their way to safety. The smell of death carried by the wafting smoke turned Billy's stomach and made him retch. He was tired, hungry, and covered in sweat, but he was alive. At this moment, looking at the carnage the fighting had left behind, alive was all that mattered.

A soldier in front of him bent over and picked up a pistol lying on the ground and put it in his saddlebag. Weapons and horses, some unscathed, littered the field. Billy picked up a few pistols along with a couple muddy muzzleloaders and shoved them in his saddlebags and scabbard. JJ did the same.

Billy's thoughts were racing. *I've killed animals for food, but today, for the first time, I took the life of another human being. Looking someone in the eyes before pulling the trigger won't be easy to forget. The fighting has stopped for now, but it's not over yet.*

"The Union can take credit for this battle," Billy said. Then an officer rode by and ordered Billy, JJ, and others in the area to round up uninjured horses and take them back to camp. It had been a long day. Billy was anxious to find Mark, but he did as ordered.

Chapter Thirty-One

Within a day after Elizabeth arrived at her parents'
home to stay while Billy was away, Quinn put his plan
into motion. "Elizabeth, will you join me for a cup of
coffee and dessert at the hotel restaurant after supper
tonight?" Innocently enough, they sat and talked of old
times and schooldays. The next night Quin asked,
"Would you like to take a stroll through town this
evening?" Elizabeth gladly accepted, and when the
evening became chilly, rather than offering his jacket,
Quinn conveniently put his arm around her waist
feigning at keeping her warm. An invitation to a church
gathering followed, then a birthday party where they
were both invited that led to their dancing together all
night. One evening at the hotel, other diners saw them
brazenly hold hands on the linen tablecloth while
sharing a piece of pie. Elizabeth's parents were now on
a first name basis again with Quinn and invited him to
the house for Sunday dinners and evening games of
pinochle.

One afternoon, her friend Mary Jane stopped by to
visit. While talking in the Parkers' parlor, Elizabeth
suddenly mused, "You know, Quinn is everything that
Billy isn't."

"What are you saying?" Mary Jane's eyes grew
wide.

"I've been thinking. Billy is content to live on his

farm and make a life with his hands, sweat, and back-breaking work, while Quinn, on the other hand, uses his mind to make money. He has invested in other people's ventures and is doing well for himself. If I were married to Quinn, I could live in town, own a servant to do the household chores, and I'd be someone." She continued rambling. "There would be events and formal gatherings every week. People would know my name. I could walk down the street with my head held high." Elizabeth smiled and let out a little giggle.

"I don't believe how pompous you are. Only a year ago you married Billy and were anxious to have his child," Mary Jane said.

"Yes, I know, but I didn't think living on a farm would be so much work. You can't imagine, Mary Jane. It's awful. My hands are rough from doing the wash and tending to the garden. All day long I clean and make meals. Then there are chickens and the cow to milk. Me? Milk a cow? And we never seem to have any fun, never see anyone, and never come to town. On top of that, we have his little brother living with us, and I have to take care of him, too. Don't get me wrong, Steven's not a bad boy, it's just that he's always there. We never have any private time, and it seems Billy's always doing things with him and not with me." Elizabeth coughed and rose from her chair to get a drink, not water, but whiskey. She found it helped settle her persistent cough.

"I don't think you should be seeing Quinn the way you are, Elizabeth. People are talking. Billy is bound to find out how you've been behaving while he is off fighting. If you don't stop this nonsense now, you might regret coming to stay in town. Billy won't be gone forever you know. What happens when he returns? Have you thought of that?" Mary Jane snatched the glass of whiskey out of Elizabeth's hand and put the glass on the table.

Elizabeth leapt to her feet. "It's none of your business what I do, or who I do it with. I'll see Quinn if I want, and I don't care if Billy finds out! Now, I think it's time for you to leave."

Mary Jane turned on her heels and headed for the door. "You're on your own then, Elizabeth. I want no part of your affair with Quinn."

"It's not an affair," Elizabeth yelled after her.

Mary Jane turned and said calmly, "Yes, it is. And by the way, everyone already knows your name. The whole town is talking about the two of you, and you can bet Billy will find out when he gets home because I will be the first one to tell him."

"Get out!" Elizabeth screamed in a fit of coughing. "I thought you were my friend. You're nothing but a gossip. Get out of here!" Elizabeth slammed the door and ran upstairs to her bedroom.

****

The following day, Mr. Parker brought home a newspaper. The paper reported movement of the Army of the Border troops. Elizabeth ran to the Postal Office to check the list of dead and wounded. Neither Billy's nor Mark's names appeared.

The following week, Elizabeth ran a fever. Her cough worsened, her throat was sore, and she became increasingly weak. The whiskey no longer helped.

When she walked into Doctor Glasgow's office her cough, paleness, and sweat-laden brow made him question, "Have you been in large crowds in the past few weeks? Or in the cold night air for prolonged periods of time."

"Well, yes to both," Elizabeth admitted. "This cough is getting worse, doctor. And I can hardly swallow my throat hurts so."

"My dear, I'm concerned. You are quite ill. You must go to bed immediately and have no visitors. Take this syrup three times a day for your cough. I've seen a few cases like yours this week. There's something going around, and it appears quite serious."

"Is what I have contagious?" Elizabeth asked, placing her hand on her chest to ease the pain of coughing.

"It well could be. If you've been close to others, have someone get word to them of your condition. If they start feeling poorly, they should see me right away. Right away," Doc stressed. "I'll call upon you at your home to see how you're doing. Now hurry along."

Returning home, Elizabeth explained the doctor's concern to her mother and asked, "Can you let my friends and Quinn know I'm not feeling well and tell them what Doc Glasgow said?"

"Yes, Elizabeth, I will. Now, you go to bed like the doctor said. I'll bring you tea and a spoon to take your medicine."

None of Elizabeth's friends were interested in coming to visit her, making excuses and keeping their distance. But Quinn didn't stay away. He sat with her, talking about the future they would have together once she was well, and urging her to take her medicine.

Doc Glasgow checked in every day as promised. With labored breath, Elizabeth complained, "The medicine you gave me worked at first. The fever went down some, but now there is no relief from the pain in my throat and chest. Can you give me something stronger, please?" Elizabeth pleaded.

Reaching into his bag, the doctor brought forth a bottle of laudanum. "This is the strongest medicine I have," he said. "I want you to take it only when the pain becomes unbearable and even then only a small sip."

After he left, Elizabeth reached out and clasped her mother's hand. "Have any of my friends stopped by to see how I am?" Elizabeth managed to whisper.

"No, dear. I think they are afraid and keeping their distance because they don't want to catch what you have. I'm going to ask Quinn to stay away now, too. The doctor says you need your rest." Bertha tucked the covers under her daughter's chin and patted her shoulder. "Rest now, dear. Your father will come to see you when he gets home."

Chapter Thirty-Two

Back at camp after the battle, Billy and JJ took the horses they had rounded up to the makeshift corral. "I'll take care of your horse, you go find your father," JJ said to Billy.

"Thanks, JJ," Billy replied and started looking for Mark. He stepped around the wounded lying on the ground. Their injuries had been treated, but many were crying out in pain. The smell of blood and fear filled the air. Many men were injured worse than Mark, with chest and head wounds and bandaged stumps where arms or legs once were. Billy said a quick prayer that Mark was still all right. He frantically scanned the field of wounded and called out above the noise. "Mark, Mark Hewett! Has anyone seen Mark Hewitt?" No reply. Suddenly Billy spotted Mark with his bandaged leg sitting against a fencerow. Making his way to Mark's side, he knelt beside him and placed his hand on Mark's shoulder.

Opening his eyes, Mark embraced him with a bear hug. "You're safe! Did JJ come back with you?"

"Yes, he's fine. He's taking care of the horses. What did the doctor say?"

"He said I'll be all right. He got the bullet out. I'll need to stay off my leg for a few weeks until the wound heals. Enough about me, though. Tell me what happened out there. I hated leaving you and JJ alone."

"You rest. There'll be time to talk about that later," Billy said. "Now that I know you're all right, I'm going to go help JJ with the horses. Where did you leave Ruby? I'll attend to Ruby for you and come back after I get some vittles."

Mark pointed behind him. "She is tied on the other side of this fence. I didn't want her to get too far away. She needs a good rub down, feed, and water."

"I'll take good care of her and fetch you your bedroll and saddle." Billy jumped the fence, gave Mark his gear, and then took Ruby back to camp with him.

Billy found Mark resting when he checked on him after supper. "Did they feed you? Do you need anything?"

"Yes, I've eaten and I'll be fine here." Mark winced. "They gave me an extra blanket," he said and gave a weak smile.

"The fighting has moved south, Father, and I don't think any Rebel troops are in the area. Try to get sleep if you can, and I'll come back in the morning to check on you."

Returning to the campfire, Billy listened as others related stories about the day's battle. Some bragged of how many rebels they killed, others told about the weapons they collected from the battlefield. Unable to fight back the weariness, he crawled into his bedroll and fell into an exhausted sleep.

Waking before daylight, Billy saw a dense fog hovered low to the ground. He threw dry twigs on the still warm embers to rekindle the fire and added dandelion roots to the old grounds to boil up a resemblance of coffee. JJ rolled out of his bedroll soon after. They shared a steaming cup of the bitter brew. As

245

the fog dissipated and streaks of sunlight peeked through on the horizon, they talked of home.

"We'd better get breakfast going if you're going to keep your strength up for Elizabeth," JJ said, grinning.

The two of them pooled their supplies and found they had hardtack, rice, and beans. There was enough for two more meals. They checked Mark's saddlebags and found a can of beans, hardtack, and a few slightly wilted carrots and potatoes that Sarah must have sent along.

Billy poured them another cup of coffee and they warmed a can of beans, adding some water and a handful of dry rice.

JJ and Billy had barely choked down their last spoonful when they heard the bugle call to assemble. They arrived to find General Dietzler giving the soldiers an update. "I'm proud of you, men. We sent those Rebels packing. And if we're lucky, they're still hightailing it right back to where they came from. Major Pleasonton's cavalry followed Price's army south, and General Blunt and his cavalry were dispatched to assist. I'm sure they've caught up to Price by now and I hope they give 'em hell!"

The men whooped and hollered, "Hurrah for the Yankees! Victory to the North!"

When the noise quieted, Dietzler announced, "In two days we'll begin marching the Confederate prisoners to Fort Riley. We don't expect any trouble, but returning to the fort will take three, maybe four days. That said, our wounded will wait and join the march later on to give them time for their wounds to heal.

"Your regiments have duties to perform until then.

Make sure they are carried out. Remember, two days. Be ready to pull out."

Billy and JJ were assigned the first watch of prisoner guard duty. They were instructed to, "Gather the names and hometowns of the men assigned to you. See to it that the prisoners get food and water. If they're sick or wounded, a medic should be called for treatment. You will be relieved in the afternoon."

"This war can't last forever," one prisoner said. "Eventually, we'll get to head home."

Fifty rebel prisoners, a subdued lot of weary men assigned to Billy and JJ, had been stripped of their weapons.

"Billy, these men don't seem like they'll give us any trouble. I'll talk to them and get their information. You stand guard."

"All right." Billy looked on with his rifle loaded and ready.

As JJ made his way from man to man, a thin, tall prisoner suddenly pulled a knife from his boot, grabbed JJ from behind, and in one swift action slashed his throat. Instinctively, Billy pulled his rifle to his shoulder and killed the man.

He ran to his friend, but too late. The gaping wound bled unceasingly. His friend JJ lay dead, staring up at him. "Oh, JJ. This wasn't supposed to happen. We were to go home." Billy recoiled from the shock of the lifeless form before him. He was stunned, unable to take in everything that took place.

Union soldiers rushed to Billy's aide. When they saw the scene, one officer asked, "What happened here?"

The prisoners answered with a detailed description

of what took place.

"Is this true? Is this what happened soldier?" the officer asked Billy, who was still kneeling over his friend.

Billy slowly stood, rifle at his side, and said woodenly, "Yes, sir. That's what happened. Just like they said."

"You will not be charged for killing the prisoner, soldier. What is your name and the name of the dead soldier's?" the officer demanded. "I'll write this in my report."

"This is my friend, John Stanton Junior, from Rock Creek, and I'm William Paul Henry, from near Dead Flats, sir. And, sir, may I have permission to bury my friend and return his horse to his parents? Not having his horse would be a hardship on his parents, sir." Billy stood tall.

"Permission granted. You are relieved from duty for today. I'll send soldiers to replace you. All right, everyone, back to your duties." The officer singled out four men. "You help carry Stanton to an appropriate burial site."

Billy knelt and with a trembling hand took the blood-stained letter to his mother from JJ's shirt pocket. "I'll see to it that this letter is sent to your folks, JJ, and I'll take them your horse as well. I know your parents don't have the means to come get you, so I'm going to bury you here."

With no coffin, no minister, no family present, Billy recited Psalm 23 before closing the grave. Exhausted and covered with dirt he slumped beside the mounded earth and cried out, "Lord, I know in these awful times I often forget everything I'm thankful for.

Thank you for keeping my father alive and thank you for letting me meet JJ and become friends. Although I didn't know him well, I will always remember JJ and hold a place for him and his family in my heart. I'll do as I promised and mail his letter to his ma and I'll get his horse to his folks somehow. I know he'd like that. He was a brave soldier and a good friend. Amen." Billy stood and brushed the soil from his pants before walking to tell Mark what happened.

By the time Billy reached his father, Mark had already heard about the shooting of a prisoner but had no idea it involved JJ and Billy. "I'm so sorry, son. I know you and JJ were friends. He was there for us when we needed him, and now you were there for JJ."

Billy took off his hat and said, "JJ asked me to send a letter he had written to his mother if something happened and he didn't come home. I'll keep my promise, and I'm also taking his horse back to his folks." After sitting in silence for a few minutes, he said, "I forgot to tell you of General Dietzler's plans for moving out to Fort Riley. I'll bring Ruby to you when I leave and then wait for you at the fort. Do you think you can ride that distance?"

"I'm not sure. I'll ride in a wagon if there's room and tie Ruby on behind. She and I have been through so much together, I wouldn't want to lose her now," Mark said.

"Do you mind if I take the food from your saddlebags. I don't know how much I'll get between here and the fort."

"Go ahead. I'm sure you're running low and they'll give me food. I'll be all right." Mark motioned for Billy to come close and gave him a hug. "I'm so proud of you, son, and I thank the Lord we will be returning home together. I pray Seth is doing well, too, and that we all make it home safely before any snow flies."

****

On the evening before the wounded were to join the march, Mark was deep in thought when he heard a loud cheer from men who had gathered nearby. A militia soldier from under General Blunt's command had returned to camp. He sat regaling the wounded with what he had seen and heard about Price's Confederate army after the defeat at Westport. Mark leaned in and listened attentively as the soldier shared details of the events.

"The evening of October 24th, we set up camp near a little town called Trading Post on the Kansas side of the border. Price's men had ransacked the settlement and the townsfolk were in a bad way.

"A storm blew in, and the night was cold and rainy. General Pleasonton's Union cavalry knew Price had made camp in the area, so he sent out two brigades to hunt him down. We knew our side had attacked when we heard the artillery blasting before dawn. And even though they were outnumbered, they hit the Rebel line, forcing them to withdraw. They had to leave their sick and wounded behind. Old Price didn't get far. About six miles south at Mine Creek, Pleasonton's men whipped him again.

"General Blunt ordered our troops forward, but we didn't arrive in time to fight. They really didn't need us anyway. The whole battle was over shortly after it began. Pleasonton's cavalry never even got off their horses, and forced Price's army further south. Blunt released his Kansas militia regiments and sent us back to our sign-in posts."

"So, are the Rebs out of Kansas?" a young man asked.

"The last skirmish I heard about was at Marmiton River later that same afternoon, and they whipped them again. We were anxious to get home, so many of us rode all day and night to get this far. Thousands of good men have died. Price lost his last four battles. We heard he gave the order to burn half his supply wagons because they were slowing down his retreat."

"What a waste," one man shouted.

"Yup, burned them so we wouldn't have 'em," the soldier said with a grin. "We can be proud, men. This is a story to tell your families when you get home. Yup, one to tell your families. The war isn't done being fought in other states, but I doubt those Rebs will ever try coming into Kansas again."

Mark looked down at his leg. Although wounded, he knew he would heal, but he wasn't sure how he'd ever get the images he'd seen out of his head. The battlefield, the smell, the bodies of the dead, and the cries for help of the wounded. He'd head for Fort Riley knowing Price was defeated and Kansas was safe.

Chapter Thirty-Three

For Billy, Fort Riley was a welcoming sight on October 29th. The regiment had been on the move long into the night for three weary days, and he was back where it all began. Once the prisoners were secure and the extra horses corralled, the bugle sounded. His regiment was disbanded. They were free to go home.

Amid the cheers, Billy took off his hat and threw it high in the air like the other men around him. Then his thoughts turned to JJ whose folks would be brokenhearted when they received his letter. He was glad he and JJ became friends. He recalled their conversations about going home in one piece, finding him a girlfriend, and how his parents depended on him. Billy could count his blessings. He would be going home in one piece when Mr. John Stanton, Junior wouldn't.

****

Men rushed about, many of them leaving the fort, but Billy would wait for Mark. He would ask the sergeant if he could bunk at the fort until the wounded showed up.

Knocking on the door, he heard the sergeant yell, "Enter."

Standing at attention, Billy said, "My father's coming in with the wounded, sir. I'd like to stay at the fort until he arrives. We fought in the battle of

Westport."

"You can bunk in C Building. You'll get two meals a day and you'll report to the corporal daily."

"Thank you, sir. May I ask, were all Kansas militia men released from their duties, sir? Even those serving at Fort Leavenworth?"

"Yes, soldier, all Kansas militia are disbanded as of today."

"Thank you, sir," Billy said.

He took Lucky and JJ's horse to the stable, tended to them, and claimed a bunk before heading to the mess tent.

Time dragged. The days came and went and Mark still hadn't arrived. *What if something happened?* On the afternoon of the fourth day, the sound of wagons and horses could be heard from miles away. When they rolled in, Billy rushed to assist. He helped carry injured soldiers to buildings, hoping to find his father. But there was no sign of Mark. A few hours later, those who were wounded, but still able to ride, arrived at the gate. He spotted Ruby, but the man riding her wasn't Mark. He had never seen this person before. Where was his father?

As Ruby got closer, Billy could see a travois dragging behind. A few more steps and a face appeared from beneath blankets. Mark was the person being transported. After a sigh of relief, he ran to Mark's side.

"Are you all right? Father, are you all right?" Billy asked as he brushed dust from his face.

Mark nodded and said, "Yes, son, I'm fine and even better now that I know you're here. I was worried something might have happened to you along the way."

"Why didn't you ride in a wagon and tie Ruby to

the back as you planned."

"I was in a wagon the first day, then we picked up more wounded. They were worse off than me, so I gave my seat to another man. Andrew here, was hit in the shoulder. He could ride, so we made this travois for me and rigged it to Ruby. Andrew, this is my son, Billy."

"Nice to meet you, sir," Billy said as he reached up to shake the soldier's hand.

"And you, Billy. Your father told me all about you and what a good shot you are, winning your own rifle and all." As he dismounted, Andrew said, "Thanks for the ride, Mark. I understand we're allowed to leave if we're up to it. I sure do want to get home. I'm going to see if I can get a horse and head out right away."

"Thank you, Andrew. Take it easy on that shoulder and remember to stop by the farm sometime."

Andrew nodded, shook Mark's hand, and headed to the corral.

"I'm going to stay and have a doc check my leg," Mark said. "I won't be able to ride any distance for a little while. You must be missing Elizabeth something awful. If you want to leave now and get back…"

"There's no way I'm leaving you here," Billy protested. "We came together, we'll leave together. But first things first. Let's get you inside to a bunk so you can rest."

That evening, Billy brought Mark a plate of food and they ate together.

"When you're better and can stand the trip, it sure will be good to head home. I had a thought. Is there anything you need to get in Dead Flats? If not, we could split up and you could go straight home to the family. I'll gather Elizabeth then meet you at the farm," Billy said.

"As much as I miss Sarah and the children, I'll ride into town with you and have Doc Glasgow check my leg. That way I could buy a few supplies and surprises for Christmas. Once the snow flies there'll be no going to town."

Billy took a sip of water to wash down the rations. "I bet Jack is itching to see Abby after being in charge of the farm while we've been gone. And most likely he has more leatherwork to sell. His workmanship has gotten really good and he seems to enjoy putting in the time and effort it takes to make a quality product."

"Yes, your brother is doing well for himself. He's saving his money so he can ask Abby to marry him when this war is over."

"Let's hope that can happen soon," Billy said, gathering plates to return to the mess tent. "Goodnight, Father. Sleep well. See you in the morning."

****

The doctor checked Mark's leg regularly. Within a few days, he was able to put some weight on the injured limb. A few days later, the doctor announced, "You're lucky. There is only a little redness and the swelling is down. The wound is healing nicely. You're free to head home, soldier, but today is Election Day. You should go vote before you leave."

The two men gathered their belongings and walked to the voting tent to register their votes for Lincoln. "I sure hope Lincoln is re-elected for a second term," Mark said dropping his ballot in the box.

"I'm sure it will take a while until all the ballots are counted, but he is the right man for the job, and I do believe he'll do right by the slaves too." Billy slipped his vote in the box. "You know he'll only be the second president to serve two terms if he's elected. The first in my lifetime."

"My leg is not a hundred percent, so we better take it easy on the way home. I figure we can reach Dead Flats in three days with breaks and stopping each night," Mark said, as Billy saddled the horses.

"I agree. A couple extra days isn't going to matter. Seth is probably at the farm by now, and with no chance of fighting in Kansas again any time soon, we know the family is safe," Billy added.

"I miss your mother, but if you can wait to see Elizabeth, we'll take our time."

When the men made camp that night, they roasted a rabbit Billy shot along the trail. This was the first fresh meat they had eaten in over a month.

"Billy, I know the family and Elizabeth will have questions for you, and the children will want to know what fighting in a war was like. But you might want to take care what you tell them. I'll confess it's hard for me to deal with the things I had to do as a soldier. I don't think I need to paint the entire picture for them. Do you understand what I'm trying to say?" Mark asked as he pulled a piece of roasted meat off the spit.

"Yup. Just because it happened doesn't mean I need tell all the details."

"Exactly. I won't be telling your ma many stories of the fighting, and those I do will be as vague as possible. I'm having bad dreams that I wouldn't want to share as a burden."

"You're right, Father. Some things are better left unsaid."

****

Riding into Dead Flats, Mark said, "I'll take the horses to the stable and bunk at the jail. I'm sure Sheriff Sloan won't mind putting me up for the night. I don't want to spend the money on the hotel room after we lost so much of our savings when the bank was robbed. I'll see you at the Parkers' in the morning."

"All right, see you then." With thoughts of holding Elizabeth in his arms again, Billy's strides grew longer as he rounded the corner to reach the Parkers' house. He knocked vigorously on the door in anticipation of the taste of Elizabeth's sweet lips and the curves of her body close to his. He expected Elizabeth to fall into his arms when he saw her, but instead, her mother opened the door.

Bertha threw her arms around Billy and said, "Oh, Billy, thank God you're home! Come into the parlor. I prayed you'd return in time."

"In time?" Billy said, looking puzzled. "Where is Elizabeth?"

"She's upstairs resting," Bertha said, holding back tears.

"Resting? Why? Is something wrong?" Billy leaned closer.

"She's very ill, Billy. Doctor Glasgow says she doesn't have much time left. I think she's been waiting for you to get back. She asks for you every day."

"Not much time? What do you mean?" Billy said, dread rising in his throat. "When did this start? How long has she been sick?"

"It began about two weeks ago with a cough and a fever, and it's gotten worse since then. She's been asking for you. We heard the Army of the Border was disbanded. What took you so long to get home? I think she's waited to see you one last time."

"One last time!" Billy stood. "I need to see her."

"She's awfully weak, Billy. She can barely talk, so lean in close."

Billy took the stairs two at a time.

Elizabeth turned her head slowly his way when she heard him enter.

"Elizabeth, sweetheart," Billy whispered and knelt beside the bed. "I'm home. I'll take care of you now. We'll get you better. You must get better. I missed you so much while I was gone. You don't have to worry about me leaving again. I'll stay right here until you're well."

"Stop, Billy," Elizabeth whispered as she coughed weakly. "I'm dying. I know I'm dying. I need to tell you I'm sorry."

Billy took her hand in his. "Sorry, sweetheart? What are you saying? You don't have nothing to feel sorry for. I'm the one who had to leave you. I'm the one who's sorry."

"No, Billy," Elizabeth managed to whisper before coughing racked her frail body. After a moment she managed to say, "You'll find out...someone will tell."

"Someone will tell me what?" Billy leaned in closer, as her voice became fainter.

"I was with Quinn." Elizabeth's hand reached for her throat, but she didn't cough.

"Quinn? What does Quinn have to do with anything?" Suddenly, Billy stopped cold. With a sinking heart, he played the words she said over in his mind. *With Quinn. This is my wife, the person I chose to spend my life with, who wants to have my child. I fought in the war to keep her safe. We were building a life*

together and now she tells me there is another man.
"You were with Quinn?"

"Before I got sick, we made plans." Elizabeth winced in pain.

"Plans? Plans for what?" Billy asked, his mind reeling.

"Plans for our future together." A tear trickled down her flushed cheek. "I'm glad you're here, Billy. I'm glad you're safe." Her voice was barely audible. She closed her eyes and Billy watched in horror as she struggled to take her last breath and exhale.

Billy gently held her limp, frail body, trying to digest what she had said and what just happened. Rage and fury and love and sadness surged through him. His beloved Elizabeth was gone, mere moments after telling him she had been unfaithful.

Billy gently laid her back in the bed. That's when the necklace became visible. He seemed to recall one similar that he found lying on the floor by the night table, also heart shaped.

He turned to find Mrs. Parker standing in the doorway. As their eyes met, he realized she had known everything. "She's gone," he said.

Bertha's face collapsed into an agony of grief as she rushed to her daughter's side.

Billy ran to Doctor Glasgow's office. "It's Elizabeth. She's gone, Doc. Can you check on Mrs. Parker? I'll look for Mr. Parker and send him home right away."

In a numbing daze, Billy located Elizabeth's father at the Cattlemen's Association Office and shared the news about Elizabeth. Next, he looked for Mark.

****

With time on his hands, Mark checked in with Doc Glasgow who pronounced his leg healing well. At the Postal Office, he picked up two letters. After reading them, he quickly penned two letters to send east letting both sets of parents know he and Billy were safe and about the loss of Elizabeth. Sheriff Sloan had insisted Mark be a guest at his home as long as he needed lodging in Dead Flats.

Billy also found a place to sleep to get him away from the Parkers. He bunked at his friend Cain's blacksmith shop as he had when he courted Elizabeth. A friend to talk to was who Billy needed right now after the shock of Elizabeth's death. Cain had heard rumors of Elizabeth and Quinn's sultry affair, but spared his friend from the town gossip.

At breakfast with Mark, strangers stopped by their table to offer condolences while others kept at a distance and whispered among themselves. Billy learned about places Elizabeth and Quinn had been seen together, and what they had been doing. News and gossip, the lifeblood of a small town, travels quickly.

****

Church bells tolled announcing the quickly planned funeral, the same bells that announced his wedding only a year and a half before. Attendees filled only the first few pews and the service was mercifully short. Quinn arrived at the last moment to sit in the back pew and left during the final hymn. At the brief graveside memorial, Billy stood in silence with Mark at his side. Mr. and Mrs. Parker were bowed in grief until the prayer ended, then Bertha sobbed, wailing, "Parents aren't supposed to see their child die. God, why did you take my Elizabeth? This isn't fair."

Afterward, a few townsfolk stopped by the Parker home, but upon learning Bertha was not well enough to receive visitors, said they'd come by later in the week.

Billy stayed long enough to make an appearance and told the Parkers he'd be back the next morning.

Joining Mark and Sheriff Sloan for breakfast, he steeled his resolve for the conversation he was about to have at the Parkers' home. He knew what he had to do.

Bertha, dressed in mourning black, welcomed him and kissed him on the cheek. After being invited to take a seat in the parlor, she asked, "Whatever will you do now that Elizabeth won't be there to take care of you?"

"Mrs. Parker, you obviously didn't know your daughter very well. I was the one who took care of her. She would help if she had too, but she didn't like getting dirty. Gardening, cooking meals, doing the laundry, and washing the dishes was too much work in her opinion. She thought gathering the eggs and milking the cow was beneath her."

Mrs. Parker's eyes grew wide and she stiffened in her chair.

"Your daughter begged me to have a child. She said she wanted us to have a baby right up to the day I left to fight. She pleaded, assuring me she'd be a good mother. But the truth is, she wasn't even kind to Steven. He loved her, did most of her chores for her, and always tried to please her."

"How dare you talk to us like this about our daughter." Mr. Parker stood in the parlor doorway.

"There's more to tell than that but, believe me, you don't want to hear the rest of what I want to say. It also appears you preferred Quinn as a son-in-law and encouraged the relationship.

"I'm going home with Mark today. The headstone is paid for. You can tell the stonecutter to engrave whatever remembrance you want about Elizabeth. I want you to know that I loved your daughter with all my heart, but now question whether she felt the same. I believe she loved the idea of marrying me and what I could give her, but when that turned out not to her liking, she turned to someone else.

"She told me she wanted to come to town when I left so she could take care of you both, but now I know the truth. She wanted to come to town because of Quinn. You must have known they were seeing each other romantically. Why else would you have him to Sunday dinners? Elizabeth told me she had been unfaithful. Her friends and others told me how unfaithful. I wish you both the best, but this is where we cut our ties." Billy reached to shake Mr. Parker's hand, but he turned away, so Billy left without saying another word to the stricken parents.

Catching up with Mark at the Dry Goods Store, a reflective and stunned Billy asked the clerk to make bags of candy while he picked out a few gifts for the family. His mind was still reeling from the scene at the Parkers'. He wasn't the one who committed adultery, and he wasn't the one who encouraged the affair, and with that realization, he resolved to have nothing further to do with the Parker family.

Mark, sensing Billy's pain, paid for his items and said, "The horses are out front. Come on, Billy. It's time to go home."

Chapter Thirty-Four

The two men rode in silence. Mark didn't push Billy to talk. He would never mention Elizabeth's actions unless Billy did first. And Billy hadn't spoken a word about it yet.

Mark was injured fighting, but Billy's wound was much deeper. He would give him all the time he needed to come to terms with Elizabeth's betrayal.

After a while, Mark said, "What do you think about stopping off at your place to make sure everything is in order? In your rush to leave, you probably left things behind that you may want now."

"Good idea, Mark," Billy said as he rubbed his eyes. "Why don't we spend the night? Your leg could use a rest, and honestly, I suddenly feel really tired after everything that's happened."

"Sounds good. It's getting late and I'm sure we can find something to eat out of your root cellar."

****

Walking into the house that Billy built for Elizabeth brought back good memories of their times together. He would never forget the feeling of carrying her over the threshold and watching her dance from room to room when he brought her home as his bride. He'd never forget their first Christmas and how she loved the dress he bought for her. So many memories, but Elizabeth and Quinn had stolen the joy of them from him. He wasn't sure what he'd do now. Mark had asked him to stay the winter with the family and he agreed. He knew he and Steven couldn't endure the coming winter alone in this lonely place filled with bittersweet memories. Only time would tell what he'd do with his life and the farm, but at least he'd have time to think while he was home with the Hewitts.

As a kettle of root vegetables boiled, Billy wandered through the house. "Gosh, I miss Steven. I hope he hasn't been giving Ma, Lydia, and Jack too much trouble."

"I'm sure he's fine, Billy, growing like a weed, waiting for you to come home. Now grab a plate. We better eat and get some sleep. Tomorrow we can fix the roof on the chicken coop and put the fence back together where the wind blew those boards off. We'll get home in time for your mother's home cooking. You know she always makes extra for supper."

"That sounds good and definitely more promising than the concoction you've got cooking there. Maybe this will help." Billy reached for the salt crock and set it on the table.

****

Billy and Mark managed to put the horses in the barn before anyone spotted them. Making their way to the porch, Billy let Mark go first. He was a little sore after the work they'd done and the ride, but managed to stand straight and tall when he announced to his family, "We're home! We're finally home!"

Sarah spun around from the stove and the children rushed to his side. Then Billy stepped through the door behind Mark, and Steven ran to jump into his arms.

"I missed you, Billy. I prayed for you every day."

Steven wrapped his arms around his brother's neck and held tight. "Don't ever leave me again, promise me."

Billy gave Steven a kiss on the top of the head and another squeeze. "I promise it won't be as long a time, but I do have a horse in the barn that I must return to a friend's parents. I promise I'll return."

The happy crowd surrounded them. Seth, Emily, and Ethan Frazer were still there as Mark expected. Picking up little Johanna, he kissed her until she started to giggle. "I know it's only been a little over a month, but I missed you all so much. My have you grown." He hugged Lydia and said, "You get prettier by the minute, Lydia. You'll be the prettiest gal in town at the next dance." Shaking Jack's hand he said, "I see the corn is already harvested. You've done a fine job running the farm." He handed Johanna off to Lydia and finally embraced Sarah in a lingering hug. Not wanting to let go, he said, "I thought of you and the family every day. I never want to leave you again." Then he whispered in her ear, "I love you so much, sweetheart.

"Something sure smells good. And I'm starving." Mark reached out to shake Seth's hand. "I'm glad to see you made it home safe. Hello, Emily." He winced a little shifting the wait on his legs.

Sarah caught Mark favoring his right leg and asked, "Are you all right, Mark? Were you injured?"

"Nothing to worry about right now, dear. Just a scratch and the doctor said I'll be fine." Mark squeezed her hand.

"Where is Elizabeth?" Steven ran to the window and looked out.

"She didn't come with us today. Get over here so we can eat," Billy said. "There will be time for explaining tomorrow."

After a hearty meal, the children played until their bedtime.

"Billy, will you sleep with me tonight?" Steven begged.

Billy kissed the top of his head and gave him a big hug. "Sure I will. Now give everyone a kiss and get up that ladder."

Once the children were asleep, Billy answered the burning question on everyone's mind. "Elizabeth passed away six days ago. Her mother told me she had been very ill. She held on until I got home and died in my arms only minutes after she saw me. She's buried in the Dead Flats Cemetery."

The women gasped and Sarah reached her hands across the table to hold Billy's. "I'm so sorry, Billy. This must be a terrible shock for you. Poor Elizabeth. And so young. You must be so sad and heartbroken."

"There is one more thing," Billy said with a somber expression. "I'm sure you'll hear all the details your next trip to town, so I want to tell you myself. Elizabeth admitted to me just before she died that she had been unfaithful. She and Quinn Harris, a friend from school, made plans for their future together. In fact, had she lived, she would have asked me for a divorce. Her parents, so I've heard, were inviting him to Sunday dinners. I confronted them, and they didn't deny they knew their daughter was in love with him.

"I cut all ties with them. Tomorrow Steven must be told about Elizabeth, but how do I explain what happened? I don't want him to think poorly of Elizabeth, and I also don't want him to find out someday what happened from someone else."

Mark spoke, "It's best to tell the truth about Elizabeth's dying, but I'd tell him as simply as possible. Mentioning the other part isn't necessary. He's young and certainly wouldn't understand. It will be difficult enough for Steven to come to terms with never seeing Elizabeth again. There'll be time for telling him the other part when he gets older."

"I agree," Jack said. "It won't be easy, but our whole family is here if he needs to talk to someone. Father's right. Tell him as simply as possible."

"I know I'm not family," Emily said. "But for what it's worth, I'd do the same. This will be difficult, but Steven is surrounded with love and that will help."

"Oh, Billy, I'm so sorry. At least we know now why she didn't want to stay on the farm with us." Sarah went to him and put her arm around him. "She didn't go to town to take care of her folks; she went because of Quinn."

Billy nodded and hung his head.

Mark patted Billy on the shoulder. "No reason for you to feel ashamed, son. None of this was your doings. This was all Elizabeth's decision. Why don't you head up to bed like you promised Steven? In fact, we all should get some sleep. Things are always better in the light of a new day."

Seth reached out and shook Billy's hand. "Emily and I will be leaving in the morning, but we'll see you before we go."

"I appreciate all your advice. I'll tell Steven about Elizabeth tomorrow." Billy dragged his tired body up the ladder.

Chapter Thirty-Five

"Come on, Ethan, tell Johanna and Steven good-bye, and thank Billy for the candy. That sure was nice of him to think of you." Emily laid a gentle hand on Billy's shoulder. Then she and Sarah carried items to the wagon.

"It's been a pleasure having your company, Emily. I'm so happy you and Ethan stayed with us while our men were away. I'll miss our morning cup of tea together before everyone rushed to the table for breakfast."

Emily gave Sarah a hug. "And I'll miss our talks in the evenings after the children were in bed. You must come for a visit when the snows are past. That will give me another reason to look forward to spring."

Jack and Mark brought a crate of chickens and loaded them in the wagon while Billy helped Seth cut his cows from the herd. The herd Billy helped brand. The herd that had the letters CHH that stood for Clark, Hewitt, and Henry. Henry…William Paul Henry.

"It sure will be good to get home. There's nothing that beats sleeping in your own bed," Seth said.

"You're right, Seth. I know what you mean," Billy agreed.

After tying on the cows, the Frazers said their good-byes and pulled out.

With the family gathered around, Billy said, "let's

go inside. Steven, I have to talk with you about something."

While Jack entertained Johanna, the rest of the family sat at the table.

Billy started, "I know you are all wondering why Elizabeth didn't come back with me. Well, when I got back from fighting, Elizabeth's mother told me she had been very sick and had not gotten any better. In fact, she had gotten worse."

"Did she have a bad cold or something?" Steven asked

"Yes, Steven. She had a bad cough and a fever. The doctor came to see her every day, but there wasn't anything he could do to make her feel better. She was very sick, but wanted to see me one last time. She was relieved I arrived home safely from the war and told me that right before she died.

"Elizabeth isn't with us anymore. Do you know what this means, Steven?"

"I think so. She got sick, and the doctor couldn't make her better and she died." Steven started to cry. "So I'll never get to see her again. Did I get it right, Billy?"

"Yes, Steven, you got it right," Billy reassured him.

Lydia knelt by Steven's side. "Elizabeth loved you. Think of some good memories of her and keep them close to your heart."

Steven sniffled. "I remember she made me an apron for Christmas and we used to bake together." Steven took a big breath. "That's a good memory."

"Then that's what you should think of when you think of Elizabeth from now on," Lydia said as she wiped his runny nose with her handkerchief and gave him a hug.

Jack stood and said, "Come on, Steven, I bet you want to show Billy and Pa what you've been working on in the barn. You know, the project Lydia and I have been helping you with?"

"Oh yeah, I want to show them the belt I'm making." Steven was off his chair in a flash and out the door, Elizabeth forgotten for the moment.

Chapter Thirty-Six

"When all our chores are finished, I have a surprise for you. I know everyone will enjoy learning about what's going on back home in Tidioute," Sarah said, pulling the letters out of the cupboard as a tease and tucking them into her apron pocket. "We can all use some good news. I'll make a hearty supper for my hungry family, and, Lydia, you can treat us with a delicious dessert. We'll make it a special event."

Once supper was over and Lydia's splendid dessert of molasses honeycomb pudding was served, Sarah pulled the pages from her pocket and began reading from her mother's letter.

October 4, 1864
Tidioute, Warren County, PA

Dearest Sarah,
I have some exciting news. I believe I mentioned that Robert Martin had asked your father for Matilda's hand in marriage. Their plan was to wait until the war ended, but they decided they could not live their lives apart any longer and had a small ceremony at the church two days ago. They only gave us a few days' notice and did not want a fuss made. I'm sure your sister will write and tell you herself after they get back from Thomas's birthplace, Busti, New York. Thomas

wanted to introduce his bride to his parents and show Matilda the old homestead, so they took some well-deserved time off work and will be gone a few weeks.

We just received a letter from Matthew. He is alive, praise the Lord. He says he is doing fine. He does not see action, but knows every detail from writing the general's reports. Of course he cannot share any information. He did write that he is decently fed, and like everyone, prays the war is over soon. He said the first thing he wants when he gets home is a cherry crumb pie and a tall glass of milk, and that he is going to eat the whole pie himself.

Emma and Abel are enjoying farm life. It's hard to believe little Thomas is already two and talking up a storm. He loves all the animals on their farm and when he comes to visit us always expects Grandma to bake him a cake so he can lick the bowl. I remember that you did the same as a little girl, Sarah. If this war lasts much longer, Abel may be called up to serve. I pray it ends soon, so our men can come home to their families.

Your father and I are doing well. The heavy chores are becoming a little too much, so we are thinking of asking a neighbor boy to help us a day or two a week. With Matilda leaving, our home will be quiet for the first time in many years.

I pray everyone is healthy and Mark and Billy do not get called up. No doubt Jack is very capable of taking care of the family and farm if necessary, but I hope that does not happen.

That is all the news on this end. I am hoping to get a letter from you at least one more time before the snow flies.

Take care of yourself, Daughter. Please let

everyone know your father and I send our love.
   Sincerely,
   Love, Mother

"Good for Aunt Matilda," Jack said, as he drank a swallow of milk. "She deserves happiness and it sounds like Grandma and Grandpa approve."

"I agree, Jack. And I just love Uncle Matthew's idea about the pie!" Lydia chimed in. Turning to Billy, she said, "Billy, is there something I could bake that you and Father would enjoy? You both fought and are back safely, so I think you deserve something special too."

Billy chuckled. "My favorite pie is apple, and I'd be glad to share with everyone, especially if you make it."

Lydia smiled. "Then I'll make a pie tomorrow and cut you the biggest piece."

"What about me?" Mark asked. "It's a good thing my favorite is apple too."

Lydia hugged her father. "Then I'll bake two apple pies and cut you each a large piece."

Sarah said wistfully, "I'm sure Emma is busy chasing little Thomas all over their farm. I'd dearly love it if we lived closer, but I wouldn't trade living here with all of you for the world."

Sarah opened the second envelope and read Mother Hewitt's letter:

September 28, 1864
Tidioute, Warren County, PA

Dear Family,

The leaves on the hillside are bright and beautiful this year. With all the fighting in our country, I take solace in the simple things in life and try to live without fear. Although people tell me the war will never reach our town, I still worry. I don't like the fact that you are so far away in Kansas with only our letters to keep us in touch.

The garden did well this year, and I put up enough food to hold me for the winter. I still go fishing on the bank of the Allegheny River a few times a month and then salt the fish that I do not eat fresh. The river is low right now, but it will rise come late fall. Every year, one of the neighbors shoots an extra deer and gives me the venison. I'm so thankful for his generosity.

Mark, I was just thinking the other day about how we used to go up the mountain and pick blueberries. I have not been able to do that for quite some time. I remember how you could not wait to get home, and I would make a cobbler. Then we would eat it hot from the oven.

I think of you often, Son, and am glad you are happy with Sarah and your family in Kansas, even though you are so very far away. I pray every day for your health and safety.

Give all the children a kiss for me. I will close now. I am going to do some reading before I blow out the lamp tonight.

Sending my love,
Mother Hewitt

"Grandma sounds lonely. Why don't we ask her to come live with us? Do you think she could make the trip west?" Jack said.

"And I was thinking the same thing, Jack," Sarah said, sliding the letter back into the envelope. "Any thoughts, Mark?"

"She does sound lonesome, and I'd love to have her with us. She'd need to wait and come in the spring. I'll write and ask if she might consider the move."

"I feel like I already know her from all her letters and can't wait to meet her," Lydia said as she took Johanna and Steven by the hand and danced with them around the room.

"Oh boy! We're going to ask Grandma Hewitt to come live with us," Steven sang as he skipped about.

"Grandma Hewitt sounds like she's a good cook. She might even make a better apple pie than you, Lydia," Billy teased, caught up in the fun.

****

A few days later, Billy announced, "It's time for me to take my friend's horse to his family in Rock Creek. JJ told me all about his town and his folks. I know it will be a blessing for them to get his horse and it will be a chance for me to share with them his last days and what a good friend and brave soldier he was. It'll be getting cold soon, so I'd best not put it off any longer."

"Leaving? You can't leave, Billy! You promised! And besides, you'll miss Thanksgiving," Steven moaned.

"I promise I'll come back, little brother. I have to do this for my friend, but don't worry. I'll be fine. I'll leave in the morning. As for Thanksgiving, I'll miss the good food, but I already know what I'm thankful for." Billy tousled Steven's hair.

"Are you really sure you want to leave tomorrow?"

Sarah asked. "Thanksgiving is only a few days away."

"I'm sure." Billy nodded.

"I understand, son. You do what you must." Mark went silent for a few moments. "I know how close you and JJ became in such a short time. And I can easily imagine how much that horse might mean to his parents."

"I'll pack food for your trip," Lydia offered. "But we'll miss you."

"Thanks, Lydia. I appreciate your help. I figure it will take me a few days to get there, so don't worry if I'm not back right away. If the Stantons need help around the farm, I might stay and work a while."

Later that evening, Lydia and Billy walked to the barn where Jack was working on a leather project on the workbench.

"Billy, I've been meaning to return the necklace you gave me to hold for you. I've gotten attached to it, but I know it was Elizabeth's, so I'm sure you want it back," Lydia said, pulling the pendant out from under her collar.

Billy looked at the necklace, a heart set with two small blue stones, and felt a shock run through his body.

"Billy, are you all right? You don't look well," Lydia noted.

"I wasn't sure until…right now," Billy managed to sputter.

"Sure about what? What's the matter?" Lydia asked as she searched his face for an answer.

"I need to tell you something," Billy whispered. "But please keep it between us."

"You can trust me, Billy. I won't tell," Lydia said,

then sat on the end of the spring wagon. "Come sit with me, Billy," she implored, patting the empty space beside her.

Billy joined her. "I know I can trust you, Lydia. I've always known that. The necklace you're wearing is one I found at the farm after Elizabeth left. I thought she had overlooked it in her rush to pack and I gave it to you for safekeeping. But the day she died, I saw the identical necklace around her neck, a heart with two small blue stones. I'm thinking Quinn must have given her a replacement when she couldn't find the original."

"Oh, Billy, I'm so sorry. That means..." Lydia touched his tightly clenched hands.

"Yes, it means that Elizabeth was in love with Quinn long before she went to stay with her folks. He had been wounded and was considered a war hero in town. I came home alive, so I guess that didn't count for much in some people's eyes.

"I think Elizabeth hung on until I returned so she could tell me about Quinn before someone else did." Billy took Lydia's hand.

"Lydia, I'd rather not see you wearing the necklace. Why don't you put it away and give it to Johanna when she's older. Someday I'll get you a different one."

Lydia squeezed his hand. "You don't have to buy me a necklace, Billy."

"I know, but I want to. You deserve to have something pretty to wear. Maybe I'll stop in town on my way home unless you want to pick it out yourself," Billy said, reaching under her curls to undo the clasp.

"No, you pick one out. Then I'll always have something to cherish from you." Lydia took the jewelry from Billy's rugged hand and slipped it in her pocket. "And, Billy, you are a hero to me. I prayed for your safe return every day and every night. The whole family did, but I think I missed you the most. I was so glad to see you finally came home, so please, don't stay away too long."

****

After the comforting solace of a few days on the road, Billy was sitting by the campfire eating some of the food Lydia packed when he remembered Thanksgiving must be coming up within a day or so.

He was away from the whispers and stares of townspeople, away from the fighting and horrific noise of the battlefield, but he was also away from his loving family.

Later, as he lay gazing at the night sky thinking of his past and everything that brought him to this moment, he drifted off to sleep. Suddenly awakened by an unseen force, Billy sat bolt upright and grabbed for his gun. His heart was pounding fiercely. Panting from unnamed fears, he had trouble catching his breath. The fire had burned to embers, but the last he remembered he had just added a log. He must have been dreaming and knew the thoughts he managed to keep away during the day found a way to catch up with him at night.

So much had happened throughout his life. The events of the war and Elizabeth's betrayal brought him to this breaking point. He needed this time away from everyone so he could unburden himself of pain and sorrows.

So many lies, so many questions left unanswered, tied his mind in a tangle.

He lay back exhausted and didn't awaken until

after the sun shined brightly in the sky, clearing away the darkness of his night terrors. Refreshed, he headed on toward Rock Creek and once in town, asked directions to the Stanton farm. He figured he could make it by dusk.

Riding up to the dimly lit farmhouse with JJ's horse in tow, a twinge of guilt and apprehension crept into his mind. *He was alive and their son wasn't.* Billy hadn't considered his presence might upset the Stantons and would understand if they didn't receive him kindly.

Knocking, he heard a voice call out, "Who's there? What do you want?"

"My name's Billy Henry, Mr. Stanton, sir," Billy called through the door. "I brought your son's horse to you. I met JJ at Fort Riley and we became friends."

The door swung open and the light from a lamp lit the face of an older man. "What's your business here?" Mr. Stanton yelled.

"My name is Billy Henry, sir. I brought JJ's horse home for you."

The man held out the lamp. "Yup, that's my son's horse all right. I never thought we'd see him again. You say you were JJ's friend?"

"Yes, sir. My name is Billy Henry, and JJ and I fought together at the battle of Westport in Missouri. We didn't know each other very long, but we became good friends real quick. I'm the person who had the sad task to send you his letter. JJ made me promise I would do that if anything happened to him."

"Well, you can call me John, seein's that you were my son's friend and all. Let's get this horse to the barn." Mr. Stanton led the way. "The missus isn't feeling so good. She's grieving something mighty for our boy."

"Were you with JJ when he died? I got to know. I just got to know if my boy suffered or if it was quick?" John asked.

Billy grabbed a pitchfork and tossed hay in the stall. "Yes, sir. I was with him. It happened real quickly. Your son didn't suffer. JJ was a good soldier and a good friend."

John swiped at his eyes. After a moment, he turned to Billy and said, "Well, son, where do you call home? Are you from around these parts?"

"I'm from west of Dead Flats. That's about four days ride from here." At the well, Billy drew water for the horses. "Would you mind if I water my horse too, sir?"

"Now, where's my manners? No, go right ahead. Did you say your first name was Billy?"

"Yes, sir. And, sir, I was kind of wondering if you needed help with anything around here. I have some time, and JJ said you might have a chore or two I could help with if I ever stopped by to visit."

"Well, I could use a hand with a few things, that's for sure. Bed down your horse then come to the house. You eat yet?"

"I don't want Mrs. Stanton to bother fixing anything. I have some food in my saddlebag, but something hot to drink sure would be nice."

"I'll fix you up some. Don't worry about Mrs. Stanton. You just might be the ticket she needs to get back to her old self. Hurry now. You're welcome to bunk in JJ's room. You can wash up at the well and I'll let the missus know a friend of JJ's has come to tell us about our son."

When Billy got to the house, Mrs. Stanton was standing at the stove waiting for the kettle to boil. "Young man, I'm sorry we don't have any coffee, but I hope you like mint tea."

"That will be fine, ma'am, thank you. And thank you for your hospitality, Mrs. Stanton, ma'am, for letting me stay the night and all. I can sleep in the barn if you like. I don't want you to fuss."

"No fuss. Pa said you knew my boy."

"Yes, Mrs. Stanton. JJ and I became friends at Fort Riley and we fought together."

"Pa said you told him our boy didn't suffer."

"No, ma'am, he didn't. I was with him. He didn't suffer."

"You don't know how much it means to us that you brought news about our JJ. He didn't want to go fight, but knew he didn't have a choice. He didn't want the Confederate army to take our farm and thought it was worth dying for. This farm is all we have. But now, without JJ here, we feel like we've lost everything. It's a good farm. JJ loved it here, but now we don't even have anyone to leave it to."

"JJ told me all about you folks and the farm and how he liked to go hunting to put food on the table."

John dropped into a seat at the table. Mrs. Stanton made tea. Hungry for company, the three of them talked until the pot was empty.

Billy was up early to get a good look at the farm and see how he could be of help. There had been damage to the coop and chickens were running everywhere. He found some tools, repaired the hole, and rounded up the clucking layers. After repairing the corral, he put Lucky and the Stantons' two horses in it while he cleaned the barn stalls and put down fresh bedding.

John came to get water for the house. "Son, come in for a bite to eat."

Savoring a piece of sausage, Billy asked, "Is there anything I can do for you around the house, Mrs. Stanton?"

The kindly woman thought for a moment and said, "I would certainly like to give these rag rugs a good beating if you could get them on the clothesline for me?"

"I'll do that, ma'am. By the way, would you happen to know what day of the week it is?" Billy asked.

Mrs. Stanton looked at the calendar, surprised to realize it was Thanksgiving. "My, I've lost all track of time. Why, its Thanksgiving Day, and I haven't prepared a proper meal."

"Well, why don't we pretend that Thanksgiving is tomorrow?" Billy suggested. "I'll go hunting this afternoon and see what I can bring home for the pot. Do you eat venison, ma'am?" Billy smiled, sure of the answer.

"Why, of course I like venison," Mrs. Stanton replied.

"Well, then I hope your knives are sharp because I plan to get a deer today, maybe even two." Billy smiled more broadly when he saw Mrs. Stanton's delight.

Billy was successful, and butchering took place late into the night. He knew what it meant to the couple to have meat. They now had food and security for the winter ahead. He'd be sure to do more hunting before he left for home.

The Thanksgiving meal seemed meager to Billy, but to the Stantons it was a feast. He was glad for his part in making it happen.

"Oh you dear, sweet boy, you took care of us just like our JJ. And you eased our minds about our son's last days on earth. You brought our JJ's horse back. We couldn't plant the crops next year without it. We so hope you'll consider yourself family now and come visit us again." Mrs. Stanton offered another helping of potatoes.

"That means a lot to me, ma'am. It's been good to be here with you, and I plan to come back again. I've been thinking. Maybe one of your neighbors has an older child who could come and give you a hand once a week or so to do heavy work and chores."

John nodded. "Good idea. I'll think on it."

Billy shared the discussion he and JJ had about finding himself a wife. The recounting brought sadness to Mrs. Stanton's face and then a smile hearing the words, "We could live with them on the farm, and Ma would have another female in the house to talk to."

Billy stayed for more than a week helping JJ's parents in the house and on the farm. By the time he left, the chickens were laying; there was fresh meat for the table and plenty more in the pickling crock, smoke house, and drying for jerky. The Stantons were good people. Billy knew he'd taken away their fears that their son had suffered. That meant a lot to them and in turn made Billy feel good about making the trip. Doing for others instead of dwelling on his own grief had been good medicine. Billy was coming to realize that for reasons known only to God, his life had been spared and, in a flash of a steel blade, JJ's had been taken instead.

****

On the return trip, Billy took his time. There was something about being alone with only the sights and sounds of nature that brought him peace. The days and nights were getting cold and the surety of snow was stronger.

Aptly named, the town of Dead Flats was filled with memories of pain and death. When he left after the funeral, he had no desire to return. But now he had a reason. He'd promised to replace the necklace for Lydia. The townspeople could talk all they want, but it wouldn't faze him this time. At the Dry Goods Store he found an oval shaped locket with the letter L surrounded with dainty flowers that he knew was perfect for Lydia.

He set out on the last leg toward home, reflecting on all he'd come to understand while away. He realized he was ready to move on. That meant making decisions about his future. They didn't need to be made all at once. He had time, lots of time. Filling his lungs with fresh, crisp air, Billy knew without a doubt that he was ready to start his new life one breath at a time. He breathed in possibility and exhaled any bitterness he felt for Elizabeth.

The war left its mark, just as the loss of Elizabeth left a wound. As Billy slowly came to understand her actions, he couldn't help but feel it appropriate that he shoulder some of the responsibility for what happened between them. She was a town girl, and he should have realized she was not prepared to become a farmer's wife. She wasn't happy far out in the country apart from everything she'd ever known. Understanding the reasons for what she did didn't take away the pain of her betrayal, but Billy was beginning to understand that forgiving her would be a step in the right direction for him and for her memory.

Billy knew he'd enjoy helping Steven grow into a fine young man with admirable goals and ambitions. Jack was well on his way to becoming a successful businessman. Lydia was smart and beautiful. Her dreams of owning her own dress shop and finding a good husband were sure to become a reality one day. Little Johanna would take after her mother and sister. Sarah and Mark were kind, loving parents. They would always be there for their children while they provided a safe home filled with love. Billy had to admit he was beginning to feel curious about the possibilities that stretched before him. He had landed on his feet more than once, and this time would not be an exception.

He acknowledged how much pain had been thrust upon his short life. He was still young, though, and knew time would bring healing. He wanted to set new goals with no regrets for the past. Excited to consider the promise tomorrow could bring, he began to understand he would always have a choice in what happened next.

While eating the last of his food at the old oak campsite before turning in for the night, he focused on his future. *Yes, I am a survivor. Nothing can hold me back, not the memories of the battlefield or the loss of my wife. I will mend and hopefully, one day, I'll be able to open my heart to another woman who will love me with all her heart and soul for who I am.*

1				1				
2			2	3				
3		4	5	6				
4	7	8	9	10				
5	11	12	13	14	15			
6	16	17	18	19	20	21		
7	22	23	24	25	26	17	28	
8	29	30	31	32	33	34	35	36

Math Pyramid

Used to count and perform addition and subtraction

By using the column 1 through 8 on the left hand side of the page easily add and subtract using the pyramid.

Also use it to count forward and backward making addition and subtraction easy to learn.

Examples:

Place your finger on the number six and count plus four. 6+4=10

Place your finger on the number twenty-two and count back six. 22-6=16

Use the pyramid as a game to learn to draw numbers, count, and do simple addition and subtraction.

A word about the author...

Judy always dreamed of becoming an author, and upon retirement from her career in education, she embraced her desire for writing. She now writes at her home in the northwestern mountains of Pennsylvania where she and her husband appreciate the outdoors, share cups of morning coffee as nature surrounds them, and enjoy the changing of the seasons.

Judy would like to hear her readers' thoughts and opinions on whether to write another book in this series. Contact her through her website and sign up for her newsletter at:

https://judysharer.com

CPSIA information can be obtained
at www.ICGtesting.com
Printed in the USA
LVHW081711230121
677302LV00044B/452